TIGHT SPACES

SINGULAR LIVES

THE IOWA SERIES IN

NORTH AMERICAN

AUTOBIOGRAPHY

Albert E. Stone, Series Editor

KESHO SCOTT,

CHERRY MUHANJI,

AND

EGYIRBA HIGH

Tight SPACES

AN EXPANDED EDITION

FOREWORD BY ALBERT E. STONE

University of Iowa Press　Iowa City

University of Iowa Press,
Iowa City 52242
Copyright © 1999 by the
University of Iowa Press
All rights reserved
Printed in the United States of America
Design by Richard Hendel
http://www.uiowa.edu/~uipress

The first edition of *Tight Spaces* was
published by Spinsters/Aunt Lute Book
Company in 1987.
Printed on acid-free paper

99 00 01 02 03 P 5 4 3 2 1

Library of Congress
Cataloging-in-Publication Data
Scott, Kesho.
Tight spaces / by Kesho Scott, Cherry
Muhanji, and Egyirba High; foreword
by Albert E. Stone.—Expanded ed.
    p.   cm. — (Singular lives)
ISBN 0-87745-665-8
1. Afro-American women—Michigan—
Detroit—Social life and customs—
Fiction.   2. Afro-American women
authors—Michigan—Detroit—
Biography.   3. Women—Michigan—
Detroit—Social life and customs—
Fiction.   4. Detroit (Mich.)—Social life
and customs—Fiction.   5. Short stories,
American—Afro-American authors.
6. Short stories, American—Michigan—
Detroit.   7. Short stories, American—
Women authors.   I. Muhanji, Cherry.
II. High, Egyirba.   III. Title.   IV. Series.
PS3569.C645T54   1999
813'.01089287'08996073—dc21   98-31803

This book is dedicated to the healing of the planet.

CONTENTS

FOREWORD

ALBERT E. STONE

 *ight Spaces* stands out as a double first among the sixteen previous volumes in Singular Lives: The Iowa Series in North American Autobiography. To begin with, this is the first reprint in the series; it's a second published look at life. Even more important, though, *Tight Spaces* is a tri-autobiography, the jointly written story of three lives. Both novel features call for explanation.

This book was originally written (often by the three writers around a table late at night) in 1985–86. It was published in 1987 by Spinsters/ Aunt Lute, a small feminist press in San Francisco. It was awarded a Before Columbus/American Book Award in 1988. This fame occasioned a flurry of interest, reviews, sales, interviews, and book tours by the astonished, delighted authors. Gradually, however, sales fell off, and by the nineties *Tight Spaces* was out of print. A year or so ago

Kesho Scott (who, it's fair to say, has been the prime impetus behind this collaboration of three strong-minded equals) called the University of Iowa Press. She wanted to see if their book could be reissued in the Singular Lives series. Since revisions and additions were needed to continue the evolution of three unique life stories, it became a formidable and time-consuming task for three busy women to consent, agree to meet, and re-create the new text. They knew this experiment in multiple authorship was both risky and revolutionary. It's by no means a coincidence that this literary and psychological feat has been brought off by three determined black women now entering middle age.

Although Detroit is the common home of Scott, Muhanji, and High and the three are related by blood or long-term friendship, the immediate origin of *Tight Spaces* was at the University of Iowa. There the three friends migrated in search of interdisciplinary higher education in African American studies, American studies, and women's studies. There all three in succession enrolled in a course, "Autobiography and American Culture." It's now clear all three were deeply affected, not only by reading ten or so American life histories but even more by the course's midterm writing assignment: to write the opening chapter of one's own autobiography. Though other class members went on to publish stories or critical essays on autobiography, none came close to Scott, Muhanji, and High in capitalizing on the discovery of their several writing voices. Even more exciting than realizing private identities was coming together to merge their separate lives. Whether the challenge was worth the discomfort and travail is one question readers may anticipate in reading the four sections — "Talkin' Real Honest," "Listen to Me Good, Now," "You Must Be Lyin'," and "Say It Ain't So." To what extent has the process of re-membering and composing together affected the structure, tone, and styles of this often bittersweet book? An equally elusive question is whether this new version of *Tight Spaces* holds together as a relatively coherent book or is inescapably a three-pronged anthology.

To repeat the second query is to raise and challenge several assumptions about American autobiography. For many readers, autobiography is a narrative of a singular self written by the person whose actual experiences have helped to shape both story and self. This definition implicitly assumes the primacy of history or memoir over literary or psychological intentions and achievements. It fits pretty well some classic American texts—Benjamin Franklin's, Henry Adams's, and

Richard Wright's, among many others. An often unexamined truth here is the culture's assumption that the individual is always more basic than the group. That's been the aim of thousands of autobiographers — to discover and celebrate autonomy. But in this century there has emerged an alternative assumption. The self can also be seen as the intersection of a whole skein of social institutions and interactions, stretching over time and space. Black Elk, the Lakota holy man, connects this wider view to his autobiographical collaboration with John G. Neihardt when he states that "no good thing can be done by any man alone." *Black Elk Speaks*, therefore, typifies other books that announce joint (and now multiple) authorship as a legitimate feature of modern autobiography. If the self as subject chooses collaboration as a way of examining the web of relationships within which she or he has actually lived and grown, why is this not a truth-seeking autobiographical device? Besides *Black Elk Speaks*, several notable texts have played variations on this theme: *The Autobiography of Alice B. Toklas* by Gertrude Stein; *The Autobiography of Malcom X* by Alex Haley; *All God's Dangers: The Life of Nat Shaw* by Theodore Rosengarten; and *Brothers and Keepers* by John Edgar Wideman.

Many of these texts were familiar to Scott, Muhanji, and High. On one level, their *Tight Spaces* simply expands the tradition. For readers to grant their claim they must recognize the many ways these three black women from Detroit and Iowa City, from Minnesota and Sweden, are dramatizing the facts of their pasts as separate but interconnected. Moreover, since dream, nightmare, and flights of artistic fancy were and are essential to their existences, these inner experiences and ineffable emotions must also find expression. As Muhanji puts it, "What if I told you that what she ever wanted was to be the girl in her dream?" Mixed-media collaboration like theirs calls into question the comfortable myth of many (white) male autobiographers who pride themselves on a spurious independence. As readers, we're nudged by this story to rethink the re-creative activity of other autobiographical authors. Whether more than one name appears on the title page may be less important than seeing the hands and memories of many who share a so-called singular authorship. Gwendolyn Brooks on the lecture circuit was fond of reminding readers that *Report from Part One* was composed at her kitchen table with aunts and cousins sometimes reading over her shoulder and urging different explanations. *Tight Spaces*, too, invites readers to a transactional view of the book in their hands. Isn't this doubly plausible since Scott, Muhanji, and High have collaborated not once but twice — and openly both times?

Energized by originality, readers are encouraged to perform a particularly complex strategy of sympathetic cocreation and critical analysis. Teasing out parallels and differences among three women's lives may actually strengthen awareness of a surprisingly unified narrative. To be sure, the title page offers a few helpful hints. No subtitle steers readers toward autobiography or fiction or into autobiography as memoir, confession, art, reminiscence, or testament. Genre borders are evoked apparently only to be crossed. Confusion is compounded when we know that Kesho, Cherry, and Egyirba are sometimes called by their girlhood names of Evie, Jenny, and Michelle. Doubts aren't all dispelled as we note the book's four section headings and forty-two subsections or sketches, stories, revelations, dreams, etc. Section titles suggest a sincere effort to speak candidly. Individual episodes articulate diversity and different inflections of common themes.

Tight Spaces is a title first glossed in Scott's new introduction. "Although we felt released from some of the tight spaces of our lives created by race, class, gender, and sexuality, we didn't know where we were going. We only knew we had moved away from where we had been ten years before." This defines a dynamic, open-ended story. Socially defined categories of feminine containment/entrapment are acknowledged (and others, too, like place and age, body and health). What's promised now are some new responses to Detroit, marriage, motherhood, divorce, heterosexual or lesbian choices, Christian patriarchy, and Sufi mysticism, with loneliness as the underlying condition of all independence. But an ongoing reality continues: again their SHE-energy, or the mysterious feminine force, promises a not very clearly specified escape from history, society, and harmful dreams. Still, autobiography remains the doorway to spiritual enlightenment.

Though personal names are attached to each essay or story, no single voice, style, or literary medium predominates. Readers must respond variously to the order and frequency of each writer's contributions. Scott's opening story, though, offers a powerful clue not only to her personal future but to others'. The girl's seventh birthday and the gift of a new dress, instead of occasions for family celebration, are secrets shared between mother and daughter behind the domineering father/husband's back. When reinforced later by a maternal family tradition of escape through "ed-ju-moo-ka-shon," Scott and her sisterhood have goals to pursue. To be sure, higher education proves as much obstacle as opportunity for Scott, whose adult identity as Black Superwoman exacts a heavy toll upon her career, marriages, family, and health. At the narrative's other end, High's contribution has the last word. Hers is a love story — indeed, a lament for romantic love that does not last. For the dreamy girl whose adult history has been to "give my heart away" is a sadder, wiser self. With the retrospective awareness that is the goal of all autobiographers, High goes beyond lament and recrimination. "I want to make real sense of things so my soul can rest, at peace." Here, the key words are "real" and "soul." Both signify movement beyond the fire dance of heterosexual love toward "that place where all intangibles exist without complication."

In between lie forty pieces of this mysterious mosaic. Among these, fifteen are written by Muhanji and constitute another essential thread in the tapestry of their lives. If winning the Ph.D. and gaining admission to the (white) old boy–old girl elite is Scott's way to escape tight places, Muhanji both follows and evades such a pattern. Unlike High, who discovers that writing a doctoral dissertation cannot be done, Muhanji perseveres. She uses Iowa's option of a creative thesis — in her case a novel. A sign of this "escape" is "Her," the last segment of the first *Tight Spaces*. By this choice, Muhanji demonstrates that fiction can help to defend her acceptance of her sexual nature and show her delight in becoming a popular classroom teacher who's "an out lesbian grandmother to my students." Still, elsewhere Muhanji confesses that she's paid a heavy price for success and independence — alienation from some of her sons, failed attachment to beloved others, rueful acknowledgment that "I am lonely." Perhaps these are some of the implications suggested by Muhanji's major metaphor of self, the fragile, light green, empty Coke bottle.

Indeed, *writing the self* into, out of, and beyond social identity provides the central unity of this new *Tight Spaces* and richly justifies its revised republication. All three writers manifestly possess skills that command readers' respect and overcome reservations about autobiography-cum-fiction. Scott's terse and touching account of running away from her family and job, only to encounter three flat tires on the interstate, and turning back to Grinnell is a vivid demonstration of her mature style. Muhanji's keynote passages are more scattered. For this reader, though, the various scenes in which an older black woman lives alone in a big, ramshackle house and entertains her imagined visitors in a haze of alcohol and music while a young girl peeks through the window combine powerful images of isolation and resistance. Still, for this reader again, nothing Egyirba High has contributed to this striking sequel matches the exquisite evocative appeal of "The Last Dance" from the original *Tight Spaces*. That piece's celebration of an experience of nature and transcendence is worthy of Walt Whitman or Thomas Merton. Yet it bears unmistakably Egyirba High's own black female voice:

> The wide, open savannah is forever my roost. I walk among the plains aware of my full essence, the territorial privilege of one as big and bad as I. I stretch my body across the straw grass, dry-fucked by the sun. Its scratchy remains irritate my skin. Still, I manage to find a comforting groove and yawn lazily. . . .
>
> Soon I feel myself being lifted slowly, magnificently up, a slow swing like a Venetian blind going up one side at a time till it gets to the top. I am being pulled. A gentle breeze blows under me, coaxing me easily upwards, Lighter now, as though my body has taken on new mass, I am relieved of the responsibility of myself. I reach the apex of my ascent and float in big, lazy circles. Black birds move past me. I am flying. I whirl and spin free to take in all that is my life. I soar uninhibited by the chains of tradition or time. Suspended by will and desire, I run through the sky, breathless excitement coursing my veins.

ACKNOWLEDGMENTS

FROM KESHO

Thanks to Annie, the *wind* behind my dreams; Connie, the *earth* bridging my thoughts; and my children, Sacha, Dresden, and James Abijah, the *water* to quench my thirst. And my coauthors, who were the *fire* behind my smile because we were the ones "who flew over the cuckoo's nest." I love you all.

FROM CHERRY

Thanks to the beautiful people on John R Street for their color. Kesho for my concepts. Egyirba for her compassion. A special, special thanks to Papusa for her comfort. MaryAnn for her commitment. Joan for her corrections. And Cindy for her comments.

FROM EGYIRBA

To my Creator and Sustainer. You are most beneficent and compassionate. Thank you for your love.

I am so grateful for the never-ending love and support of family and friends, who keep on loving me through all my trials. Mom, Dad, Lisa High Wells, Sidney High Jr., Timothy Lamar Wells, Tyrone Shawn Wells, and Matthew Justin High—thank you for also choosing me to be your kin. Thank you for your love.

Cherry and Kesho—where would I be without my lifelong gurl-friends? Thank you for your love.

To the light of my life, Vidinyu Ambani—how you inspire and amaze me! I am so happy to be your mom. You are a wonderful man. Thank you for your love.

To Jasmine Ujima Love—your unconditional love continues to humble me. You are my heart and spirit twin! Thank you for your love.

To my sister, Stefanie Cyd High—I love you and miss you so. May your spirit be at peace. Thank you for your love.

TIGHT SPACES

AN EVENING IN MINNESOTA, 1998

. . . .

KESHO SCOTT

orld conditions had to catch up with the visions and prophetic prose of *Tight Spaces* before we were able to write these new introductory essays. It has been over a decade since this book was first published. There has not been a moment in which we have not thought or been called upon to address some point about "that book," as we affectionately call it. Not only do we ritualistically read aloud the stories as we mine the challenges of our middle years . . . now being forty-five, fifty-eight, and forty-five in 1998 . . . but we call upon the stories, the She-energy, three-way telephone calls, e-mail, chat boxes, attached files, and an occasional real-time visit thrown in to do the magic and continue the saga of being black women in "tight spaces" in America.

1

"Hello, may I speak to Holly Carver?"

"Speaking." (This syruplike voice came sliding through the end of the phone.)

"Hi, Holly . . . this is Kesho Scott . . . do you remember me?

"How you been doing? Are you still living in Grinnell?"

"Well! And yes, I'm still here at the college. In fact, I'm in my office this very moment. Holly, I just glanced up at our book, *Tight Spaces* . . . and felt so bad that it isn't being read today. I decided to call you and see, I mean, well, if the University of Iowa Press would be interested in reprinting it? Holly, we know it *was* such a good book but it was unread!"

"Actually, Kesho . . . that's a great idea."

(I couldn't believe it — she blew my mind. I had just called her on a whim.)

"Holly, I just had this feeling, to call you today. It's almost five o'clock and I didn't even know if you'd be there but I had to call. I just felt it."

"Can you send me a copy of the book and some of the reviews so I can make the case with my colleagues here?"

"Oh, yeah . . . we can do anything, anything!"

"And do you have some stats on its sales? How many times was it reprinted? How soon can you send me the stuff? We'll want to get it out in our spring listing in '97. Where is Egyirba?" She said all this in one breath . . .

"I can get the information to you immediately . . . and Egyirba . . . (long pause) . . . well, ah . . . she, ah, Cherry just talked to her," I lied. "She just left California, for, ah, Sweden but we can find her, I think!" (I was panicking at this point.) But I managed to say in a cool voice, or so I thought, "Holly, I can't wait to call Cherry . . . you've made my day!"

"Well I'm glad you did call. It was a good book . . . but it had the challenges of being published by a small feminist press. Anyway, I'll look for the stuff in the mail."

"Okay."

"Keep in touch."

"Oh . . . I will."

"'Bye."

"'Bye."

"Hello, Cherry! You still asleep?"

"Yeah, what time is it?"

"Six-thirty."

"In the morning?!"

"No . . . it's six-thirty . . . it's dark outside."

"I was pulling an all-nighter on this dissertation . . . just give me a minute . . . (long pause) . . . what's up, Sweet Pea?"

"I just talked to Holly!"

"Holly, who?"

"The woman at the U of I Press and guess what?"

"What? . . ."

It began . . . and a year later . . . we had to call Holly and tell her all bets were off. I didn't want to make the phone call (I had just had surgery) and neither did Cherry (she was dissertating), and Egyirba was doing some kind of Ramadanlike thing in Sweden and couldn't talk or eat or whatever for thirty days, so we got a friend to make the call. Holly understood, but I wonder what her real feelings were. Anyhow, we kept nursing our pick-of-the-week crises and wallowing in the shit in our lives.

Cherry and I maintained close phone contact but we couldn't pull it off. As the summer passed into fall and the fall into winter, we didn't make the spring listing. I got over the surgery. Cherry finished the dissertation. I moved to Des Moines. Egyirba returned to the States and Cherry moved to Minneapolis for a J-O-B — where this evening we find ourselves experiencing the three F's: Frost, Frigid, and Freezing in Minnesota.

After finishing one of my twenty-minute, low-fat, no-dairy-no-nothing-that-Cherry-and-Egyirba-are-not-used-to-eating meals the question is upon us, hanging in the air. I know Egyirba and Cherry try to avoid it. I pull out pencils, paper, and clipboard and demand, "What have we been doing all of these years?" Cherry and Egyirba eye one another and give me that there-she-goes-again look.

We start into the black women's lament. Kesho: "I couldn't keep my marriage and family from falling apart . . . I couldn't hold it. . . . It was like being on a dry drunk . . . trying to nurture everybody and everything . . . just to get somebody to love me." Cherry: "I've been screwed over again — seduced — as a lesbian by marriage, by religion, and by the academy. . . . If only I could get it right — just once — I'm the bull in the china shop, trying not to act like a bull!" Egyirba: "I just couldn't finish it — the dissertation . . . it just didn't . . . I couldn't . . . it didn't happen . . . couldn't happen . . . didn't!"

The mood of the room continued its descent until the She-energy already settling over us — like a lover filling the room with the scent of gardenia — finally let us know that we'd had enough self-criticism. What had we been doing all of these years? We went from lament to reminiscing: "Hey girl, remember when you saw me through Vidinyu's (Egyirba's nineteen-year-old son) transition from heavy metal to rap?" (Something she encouraged him to do.) To my eighteen-year-old daughter Dresden's preteen "gangstalike" years and her change to boo-poob-be-doo — now I'm a Miss Black Thang. Then to Cherry's continual kick-in-the-ass and slow descent into deep emotional pain . . . as two out of three sons disowned her because of her lesbian lifestyle. She reminded us again that having girlfriends was the only thing that made losing her sons manageable. Yeah, the She-energy was working alright, because Cherry could talk about aging parents, now that Egyirba and I were experiencing them. In the same breath we could laugh at the time when Cherry and I went to China and Cuba in the same year and marvel at Egyirba's time in Sweden donning the veil. We managed to embrace our shifting sexualities and marital statuses and say with a smile — who is she/he to you, now? How's the divorce? And are you dating yet?

We have collected five more college degrees among us and felt more personal freedom, but had no role models for being in academe or aging — at least one that we were willing to trust. We asked many questions. Do you know what it means to be black and female and old and lesbian with nowhere to turn? Should we ask Oprah, Jessie, or Ricki, "Did my lover leave because I'm too fat?" Should I leave my husband because he can't talk to my soul? The questions made us crazy. We realized, as Cherry says, "We ain't got no side rails, y'all. We're out here alone in a culture that is suspicious of us."

So we swung into academic stardom — lectures, teaching, awards, performances, on stage and off, TV and radio appearances and book tours and from there to analyses, theories, and, finally, tears. Each time a different aspect of the She-energy would enter the maddening pace of our lives, settle in on us, and sometimes alert us to our personal health problems. We'd have to slow down, way down, and sometimes new and evolving friendships would catch our interest. But most times we didn't recognize She. As Egyirba likes to say, "You don't miss your water till your well runs dry." Through all this, Cherry, Egyirba, and I knew we weren't writing, and that, oddly enough, turned us back toward each other, lifted our isolation, and helped us know it was time to summon She.

We began to redefine the word *obstacle*: all the running and doing and doing and doing . . . but I think we tried to look at it like the Chinese *I Ching*. Instead of seeing our burnout as raw deals and bum trips, we believed obstacles were opportunities for growth; in our case, monumental growth. I went from no God to looking for God behind every anonymous group I could find him/her/it in. And Cherry? She went from "big-daddy" God . . . (her twenty-year membership in a fanatical fundamentalist Christian church) to looking for God in spaceships and ETs. Egyirba continued to roll and flow in any spiritual stream that she dipped in or was dipped into by living in the world of cyberspace and the World Wide Web.

When we started writing *Tight Spaces* in 1986 we knew we had tapped into the promise of the She-energy. We just didn't know how much we would miss She when the writing ended, nor how She had sustained us through the earlier writing process. With our academic titles and marketable-black-woman confidence, we didn't feel the detachment from the creative collective. Instead we were enchanted by the lure of our individual success personas. That didn't last long. The lumps and bumps of our daily lives and sorted realities raked our bare butts over the coals. We went kicking and screaming into personal work, that introspective and inward glance at our inner lives. This would prove to be real risk-taking, as we examined how we had been ambushed by every past unresolved issue of our lives and now by our present 1990s "crosses to bear."

Cherry, Egyirba, and I, for the last ten years, have been searching for a form, although we didn't know it at the time, toward human wholeness and spiritual consciousness. Although we felt released from some of the tight spaces of our lives created by race, class, gender, and sexuality, we didn't know where we were going. We only knew we had moved away from where we had been ten years before.

Slowly bits and pieces of our personal journeys began to fit into place. Our body parts were first. I do not remember when we realized how necessary it was to take care of our bodies, to nurture ourselves, and to learn how to stay centered. Egyirba experienced these health warnings acutely when she went to Hollywood. She told us about moving to Los Angeles, "where youth is worshiped and everybody despises the 'disorderly' body." She spoke of the pain caused by the belief that every body must have "the look," a look that cultivates a lifestyle of shallowness where total self-absorption becomes an asset. Egyirba's experiences taught us all how deep our personal work must go as she struggled to battle excess pounds both physically and mentally.

Meanwhile, I was practicing my own version of the Marquis de Sade, living in the rural heartland. I felt isolated, going round and round in a binge/purge cycle of family life and work. The noise of it all proved to be deafening; with the exercise of self-flagellation I could not hear my inside screaming for change, and that took me down a deep, dark well. I knew beating myself up was, like the Borg character on *Star Trek* says, futile, but I couldn't stop the black woman macho guilt and my save-the-world sixties-style regimentation.

Cherry, well into an academic run, didn't use her precious time to nurture her precious self. She never cooked a meal at home. She ate greasy soul food late at night and each day looked in the mirror at her graying temples and her growing dowager's hump with terror and dismay. She would turn on Miles Davis and have another rum and coke and reread every book on aliens twice.

Every once in a while, for a few days, Cherry, Egyirba, and I would manage to eat right, sleep right, meditate, and exercise right . . . for weeks, maybe . . . but we always stopped doing the things that felt good, were good. We'd shift in and out of good health and bad health — never shifting long enough to accomplish much improvement. Eventually, we were forced, because of our distrust of traditional medical pill-pushing ways, to try on some of the New Age tools, Twelve Step strategies, and ancient traditions. We were all over the map in our search for a spiritual form that would unlock our stilted muses.

We began with the scallion map, the Ouija board, and the Psychic Circle board. We studied with the Dowsers and Master Mind Circles. We tried Reiki, reevaluation cocounseling, and psychotherapy. Some of this led to exploring channeling, pendulum work, therapeutic touch, yoga, and rejoining our old church groups. We did Tai Chi and acupuncture and took long trips to far and exotic places, learning about the traditions of Candomble, Yorubaland, and Santeria. We used tarot, astrology, numerology, and palmistry to learn lessons from across the veil. We read and reread Kryon, Seth and more Seth, and did the exercises of motivation teachers such as Steven Covey, Tony Robbins, John Grey, Barbara D'Angeles, and Les Brown. We flung ourselves into Native American rituals and sweat lodges, used the Medicine Wheel, and attended an authentic Native American Sun Dance. We watched for ETs, read *The Only Planet of Choice*, and did Quan Yin, Tao, and TM. Eventually, we practiced psychic healing, past life regression, rolfing, and therapeutic massage.

One thing led to the next. We were introduced to the Crystal Skull, Kirlin photography, runes, Starhawk, Wicca, crystals, angels, candles, incense, and aromatherapy. We read about channelers such as Barbara Marciniak, the Pleiades, and Michael as we did Chinese astrology, crystal bowls, Crystal Tibetan balls, and Buddhist chants. About midway through this decade of personal work, we begin to reawaken from our dull dreams and self-induced malaise to feel the joy of L-I-V-I-N-G! We bought hundreds of self-help tapes as we explored Sufism, crop circles, multidimensionality, remote viewing, and the laying on of hands. We enjoyed and laughed as the gurus of the popular media, Deepak Chopra, James Redfield, Marianne Williamson, Susan Powter, Whitley Strieber, John Mack, Nikolai Tesla, Mary Summer Rain, and Oprah Winfrey, gave our personal work a spiritual framework. Our individual shadow sides were exposed and expunged "one day at a time." We were reignited and our personal lightbulbs were going off regularly! We had come to learn the blessed lesson that this moment and this time is all we have. Yesterday is finished. And tomorrow's pains or pleasures are not promised to any of us. We have begun to cherish ourselves, our loved ones, and our time and revere the earth that sustains us all in this present moment. When we could do this individually and collectively, we began to write again.

We believe these last ten years we have been gestating. Cherry, Egyirba, and I have been preparing, like so many writers, to take the next leap of evolutionary human consciousness that will undoubtedly manifest in our work. We do not know all that will come from the leap of humankind toward greater consciousness . . . we do know we can't stop it! We didn't cause it and we know we cannot cure it by going back to living or creating our work as if our energy, inspiration, and power came from us. We now accept the She energy as us permanently!

I began my academic run not by starting at a beginner's pace but as a graduate student. My newly acquired Ph.D. made me a cardholder in a very exclusive, white, old boys-old girls club. In my own way, I was not able to completely give up that straight-edged community tie and agenda for the academic ivory tower. I kept hearing my mother's words in my head . . . "Girl, go get that ed-ju-moo-ka-shon; bring it home and make 'em do right!" It was the making them do right that engulfed my life and my soul these last ten years. Between the phone calls to Cherry and Egyirba, I talked about my academic exploits or what we commonly called doing academic windows in my perspective programs, departments, and institution. I knew I had sat in classes as a student and later taught classes with the best of the best, and I knew I carried a much heavier load as a black woman. The idea of just being a graduate student, just being the new teacher on the block, and just "being" was not as yet part of my consciousness. In my mind and actions I had to do my studies perfectly, challenge the administration politically, and engage crucial campus questions on and off campus, while being a cultural critic about the national conversations that were bludgeoning my colored communities. I felt I had to be a warrior there, too. While I was not writing, as in the voices of *Tight Spaces*, in the early part of the nineties I was using that energy and that absolute conviction of the mother tongue — to make sure not to leave things on the campus as they were.

I was steeped in the acquisition of, at least, the academic understanding of my black feminist revolutionary voice theory and practice. I recognized I was studying a lot of what I had already lived and breathed. I embraced race, class, sexuality, and gender, American and African-American Studies and social movements, and analyses within the postmodernist paradigms with a vengeance. Armed and ready, I brought everything I knew from my Detroit ghetto into the next theoretical questions, the next epistemological questions, and the next methods of studying the lives of American minorities. My graduate classes and later my undergraduate teaching at the University of Iowa and Grinnell College became my experiments in pedagogy. The study of "Others" now emerging inside the classics of American, Women's, and African-American Studies, I treated like Langston Hughes with a six-gun. Langston and I rode into graduate school and the classes I taught, taking no prisoners and seeing revolutionary potential in everything. I drew life from studying the dead revolutionaries of Russia, China, Cuba, Guinea-Bissau, and Mozambique. I used whatever and did whatever it took to move students' minds and hearts in the direction of education for critical consciousness and education for transforming themselves and the world. I took the role on campus of inspiring and leading black women support groups, then organizing community group protest for diversity requirements in public schools and later participating in faculty seminars for expanding the canon and dialogues on multiculturalism. I took B-I-G roles in chairing African-American and American Studies, supporting student protests for curriculum change, participating in the ongoing challenges to genderization of the current curriculum, and stepping out on a limb to teach the first Lesbian Lives course at Grinnell. I was always involved in department searches for new minority faculty (sometimes as the only minority) and minority female faculty. I did library acquisition work for diversity and presidential task forces and continued my involvement in my national professional affiliations in African-American, American, and Women's Studies.

I was very involved in race relations issues in the rural community where I lived. I became a member of the Human Rights Commission for the city of Grinnell and began doing as many as twenty-five local and national Unlearning Racism Workshops, conferences, and keynote speeches a year. I took on these superwoman responsibilities to teach, preach, serve, and write as a requirement for tenure as well as centering my integrity. In the course of the last ten years, I have intellectually had to act out against the dialogues and actions of mismanaged and ill-managed administrative responses to racial incidents on campus, political resistances to whatever-it-takes methods to hire minority faculty, and national conversations to dismantling affirmative action and race-based scholarships. All this while living with the effects of Newt Gingrich's Contract with America as it ambushed the black diaspora and, recently, the academy with the highly publicized works of Alan Bloom and similar authors, and books such as *The Bell Curve* and *The End of Racism*. In doing this political-academic work, I missed my writing! I missed my connection to my creative heart and humor. But I had dreams of someday everyone reading *Tight Spaces* as Terry McMillan's *Waiting to Exhale* is read.

We realize a lot has happened since the first printing of *Tight Spaces* and movies such as *The Color Purple* and *Waiting to Exhale*. Cherry, Egyirba, and I, like the rest of the world, see the images and hear the voices of black women everywhere in pulpits, in classrooms, on convention stages, and in commercial advertisements on TV, radio, and the big screen. We see more of us involved in politics, leading organizations, and writing ourselves into the ongoing changing American cultural landscape. Sisters appear everywhere and are doing everything! We are not as invisible or as bludgeoned as in the previous decade. And with all of the exuberance we get from this, we also know that the quality of our lives as individuals and as part of the female collective is not without froth. We are still served up slight and cynical when people say, "those feminists." You can hear it especially in our community when we say, "we black women" and others believe us to be saying "anti black men" saying we are above men and other women because we are academics. Our black feminist liberation is still in the area of expanding our personal liberty and that of others. Many more of us have liberated our imaginations, and like all oppressed people, we can and must acknowledge our own choices as part of our contribution to the state of overall human emancipation.

We believe that black womanhood has always been revered in our community and continues to be illuminated by the events of this decade. We rolled our eyes, jerked our necks, and did two circles with a snap as we watched Winnie walk hand in hand with Nelson Mandela after his release from prison, we applauded Toni Morrison when she received a Nobel Prize for Literature, and we listened to Maya Angelou's poem during the Clinton presidential inauguration. We black women embraced many aspects of the Million Men and Women marches. Simultaneously, we attended to our private wounds as we had to "duck and dodge" and redefend our honor and integrity against the 1990's new media blitz against us. Somehow, in an updated Daniel Moynihan–like style, the media manages to continue to blame, to hold us at fault for gender and class tensions in our communities, and sees us as the responsible party in the legal cases of Clarence Thomas, Mike Tyson, Rodney King, and O. J. Simpson.

In the 1990s, we exist under new emotional, cultural, and economic glass ceilings. We look up and can't get out. We see the hoax perpetrated on us by those who say, "We love and need you but you're too serious, too politically correct, too strong, too educated, too demanding emotionally, too sexy, too loved by so many, and too too everything else that makes everybody uncomfortable." Alas, the bitter tongue and bloody lash of those we sleep with, pay our taxes, tuck into bed, defend at school, and work for have disappointed us consciously and unconsciously so we are forced again, like all "wild noncultured animals," to do something new. So Cherry, Egyirba, and I have begun to let go of pushing and maintaining others. We have learned that this does not mean we abandon anybody but that we give everybody time to find their own voices and energy as we have learned to use our own.

Now we know this is not a novel concept: to take care of ourselves and let others take care of themselves. We believe we all play a role in our collective emancipation. But it is a novel concept to us: three women, a decade ago, who risked airing our dirty laundry, who did academic windows, who became emotionally black bionic women, and who have been the supertits of the globe.

It is from letting go our compulsive need to be needed by our race, our sisterhood, and the people that we began to grow as individuals — not without difficulties — but as individuals whose resolved issues make us better able to give what we want and not what is demanded. In this new edition of *Tight Spaces* we are launching a few new pieces. Following our innovative writing tradition of collective and serial autobiography, biography, and as our friend Peter Thornton says, auto-fic-tog-raphy, we started creating a new set of stories detailing our lives outside the cages of our previous tight cultural spaces and our present spiritual births through personal work. We offer you our new processes, new understandings, and new directions. We have learned and lived each day in revolutionary personhood in the 1990s, and we hope our new works resonate with you and the prophetic voices in our stories ring similar bells for you that were rung for us.

Why should people buy and read an eleven-year-old book? *Tight Spaces* is an American, woman's, and African-American Studies classic because it is a text that blends genres and is interdisciplinary and multicultural by race, class, gender, and sexuality standards. For students of American autobiography, I believe it contemporizes the testimonials and protests of black women's survival and their contributions to literature and history. *Tight Spaces* is a fiction and nonfiction of postmodern America as it chronicles the continued shifting cultural landscapes of American capitalism, the American family, and the American political system. This book was innovative because it expanded the tradition of serial, black, and women's autobiography in its triauthorship with the use of prose, poems, the ever-popular laundry list, songs, biography, and fictionalized stories. I know we did not have a format when we started because we began estranged from each other as family members and friends. Within months of the writing process, "that book" had brought us together emotionally and artistically as a writing circle committed and dependent on a literary muse we called the She energy. It was from this energy and creative thinking that we gathered the spiritual authority to be critical of ourselves and society by using our many voices from our gender, class, race, and sexuality standpoints. I remind myself that we were all students when we wrote *Tight Spaces*. Cherry was completing a B.A., Egyirba an M.A., and I was in a Ph.D. program. As the book was becoming a reality, we garnered more support from diverse departments, the administration, and overlapping minority and majority communities. And to top it off, we were encouraged by our community while winning the 1988 American Book Award for its innovative style. Such a treat!

What did the book do for our lives then and now and in what context do we want people to read the book now? Personally, *Tight Spaces* validated my ability and talent to do creative writing and expanded my personal and spiritual consciousness. Foremost, writing the book brought me closer to my girlfriends and my entire family, for we were forced to talk honestly and to speak of our family secrets. Many of the awards I won from the book helped me attain other book contracts in addition to strengthening my skills as a professional speaker and performer. The success of *Tight Spaces* created an audience for my co-authors and me in the circles of public intellectuals and among the creative scholars of our day. I hope that people will embrace *Tight Spaces* today as an experiment of literature that underpins social problems and questions of the twenty-first century: identity, power, and cultural awareness. I believe the book asks us to examine our personal cultural baggage — to take social responsibility for playing a role in the evolution of our institutions and consciousness as we examine our human problems, human solutions, and human spiritual evolution.

We invite you to enter our new world of free-floating living, as individuals into worlds of personal responsibility, self-care, and diversity of intimacies. We do not take our words to the altar or speak them as the only gospel. We know our account of our lives will continue to evolve. Our hope is to live even more fully and to share a few of our spiritual lessons in our next book. We make the same B-I-G promise as before to talk real honest and hold nothing back — as we show how each story reflects a spiritual principle that we now live our collective and individual lives by. Thank you for being part of our living process and patiently awaiting our next journey.

IT BEEZ THAT AWAY
SOMETIMES

. . . .

CHERRY MUHANJI

hen John Coltrane's *My Favorite Things* entered the world in the early sixties I was a wife, mother, daughter, and sister — all the favorite things of the patriarchy. The intersection of his music with those roles became "when and where I (could) enter" creative space. I realized I hadda place. How and by what means would I get there?

In retrospect the persistent roaring of my husband, "git that shit offa the record player," still surprises me. How could he as a musician and a male with all the credentials that that offered him not hear what Coltrane was "saying" while I could? *My Favorite Things* put a crack in patriarchal space and I could feel that freedom comin' on down the line — just like the old spiritual reminds us, "it won't be long now." I was wrong. It would take years for me to consciously discern what

'Trane's invitation was all about. And, what it would cost me. His music would become the central metaphor for my dissertation, but that really is getting ahead of this story.

I entered college at forty-six in 1985. And, oh, it was wonderful! Time. Not the tick of an alarm clock (for I never allow a sound like that in my ear), but time that didn't demand, whip, or otherwise abuse. Not time filled with guilt like I'm not giving the kids enough attention, or my parents, or my God. But time that allows, time for me. Ropes and ropes of it — wrapping around me like the chain of soapsuds that slides down between my thighs as I squeal in delight, that I wrote about in "Bird Tracks" in *Tight Spaces*. Time, time for me. *You can't mean all I have to do is write papers and show up for classes — not punch a clock and work a ten- to twelve-hour day? You gotta be kiddin'*. I am, as the poet says, nearer heaven. Time, then, becomes a perfumed woman who, in passing, fills your nostrils with the scent of her, and you, despite yourself begin to fantasize about what you hope will become a long, long love affair. Of course, that metaphor is overly clever — more, perhaps, overly dramatic — it makes a point, but more than that is revealing.

For me the sounds of Coltrane produce an image of the Sankofa, an African bird whose body is facing one way while its head faces another. It is also an Akan word meaning "one must return to the past to move forward." But for now other things began to happen. I'm in a magic place at the University of Iowa. I've got the keys to the kingdom and I fully intend to use them.

Initially I move my mind and beautiful pictures pop in — content to stay as long as I like. I move my fingers and beautiful words happen on paper. I move my jaw muscles in class, not sure of this place yet, but soon I star. I am like Data from *Star Trek: The Next Generation*, the Tin Man from *The Wizard of Oz*— a robot trying out her parts. Everything works! "Testament," a poem, gets published in my first semester. I would be published again, several years later, along with my coauthors in 1987. We would win a Before Columbus American Book Award in 1988, and the last chapter of *Tight Spaces* would become, more or less, the first chapter of my novel, *Her*, published in 1990. It would win a Lambda Award for new lesbian fiction and a Ferro-Grumly Award — high drama that left me giddy.

I assure myself that the caves in my dreams mean nothing, where I'm trapped because an avalanche of rocks has blocked the exit and where the air is growing thin. On waking I am gasping for breath, and move through the day after one of *those* nights with what I'm calling "dream hangover," because I can't sober up — so to speak. Psychological stuff best left in the dark. And, I do.

In the meantime sparks of academic language descend on me — expanding my world, but uprooting the beautiful pictures I'm used to. Coltrane's sounds, which always produce the image of the Sankofa, are usurped for this new language that I'm learning. I won't let my dreams of the Sankofa tell me that something is wrong with this New World order, however.

Does something need to die "so something else lives?" Kesho asks in one of her stories in *Tight Spaces*. I was living, but not in those nights, where even the presence of my lover palls, with all the wonder of my first real awakening to the love between women. I am lonely. And I don't know why.

Tight Spaces and *Her* reveal a certain tension in my life. A raw unexamined beauty and a deep well of anxiety that let me scream, poetically. All the parts of me were speaking now, for as I said before I had fallen in love with a woman and from the scent of that I imagined myself whole.

I dutifully enter the master's program in African-American World Studies with two books and a host of readings and public appearances, and something was still dying, and the Sankofa is only appearing at night, and *not* every night and so I move on.

Aware that my life had been much like a fictional character I created in *Tight Spaces*, Miss Russell. She was a bag lady, if you remember, who collected Coke bottles with the fragile green tint. In fact, the first cover of *Tight Spaces* has a Coke bottle sitting in a window from that story. Several things happened to suggest that that story was more about something that was going to happen to me but, as of that writing, had not. For now I was becoming more than I had ever imagined, as unprepared as I was for entering classrooms for the first time where the TAs were younger than my children!

I was lucky, though. I managed, as I do most times, to get the best from any situation. (My son, the astrologer, says it's my Leo moon — that my emotional makeup expects the best.) Getting a radical feminist with just the right amount of white guilt, who saw and encouraged me, came as no real surprise. In fact, as mentioned I published a poem in that class, which won second place in a poetry contest. I fell deeply in love, the first time since my youth. My language changed — slowly at first — movin' on up, as we said in my community — less metaphor would be my guess — certainly more academic. Racial Ox!!Oxx——— gave way to simultaneous oppressions as I learn to articulate what's wrong with America, in a hundred different ways. I hang with the big girls, what's more I understand them! I can theorize, hypothesize, and scandalize in what seems to be a foreign tongue at times, and I am an out lesbian grandmother to my students. Which works! It's in the classroom where I excel, where I discover my power, but feel my students' pain. And that's all too familiar. The pinch, the pain, the Sankofa? Of my night visions? All keep returning, even as my lover does not.

My students sit in classes that so many of them are unaware of how those courses even got there. Where is the continuity? Classes that are the result of battles long fought to ensure they have Black Studies, Women's Studies, Les/Bi/Gay/Transgender/Transsexual Studies, but the struggle is different, or has it only changed so that things can stay the same? They are victims, consumer addicts as most of us are. Our flesh decomposing — skeletons of capitalism and appropriation as colleges unveil their real agenda — no different from corporate America. Students are paying whooping amounts of money, as I am, to receive a product, not unlike the latest Michael Jordan Nikes, or Michael Jordan jackets, or Michael Jordan movies. Anything that we can buy.

I move through the master's program visiting Cuba, China, Japan, and Vermont. I teach everywhere, racism — or more correctly said, Interlocking oppressions workshops. I'm hot, I'm hip, and I'm into the Ph.D. program. Audre Lorde is dead, so are Barbara Jordan and Pat Parker, and I haven't written a creative line in years. Well, perhaps, that's not altogether true. I engineer a creative dissertation, a novel, *Momma Played 1st Chair*— a clever title that came to me in one of the few magic moments I have left. But the real magic, that first magic, the one where all things are possible so they happen, has gone, and I know it. My night visions are gin-soaked, so to speak, in academe, and I know why I'm lonely.

Always there had been this voice, an ancestor? that gave me comfort. She helped me in all those years of *no* voice. It was She that I heard in the night as I made my way through the mine field of kids' toys, shoes, hanging up their clothes — finally picking through yesterday's newspapers to prime the pump for worlds and words to write a series of night poems. Sometimes She spoke between diaper changes and expected a poem right then and there. Now I smile when I think how I had to negotiate between a tub full of dirty diapers and rhyming couplets. She especially liked to take long bus rides where *lived* life is constantly passing by, or sit in the kitchen with me late at night trying to convince me that my life was passing by. *Get busy, girl— time to do your stuff,* She'd whisper through the night poems.

The first blush — in school, finally, at forty-six, is gone, I am unable to publish, most of what I write is theory, and the voice I do have sounds like a recording. I'm successful. Fat. The lean student days are over. I smile. I curtsy. I shuffle from school to school trying to find a job. Ever see a Ph.D. do the hustle?

But then — I feel shame. I have gotten my degrees at the cost of many. I feel shame. Alice Walker's "In Search of Our Mothers' Gardens" article makes me feel shame. *Women, so trapped in an evil honey,* I feel shame that *they moved to a rhythm that they themselves knew was not for them in their lifetimes.* I feel shame. I am part of that rhythm. I am their dream. I feel shame.

The Scriptures tell us that when one demon leaves a room, so to speak, it is important to fill it with something because seven demons will enter the void. The piece, this one — the one I am writing after so many drafts feels — can I believe that the Sankofa is returning? Not in the dream, but in my life. Let's hope.

My next piece of work, I am convinced, will be about a young woman's long sojourn as one of Jehovah's Witnesses, and for that young woman it may be the greatest story ever told. Watch for it on your newsstands!

WHY I DIDN'T DO IT AND HOW I FINALLY DID

. . . .

EGYIRBA HIGH

n some ways, writing the stories that became a part of *Tight Spaces* was a fait accompli for me. Though my love of words began early (I was reciting poetry at two and reading at three, my mother tells me), getting to the place where I could have my writing validated in print and receive public recognition and honor still surprised me. Inspired by the work of Laura Ingalls Wilder, I began writing very interesting short stories when I was nine years old and wrote with the dedication of a career writer, but that lasted only about two or three years. Eventually, I was encouraged to focus on getting an education, where *real* opportunity lay for black folk. After all, you had to be "really good to make it as a writer," my mother reminded me often, and the what-was-being-said-that-wasn't-being-said among other things was, clearly, that I was not. Besides it was the very early sixties, when

the opportunities for black folk seemed so much more attainable than anything my parents had experienced or, perhaps, even dreamed of (though secretly they always prayed it was really possible). The legacies of Booker T. Washington and W. E. B. Du Bois inspired legions of people of my grandparents' and parents' generations and encouraged them to value and seek out learning and training that would serve them in their lives. It was the assured path of success for themselves, their progeny — for the Race.

The realities of post-Reconstruction American life could not dampen their dreams, even if it did leave them disheartened at the hostility and hatred they would still meet along the way. But this only served to remind them about the dangers of placing their faiths in anything other than God. As strong believers and with a strong inner knowledge that they would eventually succeed, they nursed their dreams, all the while pushing their children toward the road that would lead to freedom in a concrete way. Salvation lay in education. My mother, the only one of sixteen siblings with a college education, that blessing having been made possible by the material and cultural success of her brother, former boxing heavyweight champion of the world, Joe Louis, impressed this idea upon me with such diligence and persistence that I still carry. Being a writer had no real value, no ultimate significance in a world where so much was at stake. And so, like the other God-given gifts with which I was born, I pushed my artistic aspirations aside and began a search to figure out just what I was meant to do.

In my pursuit of a bachelor's degree, I tried to find a form for the writing I had abandoned in my earlier years. Those days I turned out poems when I could find the time between classes and my first foray into real adult living. I found my inspiration in heartbreak and broken romances from a marriage that started too soon and ended even sooner, to all the subsequent liaisons I entered into every time I mistook kindness for integrity and sincerity. Still, the poetry was not enough, and I could not say exactly what I felt or meant. When I found my way back to the prose format in later years it would be the beginning of a new life, and a deeper experience of myself.

The opportunity to have the time to actually write *Tight Spaces* came in the guise of my entry into graduate school. I could leave the real world of nine to five and relax from the worries and frustrations of daily survival. Now I could hobnob with other intellectuals and stimulate my mind as I explored the really important questions of life and discover this new privileged world. I could take a little "down-time" and bathe in the feeling of freedom from real responsibility. Wowwee! It was just what I needed. Or, so it seemed.

When I began to take my education seriously a lot of things happened, not the least of which was an end to the reacquaintance with my creative flow that had begun with *Tight Spaces*. The same inner critic who had come to find a useful outlet and rightful place in analysis and critique was now honing in on my creative territory. Try as I might, I could not quell the voice that continually broadcast, "'you ain't good enough' propaganda twenty-four hours a day," as Kesho said of me in her story "The Scales of Superman." It was the internal voice of my mother and the voice of the father/academe allied now with the purpose of reminding me that I should refrain from thinking too much of myself. The more I immersed myself in theoretical relationships with Benjamin, Adorno, Derrida, Foucault, Butler, hooks, Carby, Henderson, Gates, West, and any number of other intellectuals, the less I could relate to my creative voice or validate its impulses. Like a spurned lover, it retreated to some secret dimension of my psyche and any intermittent efforts to turn a lyrical phrase or two only resulted in many pages of white space stippled with a sentence here, or a paragraph there, and sometimes, in rare moments, a few pages.

To salt the wound of discouragement I was nursing, I was now feeling dispirited about my academic pursuits. I knew I was very smart but the act of enduring what seemed a dehumanizing process, a kind of academic hazing that is often the graduate student's lot, plus the sense of having no real support or mentoring (a common situation for African-American students in predominantly white colleges and universities), left me feeling inadequate and many times downright dumb. Although I tried to make sense of what was happening in between reading, researching, parenting, and seeing a therapist, my confidence in myself and my abilities began to dwindle. There was little humor in me and even less comfort from my nesting creative voice. With all but the dissertation completed in my doctoral program, I left the safety and warm comfort of Iowa City and a sense of camaraderie with other graduate students undergoing their own personal hells, and accepted a real job back in the real world, this time to become that which I was ostensibly seeking to become: a working scholar.

If I thought a change of locale and daily routine would stimulate my creative drive, it was an utterly naive notion. I found myself thrust into a new kind of madness. My initial feeling of elation at proving myself competent after all (and being paid for it) started to subside after my second year of teaching full time, advising students, fulfilling college service duties, and working on my dissertation. It took another year of teaching before I began to see that I was approaching this thing the wrong way. I didn't know why I was doing what I was doing except that a lifelong subliminal message about the importance and necessity of "getting an education" had seduced me into borrowing a life that was not mine. Though teaching is a gift, I did not know that it was part of my legacy because I was meant (in a divine sort of way) to do it. Rather, in my search to know my authentic self, hear my authentic voice, I waited for the validation of external voices because I did not know the sound of my own.

What it took was falling in love. First with a man, then with God. At the sound of a new melodic strain playing in me for the first time in those many years, my long-buried creative drive began to show its face to me again. In the letters between lovers, in between the lines of passion, I took delight in my own renewed abilities to get to the heart of a situation in words. It seemed the more I opened up, let go, the easier it was. "What an interesting prospect," I thought while I kept writing. "Look at me." Finally, as I begin my forty-fifth year, I have begun to distinguish the other voices from my own. This simple act, this recognition seemed to be the spark I needed to use writing in a new and different way. There are many stories waiting to be told through me. But more than that for me it was the reacquaintance with an old cherished friend that warmed my heart and forgave me my neglect. Coming out of the fire of human love and into the wide enfolding arms of the Deep Love as I walk my mystical spiritual path will bring new expressions of healing, hope, and peace. This writing can save me, those who come into contact with me, and the Race, I am whispering to those ancestors. There is a usefulness in it, a practical advantage even if not easily seen. I am poised and centered in myself and ready to explore new literary and spiritual horizons.

And so I will.

....

TALKIN' REAL HONEST

TAKE A LOOK OVER MY SHOULDER AND BE HAPPY

KESHO SCOTT

 could tell it was early in the morning because the birds were singing. The birds' chirping always gave me a feeling of peace. Being from Detroit and living on the main drag has a way of drowning out the little nature one gets. As usual, I was glassy-eyed and waiting for the door to slam as my father went off to work. About an hour would pass between the birds' singing, my silence in bed, and the rambling around the house of my parents. Their dead silence during the morning inspired me (mostly out of fear) to amuse myself. I'd imagine the hour full of adventures: Disneyland and Belle Isle Park; talking to Count Dracula; birthday parties with Moe, Larry, and Curly; diving with Tarzan; taking Cheetah to school for show and tell; telling everyone Marilyn Monroe was my auntie; crying for John Wayne to rescue me; having a year's supply of Big D chips and Pepsi;

or living with Grandma, whose house had two hundred sweet potato pies, rice pudding cups, miles of backyard grapevines, and Lilly toilet water from a "real" Chinese princess.

But this morning was different and special. Today I was seven years old. My mama had planned a surprise for me all week. Between her ironing she'd say, "It's gonna be a special day on Wednesday, Evie"; or after Sunday's routine of going to church, followed by the movies for thirty-five cents, she'd say, "Evie, Mama's got a secret for you." Mama was always on edge, and everything special between us always had to be made a secret. I didn't mind. We had lots of secrets, including the way she'd keep secrets from other people for me when I'd eat up all the cookies or when I acted up in school.

The biggest secret was when I had to live with Aunt Bernice for a year, and Mama would visit. I'd tell her how Aunt Bernice cooked eggs in butter, and she'd tell me when I could come back home. We'd swear not to mention our secrets, and she'd leave me holding a teary-eyed big, big one. My tears would subside, and I'd act up again in school to assure another visit from Mama.

The night before my birthday there had been another fight. I never knew over what. It seemed Mama had done something wrong. What could she have done wrong? All she did was take care of me and John. Daddy would go on a rampage about nothing, like not being able to find something or not liking the dinner or why my mother would not force us to eat rice or Mama being on the phone or her wanting to finish high school. Once I remember him tearing up the whole house because he couldn't find an ink pen. See, it was, I guess, Mama's job to make sure Daddy had no problems at home. I think Daddy had problems everywhere.

He was also real smart. I used to brag about him, because he bought us a real washer and dryer, went to the Ford Motor Company night school, and fixed TVs in the basement. When I told my friends Buchie, Pompo, Glo-jean, Pee-Wee, Wickie, Little Bit, and especially Rudy, of the Rudy Esco gang, that my daddy had a airplane "real people" could fly in, Rudy let me carry his knife. But I stayed away from Daddy. We all did. I knew it wasn't that easy for Mama, because she had to talk to the man, sleep with him, and get beat at night. At night, I'd hear the arguments mounting, then the punches and the crying. By morning, and with the peace of the birds, Mama'd bounce back into the routine of the silent hour until the door ushered Daddy out.

The door slammed. I rolled out of bed and headed for the dining room table. We had a dining room with a big closet I used to hide in. I was a hiding specialist. We also had roaches, very little grass out front, and beige painted walls. We could look from the living room through the dining room to the kitchen and then to the kitchen nook. The nook later became my bedroom, where I'd sneak and watch TV all night. When I heard someone coming, I'd jump back into bed and pretend I was asleep. I almost never got caught. Except the time my cat kept hissing at me from the floor. He thought I was playing. So, I zipped him up in the red suitcase that was under my bed. The next morning I found him dead. I gave him the biggest kitty funeral the neighborhood had ever seen. After that, I hated cats.

What a glimpse we had from the living room. Our living had two faces: the dining room was the fantasy, as my parents entertained and toasted their friends and put away pretty dishes in the buffet cabinet; the kitchen was the work and pain place. Mama's tears and shrieks dominated. She worked there, and she got beat there. The nook is where we put the family toys: camping equipment, pastel plastic front porch chairs, and endless boxes of card games, all bought from J. L. Hudson's department store. My parents acted like they knew J. L. personally. We lived in "the house that Jack built," sang Aretha Franklin, and it was like a peanut butter sandwich with no jelly.

"Evie," Mama said from the kitchen, "are you awake?"

"Yes," I said. She asked me if I knew what day it was. Mama always took to asking me dumb questions. How could she spend Daddy's money so well, save a little change on the side for her sanitary napkins and a special gift for me, and ask such dumb questions? I played seven and said no, so she'd think I had forgotten. She said, "It's your birthday, and I have a big surprise for you." She ran off to hunt for my gift. I sat there in the dining room in the dull morning light, hungry and happy. My mother was second only to Grandma Annie in making my life a bowl of cherries suspended in cold ice cream. And I felt suspended and cold. The seconds ticked, as I heard her shuffle around in her closet. She reappeared with a big red package that had a choo-choo train bow ribbon on it. The happy birthday paper was full of teddy bears, and I held my first real birthday card.

I knew this gift was the special way my mama loved me. Mama was twenty-three. She didn't have a "real" job. If she had been paid $2.00 for the beatings and $1.50 for ignoring my father, I knew she had earned a lot of money and spent it on her own wish — me! I remember once asking her, "Mama, what did you want to be when you grew up?" She said, "I always wanted to have three kids like you." I thought, yeah, my mama is a real dummy. From that day on, I started dreaming of being a doctor to "really" help people. I knew my mama was trying to make it. "She pissed in the ocean every day," Grandma used to say, and it made a big difference in my life. Mama's dare was from her mama, who had also dared any man to dump on her. They were only sixteen years apart, and when Mama's mama got a divorce and went back to school, she started cooking all her food in wine sauce.

I opened the card and read what it said out loud, to impress my mama. We smiled together. She had a way of hugging me, burying my face in her little breast like she wished I'd been born in another place and time. I cared less as she brought me one Hostess Twinkie with a candle. The room lit up. I smiled. Mama and I sang happy birthday in a whisper-tone together. I blew the candle out and attacked the gift. Mama gave a big sigh, relieved to have pulled off the eleventh wonder of the world. My seven years was her statement too. For one moment, I thought I heard my brother wake up, but Mama had thought of everything — she had shut his door earlier.

I unwrapped the gift, swearing to myself to save the paper even till I entered the gates of heaven. Like all well-designed surprises, the white tissue paper restacked my nervousness. The suspense in my face was my mother's delight. Mama had so many ways of spending a dollar. I knew she had probably hawked the gift before it had been marked down for the fifth time. I knew her flair was special by the way she'd chosen purple tights with black and white saddle oxfords for school.

I must admit my dress in school was peculiar. It seemed my mother's dressing made all the kids laugh. I wanted to be like every other black girl striving to be cute and have Miss Shinkle, the over-perfumed white lady from Texas, like me best. I wanted her to choose my papers and read them aloud to the class. She said she was doing her civic duty to bring some correct teaching to us. But she didn't like me. I wanted her to like me. And Mama's taste in clothing didn't exactly help.

I lifted the last layer of white tissue and gasped at the dress Mama had bought. It was normal! Even Miss Shinkle would like it! What possessed Mama to buy it for me? I started to cry not because I was feeling happy, but because I was confused. Daddy didn't give Mama the money to buy this dress. He'd ask her where she got it. He not only distrusted her because she was so beautiful, but she often made him look silly and selfish. He might hurt her, I thought. This dress was gonna cause a mess. My dumb mother, I thought again, was really dumb.

Mama just ignored the thought she could read on my face. She hugged me as if she believed my crying was because I was so happy. I got angry now. I hated it when she started acting like Maureen O'Sullivan waiting for Tarzan to beat off the natives and save her. My mother watched TV too! Mama seemed like two people to me. She was a realist and an unrealist. I continued to cry.

She unbuttoned my pajamas and helped me try on the dress. It was checkered red and white at the top and had a blue skirt bottom. It was held together by a black patent leather belt. I was going to be big stuff come 8:30 A.M. I would be wearing a shiny, patent leather belt! The dress had a red heart-shaped pocket on the skirt to put special things like gum, dimes, and love notes in, all the things not permitted in the second grade. The buttons were hearts too! Four of them! I knew Mama's choosing this dress was her special way to let me look like the other girls. All the other girls had heart buttons and stayed up late with their mamas to watch *The Last of the Mohicans*, *Twilight Zone*, and *How to Marry a Millionaire*.

I quietly tiptoed to the bathroom and climbed on the tub to see myself in the mirror. I started to cry again as I stuffed the Twinkie down my throat. Mama warned me not to get crumbs on my dress. I was frightened when she said that! I thought it was a threat that she was gonna take my dress back. The red glow from the dress matched my red tearful eyes.

Had this just been a fantasy? Was Mama just pretending to give me the dress? Was she gonna take it back before Daddy got home? Was my Mama really a chicken? Was it true after all, what the kids said about her in the capping games we played at church, that she was black and skinny and dumb and lazy and scared of whitey? I cried more. I was now doubly confused.

When I came out of the bathroom, Mama told me to take off the dress and put it back on the table. Then I knew my fear was real. Hate began to well up from my feet, the way Mr. Dawson's dog growls over the fence. I stood stiff. I put the dress back on the table as Mama made some dumb remarks about not being late for school, lunch money, and going to Grandma's on Saturday. I felt the magic of the morning leave. I didn't hear the birds. Everything seemed black, and the bleached beige walls stood out like when marshmallows melt into fudge.

Mama reappeared with scissors. I closed my eyes. Seeing darkness. I thought of Stevie Wonder when he used to live across the street from Grandma. I wanted to be like Stevie Wonder. Blind. I wanted Annie. I wanted to be in her house that was at the end of the old brick-laid street where the kids stole tires from the old trains and Grandma Annie hugged me tight.

"Grandma, where are you? She's stealing my dress!" Grandma could make my mama come to her senses, couldn't she? Or if all she could do was whistle "Old Rugged Cross" in her dimly lit kitchen with all the newspapers on the floor, preserve pears from her yard trees, say "hi" to the mailman who brought her bills for Montgomery Wards Department Store, I still wanted Grandma!

"Evie, you better wash up and get your dress on, or you'll be late for school." Every syllable of the sentence stood out like folks talk in the South. My eyes rewatered, and my mother looked annoyed as she often did when I was daydreaming or hiding in the closet or writing hate words under the chairs of the dining room table. I ran and hugged her.

"Of course," Mama said, "I'll deal with your Daddy about this." And I knew she would. Now, I understood it all. She was going to finally deal with Daddy on her new terms.

Mama spiffied up my hair with two ponytails like Elizabeth Taylor wore in *National Velvet*, and I ran off to school in my dress with my mother's fate to protect. I pranced around all day.

I really felt good when crinkle-faced Miss Shinkle said, "Yvonne Marie Scott, that is a pretty dress. Isn't it, children?" I ate lunch with class, just like Mimi (my mama's mother) taught me. I spilled no crumbs, no juice, no sauce anywhere. I wiped my mouth as if using a cloth table napkin from a Shirley Temple movie, then excused myself from Brady Elementary School cafeteria.

Recess on the playground was all of a sudden beneath me. Debbie Tripplet, my best friend, followed me around not sure if I had flipped out. She always thought we niggers on McQuade Street were a little crazy. I remember using proper English that day. Mimi had popped me upside my head enough for those "dems" and "dats" and would say, "A lady pro-nounces her words carefully." I was going to be a lady that day, come hell or high water.

Walking home by the candy store, I even offered my brother two cents for an apple wine candy. I wanted to be a gracious lady as well. He accepted the two cents, and the bulge in his cheek made him think I was really crazy. This day my brother's actions didn't bother me. He could have torn up my Barbie doll, used my cat-eye jumbo marbles, or pissed in my bed and I wouldn't have cared — he noticed my dress and said it was the prettiest he'd ever seen. My brother, John, never lied, because he started reading the World Book Encyclopedia at four and knew everything. Even my dumb mother used to ask him for advice.

When I got home, Mama was settling into her tension. Daddy was coming home by 4:30. She had one hour. I thought of putting a butcher knife in my heart-shaped pocket. Mama began to get nervous. When she was nervous she'd do housework. She was really nervous now! I wondered why she didn't get Mr. Dawson, our neighbor who knew of the beatings, to come over and protect her. Mama was so unrealistic compared to the Bette Davis she loved. I knew Bette Davis wouldn't take no shit! I thought about calling Annie because she was Daddy's mother, and maybe she could make him be nice. But I didn't know Grandma's phone number. My brother would be no help. He'd hide behind the encyclopedia telling us the secrets of the lost world of Atlantis, why Rommel's army failed, about the Christian Crusades, Jewish intellectualism, or his toy G.I. Joe soldiers. He knew best how to keep himself busy.

But Mama and I were defenseless, and Daddy was gonna crucify us. We would make him mad with that dress! I ran to hug Mama as she started to set up the ironing board and watch a Count Dracula movie with John and me. She knew that with that hug I was getting into grown folks' business. It was between her and Daddy. She pushed me away saying, "Go get a snack. Dinner will be late." She was so unrealistic! I hated her. How could she talk of dinner? Snacks? Daddy was coming in ten minutes. I couldn't eat cookies!

I remember the time Daddy beat me with an ironing cord because I ate a mayonnaise sandwich without asking him. He used the excuse of permission, but really he was pissed because I enjoyed the sandwich without the bologna. Or the time he criticized me for sharing my popcorn with Glo-jean. He said her sleazy, fat mama was too lazy to get her some, and I shouldn't do her mama's work. He didn't know I really wanted to ride her wagon.

Mama offered me more food, which made me sick. I wanted her to put on Ray Charles's record "A Change Is Gonna Come." I wanted to run. I wanted Count Dracula to turn into a bat and bite my Daddy as he entered the hall of the house. Finally, I sat down. My mouth was as dry as eating a peanut butter sandwich in June. I smacked my jaws like a cow, trying to make up some saliva.

Three minutes to go! Mama closed the living room drapes, and my heart stopped. And here we all were, waiting to go mad. Or already acting mad. I was too mad to sit! I was mad enough to piss on myself! I felt mad watching my brother slowly turn the pages of volume J-K-L, and Mama was driving me the most mad! She kept furiously spraying spray-starch to Daddy's shirts. I wished it was a gun she sprayed. She was driving me mad with her ironing.

The door opened. It was Daddy. Mama glanced up only a moment, but long enough to take his eyes to my dress and back to her ironing. He stood still and stared at this room of people he didn't know, but whom he was loyal to. Daddy heard no birds singing. He had never heard the birds. He only noticed us waiting on his next move. He said all he could say as a man who had problems everywhere. He said, "Hi!"

Daddy didn't even notice my dress.

THE SECRET

EGYIRBA HIGH

ey, Yvonne . . . do you remember . . . one time you came to spend the night at my house and wouldn't tell me what you had inside your travel case?"

"What you talking about?"

"Girl, you remember. About ten years ago . . . we were fourteen. We were doing our thang. You know, talkin' about boys, puttin' on makeup, and fixin' our hair — like we was going somewhere. You even did mine in a 'Gibson Girl.' Remember?"

"Uhn-uhn."

"Yes you do, just think! Want some more tea?"

"Okay."

I went to the kitchen to boil some more water. As far as I was concerned, she didn't want to remember. But I did. . . .

"Why you locking the case, Evie?"

"It's personal."

"Come on, why you locking it — I mean, what's in it?" I kept my eye on the little brass key shining in her hand. All the times I had seen this case, it never occurred to me there was a key. I really wasn't in the mood for games, especially "Let's make Michelle beg."

"I told you. It's personal."

This time she said it with emphasis. "Some things you just have to keep to yourself as you become a woman, Michelle."

My ears perked up as the game got under way. We were, after all, the same age. Was she trying to say that I wasn't becoming a woman?

"Evie, I . . ."

"No, I can't tell you."

I studied the travel case carefully for some revelation. Yes, it was the same case she always brought to my house. It was suitcase blue — the shade all Samsonite luggage came in, in the sixties.

The sixties. I was a flower child then. I painted colored flowers on my face, decked my body with beads, and chanted love and peace songs. I even snuck down to Plum Street. Plum Street was hippie haven. I was amazed by the little shops that stretched out a mile in each direction. It was a different world to me. The little boutiques, and the people who shopped in them, stood out colorfully. Plunked down in the center of the black Detroit ghetto, a collection of mostly white, strange-looking young people wove in and out daily an overall patchwork effect on the locale.

"You know them crackers is crazy."

"Yeah — dig it."

This was the signature feeling of the black folks for whom a passing fancy was no option.

The shops' way-out, long-haired, blue-jeaned owners displayed marijuana papers, roach clips, and water pipes. Decaled peace symbols on doors invited you into taste the new feeling. The walls were decorated with posters of Jimi Hendrix, Janis Joplin, and "Make Love, Not War" bumper stickers. I remember the time and place and that shade of blue.

My eye caught a glimpse of the blue travel case again. It was the kind airline stewardesses carried. At least on TV. I had never seen any girl I knew with one. Ever. How could she afford one, anyway? It was only her and her mama at home. If anyone should've had one, it was me. But as it was, my clothes would be packed along with everybody else's in one of those giant monsters only Daddy could carry.

Evie's case was special. I always wanted one because it was just the right size for carrying things like my pink sponge curlers and Richie Rich comic books. It had a mirror glued in the lid, and the mirror was shaped like a long diamond. It was really pretty. The locked case hid all that now.

Evie sat the travel case in the corner of my room. She was running her mouth about her boyfriend, Larry. I didn't care to listen. The secret case called me. My imagination stirred up pictures of love potions, spell-breakers, and hex kits.

". . . I just told him I wasn't gonna take no more stuff from him, so he left in a huff. There's more fish in the sea, anyway."

I looked at my best friend. She tilted her head and pointed her finger as she talked. It was sort of like Miss Burgess, my ninth-grade algebra teacher, threatening us with a math test if we didn't stop talking. No . . . I had never noticed that about Evie. She did look older.

And Evie had nerve. She probably already knew a lot about how boys did it. I mean, how they really did it. I never thought to ask her. I had seen her twirl Larry around her fingers. She knew some things I didn't. Yeah, maybe she was right.

Then I remembered the little blue case again and how we shared all our secrets. What was going on? Did she find someone else to be best friends with? She would've needed to drop a clue, or was this the clue? What had I done wrong? The thought was awesome. I didn't want to think about it. We were blood sisters. Was she forgetting the bond we made as we swore to be loyal forever? She held the razor blade that day.

"Ow, that hurts!"

"You better gimme back your hand, girl. This the only way we can make it real."

I had a lot invested.

I followed her everywhere. Monkey see, monkey do. I was her number one fan. And she didn't even have a daddy at home. It didn't seem like she was going to be a thief or end up on welfare, like they said. She didn't seem strange at all. She was . . . I couldn't help but like her.

Yeah, well, even if I did, the locked case still bothered me. I tried to pretend it didn't.

"Mimi bought me an antique locket for my fifteenth birthday."

Mimi was her grandmother. She had found a comfortable spot in middle-class black life by marrying into a wealthy, black, southern family come north. The crazy things she did — like washing the dishes this way or that, ironing sheets and underwear — I figured were part of her new uppity ways. But she didn't look like anyone's grandmother to me. She wasn't hunched over, and her face wasn't wrinkled. She was sharp. In fact, all the women in Evie's family were glamorous.

Connie, her mother, was the most exciting. She was a part-time singer. I liked that. When I grew up (after college, of course), I wanted to be a singer. They lived exciting lives, made goo-gobs of money, and lived in huge homes. Like the Supremes. I wanted to be like them.

Connie was the closest thing to being there. I remember all the photographs of her, sultry and fine. Pictures of sequined gowns. Pictures of fur. Pictures of style. A beautiful small brown face, framed softly by clouds of bushy wonderful hair and earrings that dangled to her shoulders. She wasn't famous but, boy, was she exciting. I stuck around her, hoping something would rub off on me.

I got a warm feeling inside just being around Connie and Evie. They seemed more like girlfriends than mama and daughter. I liked that most of all. I found the girls at school who had young mothers exciting — they were more in the know. It must've been fun to be so close in age and have your mama understand how you feel. My mama was older, and I just knew that was the reason we weren't more like friends. I'd made a mental note to have my kids at an early age.

Whatever was in that case was incredibly important to be kept a secret.

"Michelle, you listening?"

"Huh? Oh, yeah. A locket? That's really great, Evie! I wish I was getting something special." I wanted to be happy for her but the hurt inside was growing. Evie knew it too.

"Well, I'm tired. I wanna sleep now."

"Okay. But come on, tell me what's in the case. Pleeese."

I heard myself begging. Evie was unmoved.

"I can't, Michelle." She got up from the floor and went to the bathroom.

That's that. I wouldn't be able to trust her again. This was an act of high treason. . . .

"Michelle! Hey girl, what's the matter? You must be dreamin' in here. The kettle's been whistling crazy. Are you alright? I didn't know if somethin' happened to you."

"Oh, I was just thinking."

"I remember that time you were talking about now. Was I really that secretive?" She slapped her thigh and bent over laughing. I waited for the punch line.

"Yeah . . ."

"Well, I don't know why I made such a big deal out of it. It was only a douche bag." She put her arms around my shoulders.

"A douche bag? A douche . . ." I giggled. "A douche bag! You gotta be kidding!"

Laughing, we fell up against the wall.

"Those were good times back then, weren't they?" She hugged me.

"Yeah . . . they still are."

DADDY WAS A JACK-LEG

CHERRY MUHANJI

hen somethin' ain't doin' what it should be doin' or done done already, we call the "jack-leg." The handy-dandy man come to fix what need fixin'. For a few bucks and a toot, sometimes he'd crawl 'neath the sink or break open the toilet where folk's not-so-nice stuff goes down or fix up the switch that done got too tired to flick. Everybody know 'bout the jack-leg but us, cause we got our own that nobody else had or wanted — Daddy.

Now Daddy couldn't nail a nail or screw a screw or put in a light-bulb right that done blowed, callin' me or my brother to come and "put this bulb in proper." However, Daddy fancied hisself the Mr. Fix-It of the world, and our house was bombarded by stuff dragged from the alley or from a neighbor's garbage can, 'cause Daddy felt that nothin', I mean nothin', needed to be throwed away. To the horror of my mother, who was a real lady proper, but couldn't say too much 'cause Daddy would remind her much too often 'bout whose house this was and who paid the rent.

Like I said, our house was full of every neighbor's junk redone up to Daddy's way of thinkin', which reduced Momma to her famous words said at least every weekend when Daddy was let loose to wander the alley, "You know your father's sick."

Daddy even rescued Miss Pearl's ol' rocker after she passed away; put it right in the front room where Momma talked politics to all the neighbors who come to ask Miss Annie what she thought the white folks was up to this time. Momma, havin' been a believer in the Black Star line, while Mr. Marcus Garvey was standin' on street corners tellin' all black folks to give it up and let's go home, received some kind of respect in the neighborhood. However, that respect only seemed to allow for Daddy to practice his fixin' habits even more, like the time I was fixin' to tell ya 'bout when he brought Miss Pearl's ol' rocker out of the alley after she done passed away. I say, "Lord have mercy! Lord have mercy!" Just like Miss Pearl would say, if she hadn't already gone to her heavenly reward. The rocker set in the front room with red, yeah, red blocks on the arms where Daddy, who really got a sense of what all folks say 'bout niggahs and how we all just loves red, painted big red blocks. Then he nailed big nails to hold the blocks on the straw arms of the rocker, coverin' the wo' out places and placin' Miss Pearl's rocker in the middle of the front room for all to see as Momma talked politics. Just served to remind me of the time Daddy took me to the zoo where I seen the baboons with 'em red behinds flashin' and movin' all over the place.

One Saturday mornin', Momma, with her head in her hands, was just shakin', sayin' her every-weekend speech, but what was now becomin' her what-Momma-said-all-the-time speech, "You know your father's sick." What now? I thought, gettin' a secret kind of real satisfaction out of Daddy's special kind of tom-fool-la-re. I know I s'pose to get some kind of embarrassment, but I just cain't bring myself to 'cause after all, this my Daddy ain't it? And he cain't be but so foolish. Right? Well, Momma was remainin' in one spot with her head justa goin' and her first finger pointin' out the window. Daddy was at his newest let's-get-Momma's-goat-and-fix-up-the-ol'-house-at-the-same-time habits.

Well, before I go on, let me explain how Momma and Daddy looked at the same thing but seen it different like. Daddy could give less then a damn 'bout the neighbors, sayin' in the way he said most things, "Annie they all is full of shit." Well Momma would groan and try to explain, "Old man, you don't have a sense of community," and Daddy would laugh and say, "These niggahs ain't got no sense and ain't gon' never be a com-mun-i-ty."

Like I was sayin', Momma was standin' in the floor of the room with the chair with the baboon arms, pointin' and shakin' her finger at what I supposed Daddy was doin' or about to do out the window. She got so upset she made the mistake of sittin' in the baboon chair, and wouldn't you know it, the leg give way and Momma fell on the floor. I looked first at Momma on the floor with the baboon chair on top of her and then out of the window at what Daddy was up to. And there I was in the middle, like I always was. Momma was right, Daddy was sick! Daddy had Little Tommy's wagon, and only Daddy and God (and maybe Miss Minnie, who was the local conjure woman) could figure out how he got, first, the wagon from Little Tommy who never gave his wagon up for nobody. Tommy always holdin' on to that wagon like real little kids hold on to a bottle. And second, how he got what looked like an oversized tombstone in Little Tommy's little wagon.

Daddy had decided that his half-blind pool buddy, who he beat every Saturday, had somehow passed the house last Saturday with the excuse he couldn't find the house. Which was really strange, 'cause he never missed a Saturday I could ever remember. Old Man Moore was never gonna be able to say that again, 'cause Daddy had decided to put out a marker. The marker being a large piece of broken cement that somehow had the shape of a tombstone. Daddy had decided to paint big red (you got it) numbers of our address on the tombstone.

Which was when Momma looked out the window, 'cause she must a guessed that if the address was painted on the marker fo' all the world to see, even includin' Old Man Moore, then the onlyest place the marker could go was in the middle of the front yard. And if Daddy had taken the time to get Little Tommy's wagon from him, that only God knows how (and maybe Miss Minnie), then Daddy was real serious about where that headstone had to go — right smack dab in the middle of the manicured lawn, that Momma insisted me and my brother keep up so we could keep up with Miss Chick next door. Us strivin' fo' first place in a neighborhood that was what Daddy said really had only neighbors who was hoods. "They'd rob ya blind, Annie, if I weren't always on the case." Daddy was the neighborhood Mr. Run-and-Tell-It also.

Everybody would ask Momma, "Why yo' husband run and tell other folk's bizness?"

And Momma would warn Daddy sayin', "Ol' man, people are sick and tired of you telling everything about them. Why don't you just live and let live?"

"I know what I sees and tells what I know, 'cause of what the Lord did to Sodom and Gomorrah."

And Momma would groan, 'cause she ain't never believed in 'em ol' tales. But since Daddy went to the stow-front church with the white Jesus painted on a cross lookin' paler than sin, and that plenty pale fo' a blessin', most times her groans were made to stop short in her mouth. Daddy went so he could get a number to hit, so she kept quiet 'bout what she really thought 'bout the pale Jesus in the stow-front church. But really that's another story to tell at another time.

The southern folks in the neighborhood, a-customed to buryin' folks in they front and backyard down south, out of re-spect fo' they upbringin' and Daddy's crazy ways, made sure they honored the dead. No sense in takin' any chances. The mens would tip they hats when they passed our house, no matter mornin' noon or night. And the ladies would bow they heads, no matter how many chil'rens they'd be carryin' or tryin' to see 'bout when they was passin' the front yard. And Daddy would stand back real proudlike. He figurin' he done finally gained some re-spect. And Momma would groan 'cause she knowed he ain't.

To go with our real nice buryin' place in the middle of the front yard, Daddy painted the marker (you guessed wrong) not red but white. Ain't nobody ever seen a red grave marker, have they? There I go again. It wadn't no grave marker. Why I call it that? Well anyway. Daddy decided, since he heard Momma talkin' to Miss Chick 'cross the fence in the backyard 'bout how she wished there was enough money to buy some real good paint to paint the front steps, he would show her that he really was penny-wise and not pound-foolish.

"Annie."

"Yeah, ol' man."

"Evenin', Miss Chick."

"How ya, Mr. Wash?"

"Just fine, Miss Chick. Now that I done figured out a way to save my wife some money."

"Oh God!" said Momma.

"Not God, Annie — me. I got some residue paint left in the barn (Daddy always called the garage a barn), I can use it."

"Ol' man, what colors do you have?"

"All colors, Annie."

I am still rememberin' the green color Momma, bein' kinda copper brown, was turnin' into. Then Daddy began his who-pays-the-rent speech, and Momma just went mute. And Miss Chick, with that real I-feel-sorry-for-you-Miss-Annie-but-better-you-than-me look, turned and went into the house to ring all the neighbors on the telephone to come and witness ol' man Wash and his shenanigans one mo' time.

Daddy, as I remember, went into the barn and closed the door, like Miss Minnie did when she had a sho' nuff payin' customer. Us kids would always try to peek in her house, but we would run when she came out. She bein' capable of the evil eye and all. Us kids had to protect ourselves. 'Cause Miss Minnie, Susie Simmons say, could make spiders come out of yo' mouth if she got real mad. And Susie Simmons knew all 'bout Miss Minnie, 'cause when her Momma went on one of 'em drunk spells and left fo' weeks at one time, Susie Simmons would stay with Miss Minnie. Even though she was scared all the time. So it was real likely that Susie Simmons knew what she was talkin' 'bout. Besides, Susie Simmons didn't have no evil eye but one mean fist, which she used on me every time she got a chance. But sometimes she would forget, and I was not gonna remind her she had not done her thing on me fo' that day. Daddy was in the barn fo' what seemed a long time. But not so long, 'cause Momma didn't have enough time to get to me and give me her famous the-weekend-special, which by now, you know, had become her everyday you-know-your-father-is-sick speech.

Daddy came rollin' out the barn like he was on roller skates, with the paint bucket swingin' and a new paintbrush (made outta real horses' hair) in his hand. Momma had just enough time to put her head back in her hands and groan. She started her speech, not to me this time but to herself or nobody special, 'bout how crazy this man was and how he was shamin' her face to the neighborhood and how hard she had worked to keep the old house up and how the ol' man did everything he could to destroy all she had worked so hard to keep up with.

Some neighbors had just paid their re-spect to the grave marker and was all ready to see Daddy's latest tom-fool-a-re. All eyes was on the paint bucket, 'cause Miss Chick had done all the necessary telephoning to come and view the latest act of the Barnum Bailey circus — ghetto style. People was even takin' bets on what fool color this fool man was 'bout to slap on the steps. I could see how much Daddy was enjoyin' this. He always said, these niggah's ain't never seen no real nothin' and wadn't used to nothin' — no stylin' and no profilin' either, 'cause he was the onlyest one 'mong 'em from Luzana where the real niggahs lived.

He dipped the brand-new paintbrush (made outta real horses' hair) into what must be the most important paint can there ever was in the world — then stopped. I could hear some quick suckin' in of breathin' in the crowd. He paused, careful to take the paint bucket with him, and went into the house. The crowd let out a kinda huff, waitin' and whisperin' all the time. He returned with the broom. He took his own sweet time finally sweepin' the steps. And nobody was gonna complain 'cause steps is real important to black folks. And besides, ain't no sense doin' no half-done job on yo' front steps fo' all the world to see. Folks was, however, gettin' ant-see. Anxious like I get ever' time I go to the circus and watch all 'em tigers and lions lined up with everybody pickin' at 'em. Besides, folks had they bets down. Based on what Daddy had done in times past, all kinds of money was goin' up and down — bettin' on what color the Washnon's steps was gonna be.

Daddy turned, now he finished sweepin', and looked out over the crowd. And slowly picked the brand-new paintbrush (made outta real horses' hair) into the air. He looked like he was gonna bless the crowd like Mother Williams did in the stow-front church every Sunday night, shakin' 'em smokin' incense balls in the air. Which sent Miss Ruby Brown into a testifyin' spell. Some say this gave her an excuse to raise her dress, so Brother Even-naw Smith could see what he was always tryin' to see, folks say. And what she was lettin' him see, anyway, every Saturday night. Well, anyway, where was I at?

Oh, yeah. Daddy turned 'round and started. The crowd was quiet a-gain. Then, because I was little and standin' in the back of my own front yard, I couldn't see nothin', but I could hear all kinds of sounds. Mostly, I s'pect, disappointment. The first step came out the color of all the steps in the neighborhood. And so did the next one. And so did the next. And so did all the others. Gray! Just like Miss Chick's next door. Hadn't Daddy mixed all the colors he had in the barn? He had. Wasn't there every color in the rainbow in that old barn? Yep, there was. Hadn't Daddy been collectin' paint fo' years? U-hum. How did he come up with the right color paint? Well, only God knows (and maybe Miss Minnie). But, then again, maybe Little Tommy, 'cause, as I remember it now, he followed Daddy out of the barn finally gettin' his wagon back, and he had one big smile on his face.

TAKE IT OUT

. . . .

EGYIRBA HIGH

ake it out!" His words. His solution. The only solution there was for us, according to him. His eyes looked straight through me.

I shifted my position, laughed nervously, and said, "Do what?" knowing damn well I didn't want him to say those words again.

"Take it out!" he said again, in all the languages men speak. I looked at him. No feeling. No clues. I heard the words in my head. Maybe, I thought, he has temporarily forgotten the tribal laws of Hammurabi that say "a life for a life" and only wants to finish his degree.

His words snuffed out the hidden lies I had told myself. Like how he really loved me. Or just a little more time — he'll come around. Sure, Michelle. Tears made crystal paths down my brown landscape and slurred my speech. I marveled at his composure. His spine was erect and his hands were motionless in his lap. I focused on his spiral hair. I wanted to give John one more chance for humanity.

"But I love you, John!" I knew my words irritated him like the voice behind the bill collector who calls at an inappropriate moment. He kept on sitting and staring.

Sick and frightened, I sobbed uncontrollably. The sounds stirred up his anger. He hated for women to cry. His presence grew in gigantic proportion. I felt like the inner tube of a tire rolling underneath a heavy weight.

John abruptly screeched on the brakes. "Do you think you are the first woman who's ever been pregnant for me?"

My insides recoiled, and I was jerked savagely back in time, remembering how his life was one long season of winter. . . .

On the road to Kalamazoo, Michigan, from Detroit. It was partytime. A car full of African men. And me. John always drove my car. It made him feel powerful and me, protected. He knew the road well. I sat as an African queen among his friends. They toasted my presence, weaving their laughter and Swahili with Olde English beer.

It was getting late. It would've been fun, this three-hour drive, but it began to rain and get foggy. John showed no signs of yielding to heaven or earth. He sped up, challenging even the gods. The harder he drove, the harder the mist and water retaliated. Clouds of fog began to descend upon us.

No one noticed but me. "John, would you please slow down a little?"

He snapped out of his trance and the car slowed down. I breathed a sigh of relief. I didn't like to tempt fate or anything else. But after only ten minutes, John got impatient and upped the speed to seventy-five miles per hour. I remembered a church song he had defiled, "This world is not my home . . . I'm just a bastard."

The fog got thicker and the supply of drinks diminished. This time I nudged him. "Please, John."

"I know this road like the back of my hand! I have driven it many times before! I am driving! If you don't shut up, I will get out of this car and walk back to Detroit! Besides, if we die, we just die!"

Silence fell like the still encroaching fog. The men in the car were mortified, their laughter aborted without warning. Fear stuck in their throats as cans clinked and beer gurgled in their mouths. Their bodies came to full attention, and they began to soothe and reason with him.

"Hey, John . . . it's okay . . . it's okay, man."

"She better shut up! I'm sick of this! And you too!"

"Oh, John, she's just scared. No big thing, man . . . the fog just makes it. . . ."

John pressed his foot down on the accelerator. I became still. The more they tried to reason with him, the harder he drove, till they finally stopped talking. I had seen this all before: John's bitter resentment toward life. How many times had he told me, "Leave me alone! You're young — make yourself happy. Don't waste your time on me. When I die, I go to the grave by myself. . . ." I remembered.

We sat in silent terror. I sucked in my breath, closed my eyes. Dear God, let me just get there. My hands gripped themselves as if they were not a part of me, until I noticed I was digging my nails into my skin. All that could be heard was shallow breathing and last-minute reconciliations with God. Except for John. His life wasn't worth a damn to him. . . .

I drifted back into the present. John still sat staring. Despite everything, I wanted to avoid searching an eternity for an answer. Take it out! Take it out! Take it out! demanded its place beside me, as I lay between the pillows of my past and future. I shifted again and turned on my side. Yuuch! The squeaky bedsprings, once the music of lovers making safaris of each other's bodies, resonated disapproval. The sounds bounced off the walls and wove a burial gown for my unborn child.

And so it was. I took it out and made one less mouth to feed in this world. His solution is now a scar no one can see. It floats inside me as I decorate myself in bright kangas and cowhide slippers. I create my unborn child's face in me every time I eat ugali or twist my empty belly to the Congolese beat.

Once each year I say a prayer to her. I would have named her Kesi, which means: *child born at a time when her father is in trouble.* She does not enter the spirit world through a womb but through a short moment of living in me. And through my act of prayer, which sent her there.

THE SCALES OF SUPERMAN

....

KESHO SCOTT

ll black mothers fashion a love-hate scale for the lives of their daughters. This scale later weighs our lives in grams, ounces, and pounds. The evolving nigger — colored, Black, Afro-American, African, bronze beauty — carries a hundred extra pounds of history on her shoulders as she sinks in the land of opportunity. The ounces of her stories weigh heavy, like a dieter binging on the weekend and facing a Monday morning purge. The tiny grams of liquid life begin to seep into the places where the lost pounds would go. Where do the lost pounds go?

It is a very different kind of blindness to be able to see the scale of another's life and not your own. Michelle was on a treadmill to live up to her mother's standards. She was running fast and out of breath. It tormented me to watch from a distance, the way I can't stand

Coltrane's music when I'm down. And I'm always down after a dose of Michelle.

What is really clear is why we met at thirteen. She was my step-sister's babysitter. We were introduced because they thought we'd like each other. People always hook up people who seem to dress alike. We met over the phone. I was attracted to her voice, and we arranged to meet in person. I didn't know our friendship would end up, years later, on another scale.

There is really no straight story to tell in a friendship burdened with the ghost of a mother's past. These ghosts are nothing new to women of our kind. Our options are lived like the life of Superman. We are expected to leap tall buildings in a single bound. When everybody finds out we are really Clark Kent, a phony who works at the Global Factory, they just laugh and push on with their own agenda. Remember Superman? How could his mother have known that the stone she sent with him for luck would make him defenseless. Or did she?

Michelle was sort of like Superman to me. She was birthed in black, middle-class splendor — another planet, from my vantage point. She was given the silver spoon of opportunity that lurked like kryptonite in her life. She had a hard time ignoring the mother voice in her head that broadcast "You ain't good enough" propaganda twenty-four hours a day and when the voice got too loud, she'd fly off to her fortress of solitude, which could be just about anywhere.

Sometimes Michelle would not fly. She would reject the costume and remind herself that the guy who played Superman killed himself, because he realized he was never going to be the "real Superman." There are just about a million stories of Michelle as Superman. I kept a record. She didn't.

I got my first look at her at our arranged meeting. She opened the door, smiling. This was no ordinary smile. It blinded me. She was a happy child, and I was only pretending to be — without those things that make little black girls happy. Grass in the front yard. High yellow skin. And a live-in daddy. She had that kind of queen-for-more-than-a-day presence that triggered my childish fantasies and envy. Michelle was free to be a child. She had nothing by default and everything within her ability to make a sentence. And she could really speak the king's English. She invited me into her basement, which really was the boudoir for her dreams. We built many fantasies there. In fact, it was Michelle who first taught me to have my own fantasies, not those I'd created to escape my family pain and not those packaged from the syncopated rhythm of my grandmother's lips.

I remember the day I discovered Michelle could play the piano. She was elevated to the level of angel, Annette Funicello, and Abraham Lincoln. I have always been in awe of the piano. It was a sacred instrument. My granddaddy hoarded a black, massive one in his living room. All it did was collect dust. Year after year, I witnessed its white piano keys turning yellow. Once, I tried to play it, and Granddaddy nearly slammed my fingers off. I knew it belonged to his dead wife, and he made it her tombstone. But like the Cadillac locked in ghetto garages, it just didn't make sense to have it and not use it.

Michelle and I were cooking up our third audition for the Motown Review when she reminded herself of a tune she thought would fit into our repertoire. Acting like a cross between Tallulah Bankhead and Phyllis Diller, she would beam out of the basement the way Captain Kirk leaves the *Enterprise*. I followed her to the living room, a room I had never been invited into in my many visits. A room that looked more like a mausoleum than a room. Michelle, alias "Star," opened the stained-glass doors of the patio, adjacent to this room of the dead, and there it was — a piano, the size of Mighty Joe Young. In cavalier fashion, she pulled out the stool, lifted its mahogany lid, and rummaged through it like a thief. I stood horrified. All my life I had been too afraid to invade the secrets in my granddaddy's piano stool. My mind began to blister. I knew we had entered a holy place. The thick, crusty stench was a warning, as was the light creeping through the vines that grew over the porch windows, making a checkerboard effect on the room. Michelle paused and withdrew an old yellow piece of sheet music and in a loud operalike voice sang "With . . . a . . . Song . . . in . . . My . . . Heart." I couldn't stand it.

"Let's get out of here!" I whispered. It was then that I felt another presence. My eyes glanced directly above the piano to a monster picture of a ferocious-looking black man. I'll be shit! I thought, What is the most famous black man in the world's picture doing here? It was the Brown Bomber, Joe Louis. "How did you get that picture?" I asked.

Michelle answered now in a Shirley Temple voice, "Oh, that's my Uncle Joe. He sent it to Mom from Paris!"

Before I could ask a million questions, Michelle had leaped another tall building in a single bound: her arms were raised high, fingers arched and descending "on down the yellow brick road," turning the piano keys into the sound of dreams. She sang to the most powerful man in the world, and I think he was even listening. I was enchanted. Michelle played on and on and never witnessed the great transformation she forced on me. She stopped only momentarily, when she saw me holding my crotch and said, "The bathroom's down the hall, next to the stairway." I held back my tears in loyalty to her image of being a god. Her arms reaching, in rapid succession, from one end of the piano to the other, pounding, then fast spurts of running fingers to the left and right, panting, throwing her head back and forth, shifting her weight from side to side and off the stool, bending her body, forward and back, to catch up with the keys begging to be touched and perspiring all the while. I was dizzy. Faint. Unsteady. We seemed to have flown through a time barrier broken apart by her voice. Here was Superman flying again.

I was just about to piss on myself, when Michelle bellowed, "I'm hungry, let's go get some White Castle hamburgers!" Instead, she beamed back into the basement. I flinched and jumped out of her way, behind the stained-glass door. Thinking fast. Where had I been for the last twenty minutes? Then slower, getting angrier with each word, Where . . . had . . . I . . . been . . . for . . . the . . . last . . . twenty . . . minutes? As I returned to the basement, I remember feeling that the hoax was up. I expected Michelle to have some answers. She could no longer deny her powers and hide behind the stupid costume. I knew who Superman really was.

I quietly entered the door to the basement family room. She was sitting on a beanbag chair. Her facial expression was placid, as if at an inquiry. A trial room scene flashed through my mind. She was in the witness box. "Yes, I was flying. I was really flying." Then she was the defense attorney. "Do you remember the circumstances that allowed you to reach such heights?" Then she was the prosecuting attorney. "I object to this line of questioning, Your Honor." Finally, she was the judge. "Will the defense attorney please refrain from such gross exaggeration of her client's testimony?" Look at her face one more time, I snapped back to reality. I realized that to confront her was to grab at an image in thin air. A substance that had no weight. Michelle could never afford to come out of character.

The skin around my eyes tightened to forbid the dam of tears welling up. All the rare moments I had known in my life flashed in front of me. The eclipse of the sun, the birth of Mrs. Ferndale's triplets, seeing Margaret Mead on TV, kissing Buddy Hatcher,

Florine's purple Mustang car, the cat-eye stone in my junior high school class ring — all these collided with Michelle weighing life by her own scale. For only a moment, she had broken out of the chains that bound the pounds to her back, only to be sentenced to one hundred years of hard labor for liberating herself.

And zip, a filmstrip caught in a frame. Michelle sat straight up and said, in a high-pitched voice, "You wanna call folks on the phone and talk sexy?" Asking me an obvious "yes" question to direct my mind away from the center of her pain, her ever-present movement, forward faster.

I said, feeling sick, sad, and silly, and tired of playing games, "Yes." So we picked up the phone and started pretending. We called Joe's Bar and asked for Sam. We made Mrs. Cashmere angry when we asked if her husband was home. We invited the local DJ for lunch in the name of Miss Sullivan and, of course, we just plain called and cussed a few niggers out. We bawled. We fell all over each other. We gloried in our power to be make-believers. Except there was always a tight strain in my smile, my overbearing laughter, my hugging to hang on, because I knew this was not a game but the only reality between us.

That evening, we danced up an appetite and ate a whole box of Girl Scout cookies and Cheese Twists. We slept together in Michelle's narrow third-floor bedroom and sang songs with Keener radio (the mixed black and white music station), which made us feel close.

Finally Michelle's voice, silenced by sleep, broke into snores. I tried to decode it for its secrets. But to no avail. Instead, I gave in to the only secure and natural event for the day — sleep. I slept twenty years.

I've often wanted to commit murder to whole societies, races, and peoples. Black women are no exception. The liquid life of American black women is taking no form, like mercury in a broken thermometer splattered all over the bathroom floor. They have forgotten the right temperature to cook their dreams and forgotten what it was like to be "hot."

Black women, forgetting so much, turn to their scales — Christmas gifts from their mothers — reminding them to weigh in heavy. But I . . . I will always love Michelle, no matter what she weighs.

EVERYBODY KNOWS . . . BUT MICHELLE

....

CHERRY MUHANJI

ere I sit in the midst of Africans again. And I ask myself, as I always do, why? Michelle, my friend, emerges breathless from the kitchen, sweat starting to bead on her forehead and upper lip. She surveys this happy group, catches my questioned perplexity, answers it with one gaze: why not?

Cephas, who has zeroed in on me, is now discussing Nigerian politics. Not with a passion, for he has none, at least not for Nigerian politics. Cephas really has a passion for white women. And he has zeroed in on me, because I am the closest to Miss Anne, the mellow yellow. He sings, I know, somewhere in the back of his head, "If you can't love the one you want, love the one you with." I cut my teeth on a pig foot and a bottle of beer, learned my table manners from *Ebony* magazine, and I've seen a thousand Cephases in my time, except this one has an accent.

Michelle chimes in about some past or present coup in Nigeria; Cephas falls instantly in love. Michelle is darling as she rattles on, and I'm getting sick. Michelle, in between the soup and the salad, could talk about life in Ghana, the Ivory Coast, South Africa, or the moon for that matter. Cephas has now mentally decided he's been too hasty about me and plans instead to spend the evening getting to know the Africa between Michelle's thighs.

James, the one this dinner is really for, is Michelle's man. He is a student and has, he says, never been in love till now. It's taken him all of three weeks to decide Michelle is the one for him, and they now plan a lifetime together. Michelle coos as she serves a special dinner. James, who is from Nigeria, is experiencing America's version of the Maxwell housewife as Michelle, with a song in her heart and a spoon in her hand, dishes out authentic West African dishes: fufu, peanut butter soup, and okra sauce. If, on the other hand, her love had been from East Africa, say Kenya, we would now be eating roasted meat and ugali.

Cephas is confused. Michelle is giving James the larger portions. He knows by now he is not the one. He turns, looks over at me, sees my "niggah, I dare you" look, turns and looks over at my friend, Glenda, and decides, Oh, well, if you can't love the one you want, love . . . you know the rest.

Michelle is up dancing to (you guessed it) authentic West African music. She has a whole collection. I watch the miracle that is Michelle. She reads, writes, cooks, and cares. Why isn't that enough? Always looking for the roots "over there," forgetting the legacy forged on this side of the ocean, the real drama: the American horror show. Starring: all the Michelles and company who built a world out of nothing, when there wasn't nobody — no man, no money, and no place to go.

"Michelle, you are such a pretty girl. If only my little hippo wouldn't eat so much." And with that crack in her plaster, Michelle began a life that could never measure up to a mother who had an ax to grind and who chose Michelle to ax to pieces.

I grew up (as I've said) on a pig foot and a bottle of beer. I know whores and pimps, fags and preachers. I've seen rats the size of cats and bedbugs (cinches, as they are called) the size of roaches. And roaches, out of all the scenic wonders of the Detroit ghetto, are my favorite. Did you know that roaches love beer? They do. They meet, get drunk, have babies, and get stepped on. Momma roach discovers the beer bottle first — almost empty. She crawls inside. The bottle is warm and wet. She splashes around. "God that feels good!" Then here comes Daddy roach just beboppin' down the road. Presses his antennae to the glass, picks up on what's happenin' in the bottle, then jumps! Lands with his fine brown self right in the brown beer with brown Momma roach just havin' a good ol' time!

"Say, Daddy, what ya doin' down here?"

"Just tryin' to check ya out, Momma."

"Well, Daddy, it ain't nothin' but a party."

They start into "doin' it" and soon, soon, soon, why, what do we have? Baby roaches! Who meet, get drunk, screw, have babies, and get stepped on. After all, we are talkin' 'bout who's screwing whom, or is it whom's screwing who?

Michelle, on the other hand, grew up with piano and ballet lessons, can sing like Dionne Warwick, believes she is Cinderella, and expects that her prince will come by any day now.

Gbade, James's friend, has decided he will take me home to meet his father, the village chief. I am a fair flower that will grow forever-after in his village. Dear Cephas has settled on Glenda for the evening. Michelle, high now on many bottles of beer, tunes up and entertains us. Her repertoire begins with the classics and ends with James Brown's "Hot Pants, hear me now!"

African men like their women meaty. Michelle knows this and has found a place for the "little hippo" to roam, undisturbed by potshots from Americans who love their women skinny, childlike — ready victims for abuse and perhaps a reason for child abuse. Mother and daughter look-alikes, a dynamic duo for a misogynist culture.

All of a sudden, I hate Michelle, her mother, America the beautiful, and Africans who fuck us, knowing we've forgotten our legacy. And myself, for allowing that to happen.

Cephas, by now, is drunk as a skunk and higher (as my daddy would say) than a Georgia pine. We go to his apartment on an invitation for late-night drinks, which we certainly don't need, and something he never would have made had he been sober.

He shares his time, money, and body with Beth, his very jaded girlfriend. He lives in a suburb of Detroit where all the whites and Cephases ran after the 1967 riot in downtown Detroit. Glenda, who has arrived on Cephas's arm, eyes Beth for the first time. She gets ready to call Cephas everything but a child of God. She never liked African men, anyway. "Cheap, real cheap," she'd say.

She stops suddenly, and my eyes follow the direction of her fading voice. Beth. Beth is ugly — real ugly. And as Redd Foxx says, "There ain't nothing uglier in this world than an old, white woman." Beth is both. Black women never forgive white women for being ugly. Old, yes, but never ugly. Cephas, though, never got past the white, like sudden blindness forever traps the last image seen. He never saw her age.

Beth is terrified. Michelle is straightening James's tie. I am drowning out Gbade by pretending I'm interested. And Glenda has decided that old and ugly is too much for one woman to bear; she instantly becomes our international ambassador of goodwill, as Beth starts for the toilet gagging, ready to vomit us niggahs in it. Which leaves Cephas on the loose. He grabs Michelle to "bump." I watch James flinch, and Gbade, noticing nothing, continues to drone in my very uninterested ear.

Michelle sits like a child that discards the toy and plays with the box. Glenda needs to know how much money the niggah got and where is it? And me? Well, I'm still trying to dig my way through a twenty-foot prison wall with only a spoon. And the party? A good time was had by all.

EVIE WILL BE
OVER SATURDAY

· ·

CHERRY MUHANJI

vie'll be over Saturday." No, Momma's words didn't light fires under a thousand cooking pots nor bring rain in due season but served to give notice: "Be busy on Saturday, Jenny, you're not invited."

"Evie'll be over Saturday" shoved me into corners that were my life, the meeting places where no one special lived. Oh, I had dared once to "make it." And had returned home. Lost. Late and lonely. With my dreams sifting through my fingers like sand, falling on a world that was big and scary. A world that had produced one divorce, two people who never should have married, and three babies to feed. Fear had won. And Evie had won the only thing I never had — Momma.

"Evie'll be over Saturday" meant that Annie the dream merchant, a seller of cloth, a dealer in purples, the magician sleight-of-hand, would have another chance. Momma's world was magic on Saturdays. She had hung her dreams in closets where wire hangers banged, some in mocked ritual, others alone, separated, cocked on the rod, lost at the rear of the closet forever.

Momma's world of "let's pretend" had now become the sixties. A magic time for black folks. Evie slipped Momma's dreams over her head, she wiggled, and watched them fall all over a body that had become the eyes and ears for her grandmother. She brought the striped sphinx of Egypt, the bleached bones of black people splattered on the cliffs of Goree Island, the bulging city of Bangladesh, which manages to still wrap itself gracefully in a sari, the liberated country of Libya, and finally the fabled city of Timbuktu. They would slip into trance, bend their eyes toward Mecca, move through corridors of shimmering silks and mirrored satins where charms, miracles, and strange whispers were heard among the special who stepped with golden sandals and to the swish of rustling skirts. Yes, this place, their place, gnawed at the very bowels of me. Sick because I couldn't go. Scared to go even if I could. They would vanish and so would I. Poof!

"Evie will be over Saturday" meant that one could only guess at their meanderings. Did they walk through Shanghai streets, enter Chinese opium dens, suck smoke through yellowed skins, and languish over lessons they didn't learn? Or answer the talking drums in the village and, with wild-eyed frenzy and reflected glee, enter rituals cutting clitorises of young girls with the skill and dedication of high priestesses? What is that world all about? I wondered. I knew it was not my world. A world of too many babies or one where niggahs, when they met you, said they were between women. (What they really mean is they intend to add you to those they already have.) I had no right to that magic world. Their ground was holy. My feet weren't shod and my heart not pure. I understood my place and tried to stay in it. But my need needed attention, the kid forever waiting to go to the bathroom who, with her hand up and legs crossed, just can't wait.

"Momma, what do you want from the market? It's about to close." Evie looked up in utter surprise. Momma's face puzzled, her jaw dropped. They seemed like young girls discovered with their panties down.

"Evie'll be over Saturday" made me the caretaker of the dreamers. A ghost who moves among the living, either lost or content to have half an existence. For someone has to see the rent is paid, find Al to come and fix the front steps, and make sure Momma's heart pills never run out.

"Evie'll be over Saturday" did not light fires under a thousand cooking pots, or bring rain in due season, nor bring you the answer to the question you placed in a bottle and threw in the Detroit River. But all shrines have ghosts lurking somewhere and sometimes there is a ripple in the universe. And when that happens, even ghosts dare to dream.

CHERRY BLOSSOMS

. . . .

EGYIRBA HIGH

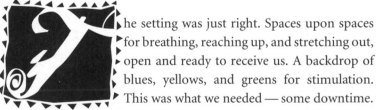he setting was just right. Spaces upon spaces for breathing, reaching up, and stretching out, open and ready to receive us. A backdrop of blues, yellows, and greens for stimulation. This was what we needed — some downtime.

It was no secret how we fought and slew dragons daily. It was part of the tradition. Girded and battle-ready, we fought and fought and never knew we were tired. When someone suggested we slow up, take it easy, we looked on them with more than suspicion. We were black women warriors, and we owed this legacy to our daughters.

For Cherry, it was a war waged in anger with God. She was convinced it was all a big joke and said so, like somebody up there was moving chess pieces, and she was only a pawn. What did it mean, this fight for self that battled husbands and lovers, children and mamas and madness? Her wounds hit the air, and she wailed and whimpered notes of quiet desperation.

She was seventeen when she got put on hold. You know, a light blinking steady, waiting to be answered. She never was. The sad thing was that it never occurred to her to hang up and call back. And we never stopped long enough to look at her or hear her cries, what with us battling our own wars. If we had, we would have seen that hers was the same war we were fighting.

The creative drive, when thwarted, wreaks havoc when it has no place to go. Cherry's ran amok at seventeen. "I don't wanna marry him, Mama. I just don't love him."

"Hush, girl. There ain't no other way outta this mess. What you mean love? Just be happy he wanna do the good and right thing by you."

She was an artist trying hard to find a form when he got her pregnant. Then he turned her inside out again and again, till she turned her fury on him, then herself. By the time she was twenty-one, she had four babies and was flashing furiously. When we met her, she was wild-eyed and crazy looking, seeing out but receiving no pictures in. She was the result of a voodoo dance stopped in midstream, left hanging and wanting.

After the babies, it was one trap after another punching or kicking her spirit into submission, or at least trying to. It was hustling for the phone company, caring for aging parents, and wanting that man back at times 'cause it was so hard and she got lonely. She painted the floor black in the living room of her small bungalow on Tillman Street and wallowed in Boone's Farm apple wine on Friday nights. But her spirit was strong. Even at the most desperate moments, she felt the raw place inside her waiting to be touched so that swallowing twenty-seven pills couldn't steal her away when she lay down squarely in the middle of a busy street. All those years battling and the battle itself a creative act in another form. It was a gift given at birth but muddled by trying to pay the bills, keep the gas man away, and other assorted tricks of living.

When we noticed her light blinking, the line had been engaged so long it looked as if the bulb was about to go. But we felt the stirrings, the rumblings, heard the sounds in the distance, and quickly captured and collected the spirit trying to break.

Where does passion go when loving no longer fuels the engine? It can, when left to find an avenue of expression, turn inward to find its mate and devour the existence of its own memory. Cherry knew this passion all her life but couldn't define it. When she turned thirty-five, she stumbled on the form and turned out mysterious lines and images that breathed life back into her nostrils. Her feeling gave new energy to words. She wrote. But the writing was too easy so she pushed it aside, trying harder to direct that unnamed feeling. It rebelled. She fought it, 'cause we know "that ain't no woman no woman, without a man."

And then there was the Pied Piper. A first-class manipulator. He tempted those feelings away from themselves. She willingly followed the sounds he played because the music was good and made her feel natural. She tried to give him her gifts unpolished, but he couldn't speak her language.

"My feelings for you have changed." Six simple notes, simply sung, and he bounded out of her life still playing his flute, still thinking she would follow. She couldn't. No, not that she couldn't — she wouldn't. He left. And when she woke three days later, the pain of her bruised ego had subsided. She reached for her pen and paper and let her fingers say what she hadn't. The passion was her.

The battles, the rhythm of the myth her life tapped out had worn a comfortable groove in her being. After forty-seven years of false security, she had begun to break away. We only stood by to hold the curtains back so she could see. She had never tested herself against herself, for herself. It seemed elementary. And now, when melancholy sets in and tries to steal her spirit, her hand quivers mindfully and soon her fingers glide over paper again. And home comes home in her.

TENDER MEMORIES

. . . .

KESHO SCOTT

hen you come to the age when you are able to think critically about the people you love, you should also be tender with your memories. Otherwise, the critical eye will flood everything precious in the mind. And you will discover the power of memories to drown you.

I loved Annie Washington as lesbians love. Passionately. Lavishly. Deliberately. Now, as an adult looking back, I realize she complicated my relationships with people who have long since survived her death. Annie was my grandmother, and she purposely kept me estranged from Cherry. Cherry was her daughter.

Cherry was always in my life, though I don't remember her. She must have been there. She was my father's sister and my mother's best friend. For years she was the fourth partner in bid whist parties every

Friday, Saturday, and Sunday at Uncle Oliver's house. (I remember his house and son, Dennis, who'd whip my ass on a regular basis.) She was the brunt of a lot of jokes about being an artist.

My daddy's family was making the quick, fast money from the Ford Motor Company assembly line. They had a sour taste for any nigger wanting to pull his weight using anything other than muscle and sweat. Besides, to them Cherry was a cream-colored girl with red-blond hair and was gonna have a good life anyway. She was to be the special-order pizza of some man's life and all she'd have to do was cough up an anchovy or two. She had no hard work ahead. I sang their gospel about her as every child harmonizes with a family.

More than the apple of her eye, Annie adored me. Her love was like having Santa Claus as your teacher every day, full of smiles, round-ness, wisdom, globs of fat, and 100 percent pure fantasy. In fact, when I was with Grandma, I didn't ever know what time it was. Other people's intrusions served as our time clock. We did nothing extra special and yet we did everything language permitted. I got a clear sense that Annie talked *with* me and *to* everybody else. She loved me and let everybody else struggle to figure out how to love her. She was a truly selfish goddess, selfish with the emotional roles she handed out to family members. Grandma was trying to protect me from my im-mediate parents and to make up for God's one-sidedness. She felt He had placed me "in a theater of life playing only tragedies." It wasn't that I was out of step with everybody else. Everybody else just seemed out of step with me.

Cherry was an extra pair of eyes in constant observation of Grand-ma's and my world. Grandma knew, but never mentioned it. I knew nothing about their relationship. But I did know that Cherry wasn't important to us. At least, I told myself that. Quite to the contrary, she was the desert root that could sprout into anything.

Once at age ten, I spent the night at Cherry's house on Maple Street. It actually wasn't her I wanted to visit but my daddy's new wife's brother, Larry, who looked like Daddy and lived downstairs. I had a crush on him and spying was the only reward for a one-way affection.

Cherry had just had a new baby, her third son, Paul. He was spe-cial. Grandma said that, so I knew it was so. Cherry had a husband but he was invisible. How I could tell was that her house was a mess, and her sons dressed in pajamas all day. She didn't take her husband seri-ously because, unlike other women, she never complained about him.

My cousins, Kim and David, were the music of the house. And I got in on their run of it. We didn't eat actual meals. This was great! We made batches of oatmeal cookies and played games until past midnight. Cherry was there but in an odd way. She was clutching a book, using her fingers as a marker. She was holding and protecting this book. It was holding her, and she was ignoring us. I watched carefully, as I pretended to watch TV in the dirty kitchen. I wanted to know what the book was, but I didn't approach her. She gave me Grandma's signal not to invade her space.

This pattern, of two on the inside and one out, was like so many scenes in our relationship. From that time on, the scales were tilted. Cherry was a sure panther sitting in the wings of my life. I avoided her. I hinted this to Grandma, and she understood my anxiety but would not discuss her daughter with me.

Cherry was invisible only as long as I was busy growing up. To Cherry and her family, who lived with Grandma by then, my visits were grand entrances. I entered like a queen and watched them scatter to other parts of the house and freeze until I departed. Besides, Grandma and my afternoons together began to take on a richer meaning. She was the bouncing board for my stories about pimples and real love. The older I got, the more adoration I received from her. However, I did sense she was expecting something from me.

When I was about nineteen, I realized my grandmother was getting old. I didn't know her actual age, but she now spent some of our time complaining about little things. My only consolation for her was to replay a fantasy she gave me at ten and live it out at this age. I lived all of Annie's fantasies. They were the dictionary of my life. I knew how to look up words and change the world. She liked that! I was a celebrity in the family. I never knew or cared if my status affected others or if the gifts of Grandma's love had a hidden agenda. But the space between pure fantasy and reality had a kind of out-of-body feeling and often filled my stomach with butterflies. I'd feel them most when I'd say good-bye after a Saturday afternoon visit. I'd walk down the hallway stairs. They seemed to move. As soon as I'd adjust my mind to the time of the bus's arrival, the butterflies would disappear. Butterflies didn't register as harmful to me until the day we made Mexican pie at Grandma's.

The intersection of Annie's relationship with everybody was her kitchen. It was a place to be nurtured. She gave to everybody at the level of food. This hypnotic relationship directed the living we did at Grandma's into a fine sequence of groceries in, hot stove on, table-setting rituals, magnificent meals, and a temporary relaxing of our guards. It was at one of these Saturday midafternoon rehearsals that the butterflies attacked me.

Cherry, as usual, brought in a bag of groceries. But this time she also brought in a dream she had not deferred. Her trip to Morocco had to be served with the food. She sat down at the table next to the refrigerator, in Grandpa's authority chair, and scrambled our minds. Everybody's movements seemed to be in slow motion and less hypnotized by Grandma's food. Cherry could have spilled milk, and we wouldn't have realized there had been an accident. Our cooking together was replaced with her one-act play in which she produced, directed, and starred. We were at her movie: amazed, scared, observing, and held. Having selected the recipe and in control of the temperature, Cherry served us an artist's interpretation of existence. I realized immediately that Cherry, as panther, could chase my precious fantasies. I felt connected to her as though we had been flip sides of the same song, sung in two different parts of the world. Grandma was disturbed by our not cooking the Mexican pie. She was shaken. She knew there was a new cook in town, and it wasn't her. She was desperately disturbed. She retreated to the living room where the living never lived. From this day on, she retreated whenever mysterious food was being cooked. She became the observer. It was only around cooking that Cherry and I nourished our awkward relationship. Butterflies began to fly free and land on Grandma's shoulders.

Since we very seldom cooked together, Cherry and I seldom digested together. But the possibility of the act was always available. There was the trance we slipped into while cooking chili, sharing the spotlight. This was also the visit that I noticed Grandma was growing weaker and tired of something. I felt the connection between our growing relationship and Grandma's growing weakness, but I denied it, as I had the butterflies. And Grandma's pathetic poetry, that somehow told me someone was dying for someone. Or maybe, someone had been living less for others always.

How do you make sense of the past? How do you understand the meaning of gifts, fantasies, feelings of specialness, awkwardness? Or the power struggles in a three-way, unequal love affair that was balanced by an emotionally fragile and physically crippled woman? Tenderness now answers all the questions I have about the "whys." Tenderness is the common denominator of Grandma's will, written and administered by herself before her death, as a guideline for living less. When a woman cannot grow in the flower bed of her choice, she continues to take in the water and sunshine but may refuse to bear fruit. Cherry was her water and I, her sunshine, and each never knew the connection or underpinning of our roles to this woman. What does it mean anyway to be the water and sunshine to something? Water and sunshine are not human or alive. They are conditions for making existence existence.

Cherry and I knew within the private circles of our minds that we compared as apples to oranges, but were really the recipients of Grandma's soul reincarnated. It was as if she decided out of the frustration and humiliation of being an object, a wife, a nigger, a grandmother, all servant roles — to play a trick on life. She divided herself and gave halves to whom she believed would someday be wholes.

Looking from her vantage point, I can now understand the choices she made for her life. She accepted a pinhole peek in exchange for a laugh with God. It now makes sense, her senseless suffering. She was playing a waiting game.

The first third of her life she tried to be a woman acting out visions of an age, in the bandages of her race, with the skills of a child fighting to get out of a garbage can. She was stopped cold by the American version of humanity.

The second third, she fished in life's pond and gave birth. Only to find in love that her body, acting on the signals of a nonsupportive society, had to be sacrificed. As she lost her fingers, hips, and ankles to arthritis, agitated by the lack of man-made social medicine for her kind, she stopped touching and being touched. This is when Cherry entered her life. What is to be salvaged of a mother-daughter relationship imprisoned by a diseased touch? Isn't the beginning of life a result of touch? A touch from a tit, a touch to smooth the goodbyes after marriage, and more, a touch to identify one's sameness with the source? Annie's touch did not give off signals. She was already numb. So she chose not to touch Cherry. This way Cherry would always know she was different from Annie. Cherry inherited from her mother a passion for touching life in the raw and unscrambling it into poetry.

I entered my grandmother's life when her body was merely a vessel for a museum of dreams. The sweet first grandchild of a son she had out of love. But then her second marriage of convenience had passed its winter stages, and Grandma whistled instead of talked. She chose to unload her saved-up dreams on me. (I would later become a Pandora's box of her creations and plague all nondreamers.) But what is to be salvaged of a grandmother-granddaughter relationship imprisoned by fantasy? When will it ever be safe for a nuclear bomb of dreams to explode and harm no one? Annie's gifts were always wedded in her need to fight the demons and to help me not focus on my own. So, she filled every cavity of my soul with her adventures. I never asked what would become of me when I'd question what dreams I'd created on my own.

Her gifts have been delivered by now, and her plan to trick life is the laughter Cherry and I make. The end of her own life was spent in waiting. And she waited as women with stripes of all colors do. They operate like minerals, neither dead nor alive but there to be used.

When the dim light in my mind now surveys the memories of the people I have loved, I remember to be tender, because I know I survived the flood.

BIRD TRACKS

....

CHERRY MUHANJI

 omma washed me but bathed my brother. Within the tumble of the mind, I move. My life, a thesaurus of my mother's synonyms and antonyms. An unsteady voyeur, in need of a tonic, searching for treasure while trembling under the glare of my own passion.

"When will you bathe me, Momma?"

Somewhere a camera flashes and I am caught — frozen in the frames of my mind — and I remember, I remember, I remember you, Momma. . . . You bend under shoulders yoked and laden from not enough love, or was it too much love remembered?

"Was he that important, Momma? Or was it something else?"

Fingers knotted into corkscrews, snarled crowns, swollen joints, ill-fitting skin hiding a skewed skeleton that reaches toward the child that you now bathe with tender touches. . . . I can still feel cool water along my spine and the sponge from warm soapsuds that winds around my body and slides down between my thighs. I squeal in delight. And I swear, if I close my eyes real tight and press my face in the warm split between your breasts, I can smell the milk that was mine.

"Tommy, that you?"

"No Momma, it's only me."

I explode. My passion in a thousand pieces flares in the night. One flare. Two. Then three — here I am — here I am. Momma, can you see me? I tear the head from my momma doll for the hundredth time, run wildly through the neighborhood jumping in mud puddles, shooting at bad men, hanging from trees — upside down trying to build a world right side up from ABC blocks. In search of a feeling — any feeling — my feeling, your feeling, Momma. Tired, I come home again.

"Where is feeling, Momma?"

Is it in the piano you play somewhere in your head? — the one you play because your world is full of low notes, and you know there are other notes to play — those at the far end of the keyboard that tinkle and fill you from the brook that isn't there because the garbage is and poverty is and the man that kept you there, who was my father and not the man you loved or wanted, is . . . and then there was me.

"You always loved your father better than me."

Thirty-five years fall from my eyes. My jaw muscles start to work. But nothing will come out. Nothing. Nothing. You turn, light another Pall Mall cigarette — tune into the six o'clock news. I swallow hard. "No, Momma, I loved you better." I guess the television is up too loud.

"Who are you, Momma?"

The old gray sweater. The one that lay on the back of Mary's chair, your teacher. The chair in the front of the classroom, alone and unattended — by the teacher who limped. She fed your dreams, hope — and then your heart.

"Why do I remember the chair now?"

The teacher with the limp? The one you spoke of . . . the one in your dreams. "Guess who I dreamed about last night," you would say, unaware of how many mornings you awoke asking the same question . . . as I played at your feet, more interested in the dream than my new doll.

"So where are you now, Momma?"

"Hello, this is Mercy Hospital calling. The bed for Annie Washington is ready."
"Annie Washington dropped dead on the kitchen floor early this morning. This is her daughter speaking."
"I'm so sorry."
"So am I."

I hang upside down, pinned to the clothesline — a shirt left blowing alone in the breeze. You crowd my dreams and bump into my daylight. In each little girl you soothe chocolate wrinkles, sigh over the spills down the fronts of starched yellow pinafores, straighten bows, place rock candy in the center of tiny palms, and take all the hurt away. I deposit that hurt in my pocket, carefully, rush home to the wide, skeleton structure that is my life and wait for you in dreams, Momma. The nighttime-daytime ache floods me.

"Is that what life is, Momma, one long winter?"

Meant to wrap us in rags while the silver birds with the silver beaks strip our bones and desecrate our shrines. No marker no flower no flame no one to say, "And she was here." Not even a plot number.

"Who builds monuments to memory, Momma?"

But I remember you . . . follow your tracks through the snow. Why do they end in the marsh where the cattails and evening birds vie for song and comfort? Where are you when the wind is high in the trees and the winter geese cross the moon and I call out in the stillness,

"But, Momma, I loved you better."

DEAR GOD

....

KESHO SCOTT

hen my mother said, "I've committed my life to the Lord," I thought of the TV peacock. His colors are vivid and bold. But his preview isn't always so entertaining. Why do I feel so shitty? I, in fact, was the one who had always leaped to congratulate change and spread my wings over Mount Everest. I refused to narrow reality down to a manageable stream repeating itself. So, why am I in so much pain?

Some folks said it's because I won't seek the Lord in their way. Now God, how can a life so full of opportunities as mine seek God in their way? I don't want to starve myself from living! Nor have any of my sins caught up with me from life in the "fast lane"! I don't want to give up on myself yet! And I certainly am not gonna let my mind be poisoned by "their religion"! Come one, God! I know you expect me to do better than that, or you wouldn't have sent those early space travelers to Africa. I know black folks got a special con-nec-tion with the "Connector"! You can see it in the way niggers wear their clothes, comb their hair, and move their body to their music! You know that! That connection has carved a mood in us. That's why we are so cool. The coolest people in the world. So, why is my mama acting so uncool? I know living in this here A-mer-i-ca is like a rat maze that turns niggers into mummies. Seen my mama walk with a limp on more than one occasion. She was walking head-on into walls.

Then she started kicking them down, and I enjoyed that. But Mama has decided to look up to find heavenly intervention. That ain't bad in itself. But there's a lot of unidentified stuff up there giving away "personal assistance." And I'm wondering if you really communicating with her, or is she on some kind of freaky-deekey paid cable? Someone or something is broadcasting to her daily, and me and the rest of the family can't buy in. Now look, I went to Sunday school for years, and I know your "words." And it looks to me you made a lot of promises about "if you folks just do this, I'll handle the rest." Dammit! You broke your promise. You got my mama on this here um-bil-i-cal cord that nobody can cut, and she's turning back into an ugly duckling. Born again, my ass. Blown away, is more like it! You expect her to throw herself out? Her family? And me? Look here, she was my mama first! Her tits were all mine! When I hurt my knee at seven, she was a wonder woman to the rescue. She did not call for your help. When I married and was with child myself, she buzzed on the "A" train — a ditty-bop, to the jazz of Rasahn Roland Kirk and Pharoah Saunders. She traded in her lizard skin of mother and took the shape of a butterfly, causing us all to notice her flight. We enjoyed picking her up from airports and kissin' in front of white folks. I knew then what I always wanted to be as I grew older. Just like my mama. I suppose flying was too scary for Mama and felt too good. Ugh! A nigger living a happy life in A-mer-i-ca just don't seem right. Probably made her feel weird among her friends. So she asked for a heavenly audit. Did you have to take her all?

Why can't you get your victims when they're not weak? I am not gonna forgive you for this! Now my mama lays no more golden eggs. And as it is, all niggers talk about is who robbed who. This complaining, of course, is said to be my selfish and childish imagination. I expected Mama to be Mama. I am having a temper tantrum, because she won't be the clown she was to keep me laughing in the ghetto. She won't pull any more rabbits from her bushy afro to feed or please me. She clings to you, because she raised me to leave her, anyway. I hate you, or Mama's need for you, that keeps her from snuggling me into her treasure trunk when I need to feel like a jewel. Instead, she says, "Child, the Lord has a wonderful plan . . . read Revelations." I've read Revelations, and the only rev-e-la-tion in that is the feeling of being aborted by your own mama. You reread Revelations and tell me why must I die for her to be born again? If I was a snake I'd suck you dry. I'd stalk you in the dark because my most prized possessions is possessed, not by me. And yes, I'm jealous. And I'm gonna get revenge. The preview of your "coming" is a cheap media trick we will be able to watch on TV this fall. As I watch, my eyes glued to your cartoons, laughing and eating popcorn, I'm gonna remember that I can do more than unplug you. I can kick your face in! And when everybody in the room looks at me like I'm crazy, I'll whisper you a little question. Dear God, why didn't you simply admit that you could have used Plan B?

ODYSSEY

....

EGYIRBA HIGH

or the first time in my life I was riding for me. Not like the many places I had been. Not like the things I had done before. It was different this time. I was riding toward myself, and the fear I felt was exhilarating.

I remember the first time I rode the rolling stairs without holding Mama's hand. I was six years old. The stairs were like magic. I was sure something would happen when my feet finally touched down on the escalator. Like my heart was going to stop and leave me pinioned forever.

"Come on, Michelle. Get on." But I couldn't. I stood debating the possibilities when I noticed Mama halfway down. I closed my eyes . . . sucked in my breath . . . grabbed the handrails . . . oh, I'm scared, Mama . . . as my feet touched down for the journey to the unknown.

76

Lids squeezing the eyeballs back till there was no more shutting they could do. I waited for my destruction.

My breath, suspended in my chest, waited for a sign. But I was floating. Caught by surprise, my held-in breath whooshed out in thanks. Even my feet took delight in the discharge of their duty. My grip on the rails opened slowly, my palms wet and sticky. I was safe. When my eyes opened at last, it was in time to calculate the descent and next horizon.

On the road again. Not like the times I wanted to try out for plays in high school and was too scared. Or when the musical *Hair* came to Detroit, and I didn't audition. Or maybe the reason that Marathon Oil commercial didn't sell was because I listened to voices, not mine, protecting me from the big, bad world. The ones that said it was nice I could sing, but singers were a dime a dozen. Or, yes, I acted well, but I needed to think about a real job. Or, go to college and help uplift the race.

Mama, if you had known I only wanted your closeness, what would you have done? School . . . work . . . all the sacrifices you made . . . for us. . . . Weren't you scared, Mama? I mean, if you had followed your dream, would you have married Daddy?

Uhmmm. Remembering. My lungs refusing me the pleasure of smooth, easy breathing. Jerking in my chest, scared like when I was six. I remember . . . some good times. Hearing Daddy's voice.

"Michelle, you're such a clown. Play that piano, girl!" Daddy doing the Madison, me pantomiming Duke Ellington or Count Basie on piano . . . while the record played. Daddy laughing. And me and my sisters. I remember shuffling them behind me to do-wap. Me singing the lead to "What Becomes of the Brokenhearted?" by Jimmy Ruffin and "Don't Mess with Bill" by the Marvelettes. And through the looking glass, at me and my best friend, Evie, on our way to Motown, representing a fine young thing named John Brown.

The bus ride was wearing on me, flooding me with my memories. I couldn't ever recall a time I'd left the driving to Greyhound and didn't enjoy the journey. I looked around at the other passengers. Unimpressive, I thought. I opened my novel, but my eyes went wild over the page. The woman in the seat across the aisle noticed me, while she tried to calm her fussy baby. I glanced at her. Her other two children were squirming. Both she and I were doing a balancing act. She and her baby. Me and my thoughts.

Grandma was wonderful, you said, Mama. I know. She did what she thought was best for you. It was all she knew. But . . . you still needed. And 1935 was a hard time to be. Independent. Beautiful and an artist. And black.

Two in the morning. I closed the book and looked out the window. A sheet of coal blanketed the sky. The voices of the people behind me rose and fell with a persistent, edgy twang that scraped against my ears like fingernails on a chalkboard. White, southern accents always made me nervous. Damn! I couldn't even see the moon. Disgusted, I turned away from my reflection.

I have always loved you, Mama. I watched you. Every move you made. Careful. Thought out. I watched. You survived. How to pass that on? You planned . . . I took . . . and held on. What could I give you back?

The passengers were finally getting sleepy. Even the woman and her three kids were quieter now. I left my reading light on. No more darkness. No more pain. A sign of the goodness to come. The price for trading dreams had been so high. . . .

Mama wanted to be a singer. She always sang. I loved to listen, while she washed collard greens or dusted her mahogany end tables. I hid in corners or peered out from closets to listen. She sang blues. I was hypnotized. "I wanna drink muddy water, sleep in a hollow log . . ." or "I wish I didn't love you so." She gave me my dreams, never knowing that every time she sang and rocked me, I listened. She sang and rocked me.

"Good, respectable girls don't go into show business, only fast women," my grandma told her.

I inherited Mama's love and talent for sweet melodies. It was her dream. It was born in me. But I pawned my dream like she pawned her dream and we settled.

But oooooh, Mama . . . if you had followed your dream, you would have been a star. A voice like aged wine. Pulling up that passion. Where did it go, Mama? The world would've loved your melodies. I might not have been your daughter, but I would have bought your records.

The bus pressed on, and I listened to the purr of the engine. Tired. Anxiety swelling up in each nerve. The baby was crying again. Thoughts of Bishop crept into the purr. How many men like him? He wasn't going to understand. Hell, when had I ever understood, back then? I was happy to have someone love me. Take these bits and pieces of me, I told the men I had loved. Bishop. I hardly knew him. Will you marry me? he asked. Yes, I said. He was nice. As the bus moved toward

Iowa now, I thought of how I had gone to be with him. I flew to Manhattan, already regretting.

"Oh, honey, I'm so happy. You'll see. You can have your space here. New York's the kind of place where you don't have to deal with people if you don't want to. It'll just be us." Such a sweet man. His voice waxed and waned, making love sounds. Another detour.

What can I say about loving like that, Mama? It's noble, I guess. But it's dumb. The years press the love down inside us. You did it for Grandma. I did it for you. Turning love into duty. Before you were my mother, you were a woman. And that will never change. Before I was your daughter, I was a woman too.

The lady with the baby was fumbling in the bag at her feet looking for a bottle. Sleeping bodies twisted and turned in their seats, imagining themselves about to be awakened by the baby's cries. The mother placed the milk bottle in the tiny girl's mouth. She sucked greedily.

But even while I was escaping to New York, I was moving toward this moment. The years I had been trapped inside myself stopped, moved backward, and rolled over the crusty layers around me. And the shell cracked. I peeled and scraped the layers away, because boredom and self-pity were the final straws.

I have learned some things, Mama. From your life. From your sacrifices. It is not enough to be a mother when you want to be a singer. I can do both. Or none. But I can't deny the life in me. And it is not possible to forget how you tried. I know now. There is no glory in suffering. There is only pain.

My friend, Evie, all grown up like me, had become Kesho (which is Swahili for "tomorrow"). She was a woman who had herself begun to leap the many mountains of her childhood dramas, those skeletons that loom inside to later bring us grown-up fears. She said, "Come to Iowa and heal yourself."

Thank you for your lessons, Mama. Thank you for the way you tried. I have come to see that it is my birthright to be free. Even in your sacrifice, I have seen this. Before we were women, we were Love.

So, here I was on the bus riding. The clouds were breaking open. Morning was dawning. The sun stretched a yawn of color through the cracks. I felt a tinge of relief. The passengers around me stirred. I wished them back into their dreams a while longer, so I could greet the day alone. The sun brought a smile to my lips. She winked at me and pointed her arm on down the road toward Iowa. I winked back. I was riding again. It was a new day.

MARKIE

. . . .

KESHO SCOTT

 filled the tub for the drowning of Markie. This was nothing new. I had given him a bath a million times and heard that voice inside of me whispering, "Leave him in when you pull the plug. Watch him get sucked down the drain like all the stories on TV that have a happy ending. See the fright on Markie's face? But don't laugh out loud." The voice would continue. "You might crack your face and mess up the makeup that covers the real animal you are." There raged inside me a seething, giant beast ready to murder. It had gotten tired of life in a ghetto cage, barred at every turn. It was overfed, and the snapshots every Christmas showed that it was getting too big to keep hiding its fierce jaws behind my tightrope smile. Somebody would say, "Smile for the camera!" I always did, and its two-dimensional view would just barely keep my giant freak in

check—still unseen, unknown, just under that layer of life called wall-to-wall carpet.

The dictionary defines "ambiguous" as having mixed feelings about something or someone. Having a child gave it another meaning for me: Am-I-Big-Enough! The answer never changed the reality. We were in prison together for whatever the crime we committed.

I filed the tub, anyway, and even added bubbles to make the drowning smell sweet. Floral scents always reminded me of being smaller and running through Grandma's grapevines. At the end of the summer, we'd smash those grapes and make enough wine to make everybody high—high enough to think we were rich and white and president of the United States. Grandma's grapevines got us all confused.

We made jelly too. We spread it to the edge of Wonder Bread and knew that it was the only edge we'd have in this life. We lived between the crusts of poverty, ignorance, racism, and pain.

"Markie, take off your clothes and come get in the tub," I said softly. I wanted this night to seem like any other. I turned off the water, testing it just one more time. There was no way he was gonna screech and attract the other birds nesting in the house. I even threw in his rubber boat, so he'd jump to his drowning as he laughed and splashed.

I drew back to take a long last look at his beautiful brown body, silk-spun from the lovemaking of two ignorant niggers. I wanted to remember how his coming into my life was by pure accident, the kind that leaves the whole family crippled. Markie didn't notice my probing calculations. And anyway, I wanted him to die clean and look good. A thought that always ran across my mind at funerals.

I soaped the rag with bubbles and covered Markie from head to toe. He stood in the tub, innocent and unaware of my predilection for murder and toyed with his rubber boat. I made his sculptured face into a continuous brown glob. This way, I could see him the way I felt him—a weighted object, like something I'd put in a garage sale; people discard objects every day.

My shoulders were holding up the seams of the family. I was used to turning myself inside out and pressing down the bulges made on the outside of my dress. The seams had to be starched down now. For Markie, the bulges signaled the moment of his demise.

He was appropriately slippery with soap. Many a nigger had lost his life from a slip. I had overheard the old folks say, "Boy, one of these days you gonna slip." A slip had a lot of meaning in the ghetto. You'd slip when you cussed out the welfare lady for accusing you of working on the side; or when you cussed out Miss Mary, who gave credit at the corner store, for padding your bill; or when you told "the white man" you'd kick his mother-fuckin' ass if he did so and so again. Yes, Markie was gonna slip . . . with a little help from me. He was gonna slip hard. He was gonna pay for that bad word he was so free at saying. He was never gonna say "Mama" again.

I shifted my weight as easily as I had lost recollection of the past three years. I saw no reason to think of his thin body frame as cute. I didn't have any snappy little anecdotes to repeat about him, like the women at children's playgrounds — all of them hiding the boiling steam beneath their cracking smiles and most of them not noticing the last time they'd caught a moment for themselves. They wouldn't have recognized a moment if it had been wrapped in aluminum foil and had given back their reflection. It was the same moment they crammed in twenty diaper changes a day, three full meals from scratch, eight hours of housework, twenty-four hours of child care, and two seconds of affection from their men, which wasn't enough to give them a postcard view of life in the Beaver Cleaver house.

I searched my mind for one last thought that might make me reconsider what I was about to do. Inside, I felt like my mind was moving at ninety miles per hour and said, "Markie, sit down in the water and let me rinse you, sweetheart." I couldn't even utter a harsh word because it would sound to me like I was crazy. I wasn't. I was stopping the invader in my life. I was defending something in me that spoke louder than the message I received by osmosis, a sneaky message that had crept through the tiny holes in my skin and had something to do with duty and responsibility. But it wasn't a rhythm I could mellow to.

I began washing off the soap, conscious that the water level was at his breast. My hands anchored him down in the water to keep him from floating. I remembered history lessons from the past Salem witch trials: if Markie floated he was a witch; if he drowned his soul was reprieved.

The water was now resting comfortably under his chin, and the giant within me was about to rise and unplug the force behind the dam. Glancing down between his legs, I noticed his little penis was excited by the pleasure of my soapy touch. I shook my head in amazement. Markie had a hard-on even as he approached his death.

The face rag fell from my hand as I grabbed his shoulders to push him down. I heard that voice say, "Now." So, the giant pushed Markie under the water and I watched. I wasn't afraid but very quiet. I felt lighter than I had in three years. I watched him watch me as the soap on his face disappeared under water. So did his smile. So did his heart. So did his life.

Markie suddenly awoke from childhood to an age he's been ever since. He made no cry but took the giant by the throat and clinched him with a hug. The two fought each other the length of the tub. I heard the Mama cry come up in bubbles . . . but the giant didn't, he was already too weak. Markie squeezed and squeezed and, victorious, was left hanging onto my neck. He hung and collected his breath, as I stood up and set us both on the toilet seat. I covered us with a flood of salty water and moaned the loss of a secret friend. I no longer had the companion whose voice would say the things I could not say or feel the feelings I had ignored like I do roadside pop cans. Markie held onto the Mama left in me, and I folded back into the neat creases I'd had all along.

I don't know why the giant failed to drown Markie. The voices were strong enough. The rage was intense enough. And bars on my cage had finally bent enough for the giant to let out my secret: I was Markie's ten-year-old sister.

WHO SAID THAT?

....

CHERRY MUHANJI

addy was a big butter and egg man up from New Orleans, and he didn't care who he ate his breakfast with. When he dropped into Momma's hole and I popped out, he knew he was home, and Momma knew she had the niggah by the balls. 'Cause here I was hi-yellah and red, just like Miss Emmalean (Daddy's momma) with the long starched skirts that made her wiggle when she walk and make a hound dog talk.

I stood real straight in Daddy's eyes, a real re-peat of Miss Emmalean. That was okay, but I wanted to look like Momma. I couldn't believe all that stuff about my grandmomma 'cause, for one thing, Momma didn't look like Miss Emmalean. And when she wrapped them North Carolina thighs around Daddy and started spinnin' silver threads with those long copper-colored legs, Daddy stood still, real still, while she took big chunks outta him. And he didn't pay no mind to Miss Emmalean then.

When Momma saw me, she asked, "Why ya body always in a state of jackknife? When ya gonna spring open? Ya look like a rat that cain't git outta the trap." After that, each day I'd take my jackknife body and will it straight. But nothin' nevah happened. It was hard gittin' in and out of spaces with a body on bent 'cause then the blood cain't flow up; it flow in circles till it git so confused it jump the track and spill all over. Then I got a body on bent and bleedin' too!

I don't remember the exact date I wished fo' straight, but my body kept on bent. I only know Momma kept lookin' at me, that is, when she weren't spinnin' silky webs, to see if my jackknife spring open. It nevah did.

My brother talked in e-quations. Asked once if I wanted a ride to Antaria. "Maybe," he said, "they got bodies like yours. Then you won't feel so bad always goin' a-round in jackknife. Besides," he managed to say while fiddlin' with his decoder ring, "I cain't always fight the Martians 'cause I got a sistah on bent who look like the Antarians."

I finally found me a man who used to rub my bent. Settled down between my legs and rub and rub and rub. When, though, he git mad, he mock and laugh, "Ya ain't nevah gonna git out of jackknife." I pound my temples and squeeze my eyes real tight, and I will he shut his mouth. He nevah did.

My children see my bent every day, and since they ain't seen nothin' else, that's all they know to see: me doubled up in a knot.

I went fishin' in a pond once to catch me some good looks. And when I see my re-flection in the pond, why I ain't got no bent. Leastwise, in this pond I ain't. I look again and again. No bent. No bend. No jackknife. I so happy. I feel like flyin'. I look again in the pond, and wow! I really look like a firefly! Fireflies sit inside the bushes and wait till night. And look what they do: they turn they asses on neon and light up the night!

Why my folks see me on bent? Well, Daddy ain't nevah said so, but he ain't said much else either. He so busy bobbin' and weavin' inside Momma's web. And Momma, needin' to feel some power in a world where she ain't got none, needed to tell me somethin'. And my brother, chartin' the skies 'cause he cain't stand the stench down here. No wonder they cain't see my ass light up! I know I pretty 'cause who ain't nevah heard a body say, "Oh, look, a pretty firefly!" It great havin' a ass that glows!

A RAM'S HEAD NOT
A RAM'S HEART

- -

KESHO SCOTT

very Saturday John kicked the soccer ball with precision as if it were the ball in Michelle's stomach. She'd attend the games, as each month passed on to the next, so he could see his child growing inside her. John ignored her presence because winning was all he wanted. She rationalized that maybe a combination of peer pressure, her refusal to disappear, and his African ancestors, who glorify the birth of the first son, would drive John Muhanji back to his senses and into her arms. The first son was born, and John Muhanji left for Africa, leaving another black child bumping his head against an American wall.

Vidinyu, an odd name for a nigger, means "difficulty." That goes without saying for black children, but to be named it goes with the African tradition. We hope our children will live up to their names. Watch out, John Muhanji, Difficulty will come into your life one day, and you'll wish you had been there to set his sail. You left it up to that half-African whom you fucked. Funny how full Africans look down their noses at us mixed-breeds and yet breed with us — and for more than green cards.

I heard of Vidinyu before I actually met him. I heard more of his mother's woes to recruit him a full-blooded African father. He's got plenty of uncles. Somehow that crazy momma saw fit to disqualify many applicants. She'd say, "I'm still waiting for my African prince." A prince is what Michelle wanted. Vidinyu needed something else.

After years of not hearing his name, I next heard that he was Joey. Another no-meaning name of the Afro-American tradition. We don't burden our children with names of dreams that will never come true. We just want them to survive and get rich. As if "Difficulty" didn't have enough difficulty trying to balance this tightrope act, as if a name change could give Vidinyu a vacation from the African dreams his father denied his soul.

Difficulty plays like other kids, eats fudgesicles, loves his grandma, spreads his arms when he needs, and never asks his mother the really tough questions like "When did you and Daddy get married?" But in fact, I think a few of his friends, the Captains Fear, Damage, Pity, and Death, chase him around the playground as he sings the victory songs of the Saturday morning cartoon He-Man. He is He-Man. And He-Man always wins. And He-Men are given everything else from their mommas 'cause they can't make their births the way they should have been. Vidinyu has stopped trying.

When I finally met He-Man in the flesh I looked for signs his momma said were red flags. He had been renamed Vidinyu and, of course, was light-skinned like her. An American high-yellow with sculpted African features. Why was John so cruel to deny Vidinyu and leave him to find his reflection in the eyes of another? John thinks to himself, I will abandon what I do not have to claim. John says, "He is *her* son!" John knows that somewhere is his seed. He refuses to validate it. He says, "I am king! I am first!"

Vidinyu has been told all by now. At five, he has been to Africa to search for his runaway father. Father is still missing. As Americans, we live with the nightmare that someone will steal our children. Do you remember Atlanta? It occurred right after slavery! No one is gonna snatch Difficulty. He knows that. Yet, he awaits a kidnapping.

Vidinyu is that crazy woman's son alright. Ninety-five percent Michelle. Thank God. She isn't cruel, doesn't abandon her seeds, won't kick or deny the challenges brought on by birth. She knows that by giving life she gives back. So she smothers without a return. She acts out a million faces as therapy to a single sullen heart or to a multitude. She truly believes in the international "niggertude." Personally, I think she's sick. I've seen her take her lickings hard and still look for compassion in all of God's creation.

Her son has soaked in her goodness. His smiles tell you that and more. The way he tilts his heavy head is a just right disclaimer that you will get a power struggle from him. Sure, he fusses like a grandmother, old and feeble, and really wanting to give in to the candy treats in the kitchen. He gives in to the natural movement of all things that pass him by. He gives and gives and gives in silence and twinkles his eyes, asking only that he be given a more difficult task. "I'm Difficulty," he says in the He-Man voice. "I'm just difficult!"

Then there is the 5 percent John Muhanji in him. The fragile African boy who digs holes with nothing to plant and who wants an ultimate question answered without the work. You can see it in Vidinyu, by his clever use of personal distance and busybody qualities. He thinks to himself, If I wait, they will come to me. He says, "Can't they see I'm not really too busy?" And he knows to keep out of everyone's way. Vidinyu's 5 percent loss can shadow his equations to figure out the world, his lifelong vulnerability stalking each solution.

The other day his 95 percent and 5 percent sides came together as he showed me pictures he drew in his He-Man book. Like all American boy-kids, Vidinyu has received the call of masculinity, an enlistment against those "feminist bitches" gone wild. However, Vidinyu's pictures weren't of women Amazons stealing masculinity; they were of men fighting boys. He told me about the battle and quickly said, "The End!" I read in his eyes "my end." I could find no words to assure him that masculinity had been replaced with humanity. I gave him a strained smile.

I now watch Vidinyu very carefully, as he has an affinity for kicking balls. His precision, his wanting to win, his cautious smile before netting the ball. He instinctively stops and surveys how much difficulty his kicks will bring to others. What a man already! And yet, it is hard for him to be that man without being Difficulty.

HEAD DROPPERS

. . . .

CHERRY MUHANJI

 come from a long line of head drop-
pers. Trouble is, we thought we was jug-
glers. We never seen ourselfs as no head
droppers. Lawd, Lawd, Lawd, how we
could juggle! We start tossin' and spin-
nin' all them chil'rens in the air; then there is the rent man; and us
always tryin' ta spook the gas man. Then, too, us commencin' to stop
our legs from openin' on cue and closin' befo' time. Make a body
dizzy just thankin' 'bout all that. We worry, too, cause we hear tell of
folks droppin' folks. And they say it always be the one least able, most
times.

Fruzzie, my grandmomma, drop my momma on her head. She
never own up to that, though. She be the best juggler of them all, jugglin' two husbands, two sets of young'uns and sharecroppin'; cookin'
clothes in a iron pot with all that lye stingin' and burnin' her eyes;

89

keepin' the roosters away from the hens; and easin' down 'tween burlap sheets with those two husbands, one a drunk and a sinner fo' real, and one saved, sanctified, and free from sin, except, of course, where the good sistahs of the church is concerned. Whew! She sit down once under the apple blossom tree, wo' out, and who is up there justa swayin' and stretchin' her body out on them long lean limbs? Momma!

"Gal, what ya doin'?"

"I re-peatin' my lat-in verbs."

"Up in the apple blossom tree? Ya know what the apple blossom tree git ya."

"I up here re-peatin', not moonin', cause moonin' gits babies and babies gits jugglin' and I ain't gon' be no juggler." She pout and push her mouth out — pearin' sounds just start ta rollin', them lat-in verbs just flappin' in the breeze real prettylike.

Momma was good in the alphabets. She talkin' just like white folks. Talkin' real chop-chop, Fruzzie say, not like slow movin' syrup on Sunday mornin' that come out just right fo' soppin' them good buttermilk biscuits. But chop-chop, just like white folks, Fruzzie say.

"Lat-in verbs ain't gon' warm yo' bed, gal," Momma laugh.

"Lat-in verbs gonna buy me a heater fo' my head. Don't need no other warmin'."

"Ya gon' need some warmin', gal. Ya been put here just like the rest of us. Gonna want some lovin'; gonna have them babies."

"That's what ya say. That's what y'all all say."

"Watch yo' mouth, gal. Maybe ya bettah do some listenin'— pay some a-ten-tion to how you be talkin', 'cause life gon' do some conjurin'— don't never say what ya ain't gon' do. Fo' the Lawd is my witness. Ya gon' do just what ya say ya ain't."

John Arlane stuck a ache in Momma's side and all them pearin' sounds just spill out and roll all over the ground. Momma went mute, even when he was painin' her the most. "John Arlane is a need that needin' a place to go," Fruzzie say. He went, alright, and Momma could never pick them lat-in verbs up again. So, she went north to get her a city man, one who didn't care fo' no particular talkin' woman. And just maybe, he don't notice she ain't doin' no good talkin', 'cause the pain fo' John Arlane keep gettin' in her mouth. He notice, alright.

"Why ya words keep comin' out on a slant, woman? How a man gon' com-mun-i-cate with a woman who be talkin' and slantin' at the same time?"

She try. But he git tired, and spend his sleepin' time with Miss Bessie Mae, 'cause she got hair that pomp-pa-dew in front, and Daddy like to always be up in front, at least with Miss Bessie Mae. So, while Momma be tryin' to com-pete with Fruzzie fo' the best jugglin', her spirit go out. She twirl fo' a while but she lose the beat. Twirlin' get real empty after awhile; ya fo'git what be spinnin' and what don't. So, I be dropped on my head.

By the time Momma reach down to bear me up, she discover I already doin' a jugglin' act!

"I too busy to stop and talk now," I say. So, I let myself stay lost, 'cause I don't wanna be found. Me, Momma, and Fruzzie coulda been a sistah act. You know, the ones be up on the television set. Them with the big row of white teeth showin' up in front all the time, tellin' how they be owin' everythang to they mommas, and if it wadn't fo' they mommas, they woulda been real lost in the world. Course, the truth be that one head dropper be droppin' a-nother, and since that be happenin' all the time, how we gon' learn to stop droppin' one and the other on they heads?

In the act of jugglin', the one be dropped can never be a-counted fo'. Ya count them in alright, but they start off sittin' in the back, in the corner, in the dark — justa wonderin'. And since they ain't got nobody to be talkin' to, they gives up and out bein' lonely and just plain scared most of the time.

My David fell 'neath the first and third spin. He hit real hard! I can still hear the sound in my head. The sound make such a ruckus, I go all but dumb in one ear; I keep twirlin' just like he there all the same. I finally recognize he ain't spinnin' no mo' when I re-turn from buryin' my own head dropper. David ain't too particular 'bout doin' no talkin', now that I thank I finally got some talkin' to do. He just ain't too particular.

David sits in a tilt. A kinda funny leanin' now. He got real dizzy seein' all my spins, like watchin' all them shiny folks in the Ringlin' Brothers circus who puts plates up on them long tall poles and turns them in all directions. It ain't that he ain't no juggler, but it be different. He be jugglin' alright, but it be his thoughts. I ask myself, "Why that boy be jugglin' his thoughts? Somethang all of us ain't never had no time to do." Us bein' so busy and all. I read once that all us busy made it possible fo' some us chil'ren to slow up sometimes. And we made room fo' them to do some sho' 'nuff thinkin'. Maybe 'cause this be the first one in our line to have some thinkin' time that be why he look so funny. He toss one thought up, it fall. He toss two thoughts up, they fall. Seems like the boy should be knowin' if one fall, two sho' 'nuff gon' fall. He try and ex-plain hisself, but I shakes my head, 'cause ain't Fruzzie, Momma, and me knows all a-bout jugglin'?

I be worryin' 'bout this boy. And this his new way of jugglin'. He says, "Don't be worryin' 'bout me now." I tell myself I ain't, but I wonder where all this thinkin' gon' lead. Fruzzie woulda laughed at the boy, if she still be livin', and excuse him 'cause he a man, ain't he, and what mens know? Momma woulda said too, "Leave the boy alone. He just need some mo' room." Mo' room? Ain't he had mo' room than all of us put together? How the boy need mo' room? 'Cause we womens and he a man don't seem no reason fo' him to have mo' room than us. Somethang real wrong if we keep s'pectin' our daughters to do mo' jugglin' than our mens. I needs to sit down and thank this thing over again.

SCARS

....

KESHO SCOTT

 herry and Paul had arrived in Iowa to claim the keys to her future — a mind expanded by a university education and a spirit set free to challenge "the man upstairs moving the chess pieces" in her life. Opening my life to Cherry was odd enough, but Paul was her seed and also had a touch of Annie — alias something. Twenty years ago, they had taken a detour in the ghetto called "re-li-gion" and I wasn't sure if I was gonna enjoy their "coming out party."

Paul, as I said, was "touched" and his face was covered with grotesque acne. It hid his other facial features, by contrast, and sickened my stomach. I was scared to look into his small hollow eyes that shadowed the monstrous pit beneath. His presence was strange. I had never ever really talked with him when we were kids. He was no longer the boy with the "big head" who used to sit and talk with

Grandma. This time, I decided to watch Paul closely as I carried, in script, the memory of the grandmother we shared. What I was to learn soon explained the meaning of the scars on Paul's face and who gave them to him.

Traveling down canals in Port Harcourt, Nigeria, across the land of the Ibo people, I learned how important it was to read faces. But as an American black, I interpreted the facial designs on African faces to be superstitious mumbo-jumbo and handicaps brought on by ignorance. I remember staring at Akwapon's face with contempt, embarrassment, and pity. Sitting next to him, I asked myself, Why do these fools let this happen to them? Must they bear these markings for life? My arrogance seeped through my skin, filling the jungle air, and all the animals turned away from my smell. I was acting like those white people who specialized in tilting their noses up at darkies. My nose pleaded innocent. My European-American education taught me that these facial disfiguration rituals were really barbaric and perpetrated on helpless African children.

I could see it clearly — an hour after the child is born. The old high priest of the village takes the baby and cuts tracks into its delicate skin. He throws salt in on the wounds and renders the child unconscious. This is the sign that the child has sacrificed enough to the ancestral gods. Later, their dear mothers peel the scabs from the wound and invite the flies to suck the pus away. The scar eventually heals like rugged mountaintops.

Scarred for life, I thought. It was bullshit! They were scars that could not be hidden. Scars that were like paintings that immortalized the human experience by whipping the canvas with brushes. It was the message (for eternity) from birth: you are black and wicked and ignorant and ugly and one step out of hell and jungle-bound, and you were scarred by your own people. I got up and moved away from Akwapon in the boat. But my disgust with these ignorant African niggers was challenged and cleansed the way Akwapon kissed me. This was also the day I tried to kill myself — my white self.

Akwapon, seated next to me at breakfast, simply leaned over and kissed me. I slapped him. Immediately. Naturally. Indignantly. He stood up and stared at the twenty-two eyes turning him into stone and dismissed himself. Those of us from the "fifty states" were appalled at his absolute stupidity. I had to put him back in his place. I had to reteach him a twenty-first-century lesson. I could feel them cheering me on, as I crossed that black face (the black continent), and said: HANDS OFF OUR WOMEN! The smell of my own perspiration seemed foul and made me dizzy. I began to tremble. Something felt terribly wrong. Was the voice in my head mine? I asked myself, Girl, what women are you talking about? How dare *what* savages! Somehow, I had felt the deepest threat of the white girl. It was a foreign sensation. I didn't feel like this when I walked through the ghetto streets. Why now? Shivering away my dizziness, I stood erect like most martyrs do. Tall. Frozen. Dead. The power of the moment spooked away my confusion.

The morning hours slipped into afternoon when Karibu, a "better-mannered" African, came to pass me a note from Akwapon. It read:

> Pardon,
> I wish to make my sincere
> apology. Please meet me at the
> Fountain Tree at 8:00 this night.
> Yours,
> Akwapon

"You damn straight you should apologize," I said as I hurried to assert my golden moment on his slower pace. As if leading a pack of stampeding elephants, I wanted to shake the jungle. When I arrived he was slouched over the tree trunk. As he looked up to catch my eye, his nectar black skin was a sharp contrast to his bloodshot red eyes. He had been crying. I'd never heard of such a thing. I had never read or seen such a thing. Africans smirked, mooned, moaned, sang, and carried placid, serious faces but never tears. Akwapon gestured that I sit. I sat. He drew in a deep breath that he hoped would last long enough to finish his explanation. I felt doom approaching, not from him, but from directly over me. I was not his victim. He had come in the jungle this night to save me.

"Miss, I deeply apologize for my stupidity. I am an African man and decided to express my feelings to you in an American form. My kiss was so you'd understand. I see you did not. I did not follow the custom in my country to express myself. I doubt that you would have understood."

I interrupted him because I knew a come-on when I saw one. I felt sorry for this captivated fool. "Akwapon," I said with a snap, "I don't find you attractive." He laughed. I snapped again. "Besides, I have a man."

He continued to laugh softly and then abruptly stopped. "Miss, my actions were to extend the utmost respect, not intentions of matrimony. I was trying to accommodate *your* ignorance, not mine. You see, if you could read my face you would know that my scars declare who I am and how you were to react and relate to me." His soft-spoken mockery hit like a firing squad. I took off my blindfold and he said, "I am a man with the destiny of my people marked upon my face." He pointed to each facial scar and bludgeoned my ears with the tales of centuries past. Yoruba lineages . . . Ibo conquest . . . and sacred dances by Ife women at the water. The air thinned as my cold tears danced in coordination with his sounds. I had been blown away on African soil . . . pieces of myself all over the ground, all in movement, eyes rolling, hand flickering, heart racing, mouth opening — making no sound. And as my body pieced itself back together, I knew that I had insulted not just one man but a continent of people. How was I to know that his scars were designs for his destiny? Akwapon dismissed himself with a handshake that steadied my world. He wished me greater understanding and left.

I felt like the slashing of my wrist was an easy punishment for my insidious script — white inhumanity in black face. For the remaining summer in Nigeria, I ached at the thought of my drama. I ache now each time I forget I am African and must wait for my clan to pass on to me my destiny. I ache when I realize that we have forgotten our scars.

Paul, the small one, was sixth in the ancestral line of Annie's clan. He, like the rest of the ancestral core, came from a non-African queen who bore the cast of the "southern high yellow." He, dark like Akwapon, has the scars we don't know how to read. Strange how Annie made more bones over those carmel to black grandchildren of hers. Proves those white folks' science wrong every time: that black comes from white — 'cause we all know that white comes from black.

Paul was not like me, Annie's first special grandchild. I was unlike "this short man with a large head." I was an emotional dwarf. For me, a kingdom of DREAMS was my destiny and legacy, to counterbalance the salting of internal wounds. I was kidnapped by the high priestess and then abandoned. My hidden scars work like a layer of skin. They filter, in and out, the powerful "rays of living" and protect my imagination. My potency is camouflaged. And no one knows that I fly around at night and whisper ideas in the heads of sleeping children.

But Paul is a different kind of special child. He is from the direct genes of a richer soil and has the gift of fertility for a different harvest. When he stands, so do scattered parts of a race forced to be international. He is the remains of this race from African soil, carved out of limestone, massive heads and torsos of kings mounted on animal limbs. What were long legs needed for in a kingdom where wealth was a foot away? (It was long-legged westerners who ran into our caves to find slaves in panic, and who sledgehammered the remnants of our empires to hide the secrets that the black man was first.) These African soils hold the permanent writings on stone of histories of child kings and queen mothers who acted from birth as gods and commanded the world through their minds. Blood lines do not lie, they burden.

The first, the sixth, the twelfth, and so on, becomes the pattern for reading the heavens and our family's destiny. Have you noticed the pointed edges of all the constellations? They have direct lines from one star to another. They cannot curve to make pictures in the sky. It is not their nature as stars. Stars light up the navigational pathway from one universe to another. Stars are but chips of the one single source that beams coordinates from heaven to the center of our brain. No wonder our eyes point to the heavens first.

Paul has recordings on his brain that will navigate us out of this universe like our Egyptian ancestors some 7,000 years ago. They used to climb Giza and open their skulls to the glory of time-mind flight. They left us a solid record that someone had taught them about the limitations of the body and the light within the spirit. Africans of all kinds (and their lighter-skinned kin) have been telling about the great journey ever since. Stories were told about the creation out of darkness, of flying ships, Timbuktu, mystical jungles and talking animals, mountains of gold and ivory, slavery, kings, queens, and greater gods than Jesus. Africa was the spiritual light — an earthly reflection of a supreme mind. Through our minds we created it in our image.

I can remember the presence of light on Paul when he was a child. He was in endless training. Paul's head grew as Annie and he communicated. It underdeveloped his body and blew up his head. What was he to use his body for, anyway? They dialogued and discussed and "problem-solved" themselves into a heavy state of constant, inconsistent gloom that made it rain and thunder in their minds always. They, most times, were silent like those African men. They didn't cry; they thought. They thought together like smug aristocrats ignoring the uprising in the ghetto. They lived within. Their mind was never a place for them to get lost in, because it was not anchored or committed to this earth.

The biblical Paul was the zealous nonbeliever who persecuted Christians as they risked death to worship in Pharaoh's tombs. Converted and blinded by the "Light of God," Paul was whipped into faith. He bore scars after that, and lived his legacy. Paul understood the tensions between mind and sight, spirit over body, and faith over reality. In essence, there is no sight, body or reality. There is only the one mind transferred from clan to clan, universe to universe. And in only a few minds is planted — from birth — the original score of music one is to make in this life.

Small Paul withdraws from the music he hears in his head and has yet to sing for this world. Like the artist who has a feel but no product, he savors, very uncomfortably, that gnawing urge to look to the heavens. Let us have pity, for he was chosen and it is a burden. He does not remember when he lived with Zac-Nité, Hannibal, Kwan Yin, Mohammed, Malintzin, Buddha, or Lao-tsu. He does not remember when they kissed him good-bye and transcended for a higher mind. Ten years later, *Newsweek* would only report that deep down inside Paul was a fag and in love with his mother.

"I really want to go to graduate school, so I can find myself," he said. I hope he isn't lost, for our sakes, I thought. I replied to him, "Hey, I can understand." Words to make him a little more comfortable hiding his scars.

As Paul left for Detroit to absorb his salt wounds, I knew that he would return. If not to Iowa, to the destiny in his scars, because he must look at himself every day. His long drive home is a thunderstorm in his head, like all the headaches he had learned not to fix. The storm will eventually muster up a bolt of lethal lightning. Where or who will it be directed at? Paul knows. He is deciding now. And the next time you try to judge a nigger by his color — judge him by his scars.

BOOZER'S STORY

CHERRY MUHANJI

here he git that hard knot little woman? Cain't the boy do no bettah?" they asked. She moved in among us, crawlin' in, a lame draggin' a clubfoot, "a real ugly," they said.

"Why dat boy marry that hard knot little woman?" they asked, mutterin' in clustahs, raisin' eyebrows and pattin' feet.

"Good fo' him," I say. My brotha gittin' what he s'posed to, growin' up in North Carolina where the darkies chaw tobacca and spit through brown teeth and thin lips. I could really give less than a damn. I was already pullin' around my own un-even. My grand-momma dumpin' herself in my blood puttin' me on overload. I drown in yellah but surface in black-git-back features and red nappy hair. A real embarrassment to southern Negroes, still hair slick and mind slick, by white is, after all, always right.

"Hi! My name is Connie Boozer; sorry, Connie Scott," flashin' a real pretty smile. I was surprised. It walked, it talked, this hard knot little woman, who I half expected I'd need to poke a stick at, thinkin' her knot might open anytime, and I had to be ready. Nevah can tell, I might have to protect myself. Black ain't never had no special appeal to me, anyway, since Susie Simmons with her black fists whipped my yellah ass on a daily basis. Still, though, I 'spect somethin' ain't right. I ain't black (leastwise my skin ain't) and I still fightin' and strugglin' to be included, somewhere, anywhere, but findin' nowhere.

"You're John's sister?"

"Yeah, I his sistah." The one Momma had by de-fault from the husband she got when she came north. I thought, Momma's embarrassment but Daddy's delight. I place no store in daddies, cause daddies love anythang, especially they daughters. But what do mommas love? I asked in my thinkin', feelin' one long searin' pain.

"Jenny's your name," Boozer say, payin' no nevah mind to my thinkin'. "I hope we can be friends." She was the one start that feel-talk, feel-good feelin' that served up hungry pieces of myself on steamin' platters, where I, with knife and fork, carved my mix 'n' match dreams. Her feel-talk, put-together laugh, chiseled my inservice nerves to zigzag, as I tried to answer why that boy marry that hard knot little woman? Boozer just smile and say, "Tell them to ask me." Yeah, I like this hard knot little woman.

Months later, we stood inside that hot North Carolina kitchen. "You gals gonna go to the dance tonight?" they asked. (Boozer decidin' fo' me to go with her and my brotha to visit the southern re-lations.)

Boozer smiled, "Yes, but we have to press our hair first." I understood that smile. Inside, that feel-good, pop and snap, shimmy and shake feelin' got started, slidin' down between my legs and bumpin' my un-even into straight.

"We *are* going to the party tonight, aren't we Jenny?" Boozer say with a wink. Boozer was gonna drop Dee-troit on 'em at the dance. And they ain't never seen Detroit smokin' the dance floor till they seen Boozer dance. Yeah, even the skinny leg gal gonna jump and jive, shimmy and shake, and it ain't gonna be like they sistah Kate . . . tonight.

Boozer passed the hot comb from her hand to mine. Naps leavin' a trail with each pull of the comb. The woodstove doin' double duty:

heatin' the hot comb and sweatin' our hair back—all at the same time.

"What ya gals doin'?" The North Carolina re-lations asked. They was niggahs with "good hair." Me and Boozer in the kitchen on that hot day down South, with a fo' sho' 'nuff hot comb passin' 'tween us, was some real freaks to them.

At the dance, Boozer eased onto the floor with Cousin Bill, her hips doin' one motion, her thighs doin' another. Cousin Bill stopped cold. Boozer never noticed. Every cousin in the place, and some that ain't, got stuck, mens and womens, on them be-boppin' hips. She was a snake charmer—a call from the wild. My brother freaked watchin' his hard knot little woman uncurl to the tune of "See the lady with the red dress on . . . she can shake her thang all night long . . . hey, hey . . ."

I hollahed, jumpin' on the floor doin' the Booty Green. Boozer cut her eyes; my head snapped back, and I landed on all fours. They was stalkin' us now . . . smellin' 'em bitches in heat. Then Boozer and I paired off. . . . Wouldn't ya know it, somebody called the dog catcher just as the two uglies shimmied into shape.

That night our ugly began the kick, strut, and grind of our lives—a crazy quilt. Her reds would drown my blues. My yellows, flood her browns. Our quilt covered our lives and warmed the space. We had nobody, so we became each other. A crazy quilt stitched in need, signed in love . . . by ugly.

THE LION SLEEPS TONIGHT

EGYIRBA HIGH

In the jungle
the mighty jungle
the lion sleeps tonight. . . .

Eloise Carter wasn't my blood relative. She was just Aunt Eloise.

In the jungle
the mighty jungle
the lion sleeps
tonight.

She was the odd one.

A weema way, a weema way
A weema way, a weema way
A weema way, a weema way
A weema way, a weema way . . .

At least that's what the folks wanted us to believe — that Aunt Eloise was crazy or something.

Bright orange or yellow caftans flowing, purple and brown and green turbans sitting stately upon her head. She was regal. Her face was not extraordinary, but bathed and dressed in Africa, she was exquisite. She was all Africa. She was out of step. She embarrassed them.

Sometimes, after church on Sundays, we'd go to her home. I remember once smelling something good in the kitchen and then jumping back ten feet when I peeked in and saw a large cow tongue in the pot. I grabbed my throat and wondered how painful it must be not to be able to talk.

Then there was the time when she cooked hogshead cheese. I looked at the finished product and tried to figure out what the head of the hog must have looked like.

"Go on and taste it."

"It looks ugh, Aunt Eloise."

"Come on, take this little bitty cracker and put some cheese on it, just a little itsy-bitsy."

I looked at her intently to see if she was serious. Her face bore a deadpan expression.

"Okay, just a little." My mouth turned up, imagining the worst, as I bit into the jellylike substance.

"It's still ugh."

And peals of laughter came bellowing out of her mouth.

"Well, good, then. More for me."

"You can have it."

"You know, Michelle, that's how Negroes had to survive in slavery times — with what they had."

Those conversations happened on her more subdued days. She was a teacher and always teaching me and my sisters when we came to visit. But the most curious, exciting times had to do with African dancing.

Aunt Eloise would sit and chat for a while and then, as if by cue, she would glide over to the record player. This was the signal that there was about to be a show. Stef or Lisa would giggle, "Uh oh, she's getting ready to start," and I'd turn toward the grown-ups to catch their reactions. Mama and Daddy would sigh a big here-we-go-again sigh, and the voice of Miriam Makeba filled the room.

She danced. My sisters, Stefanie and Lisa, stood by and watched her with great curiosity. None of us had ever seen dancing like it before, and nobody did it except Aunt Eloise.

All the time the music played, Aunt Eloise danced. And danced. And then as she danced, she remembered us.

"Come dance, girls."

Timidly, Stef and I would get behind her and try to copy her steps. Lisa hid in the corner.

The grown-ups, Mama and Daddy, her husband, Uncle John, and their daughter, Brenda, were always ashamed.

"Woman, sit down. Don't nobody wanna see all that spook stuff."

No response.

"Eloise, come on over here and talk to your company. You can't leave these people just sitting here."

Still no response. Only the beat of drums growing louder in the room as the silence of discomfort grew, and Uncle John quit trying to reason with his wife. He'd look back at Mama and Daddy, and then they'd play the eye game, which was also known as the what-can-I-say-you-know-how-she-is look.

Mama would pick up his cue, glance back at Uncle John with "I-know-but-you-have-to-let-her-be," while my daddy just grunted, to no one in particular, his feelings of disgust. Brenda, who had no patience with her mother's shenanigans, would sigh loudly, turn on her heels, and walk quickly out of the room.

"Ahwoo! Ahwoo! Ah! Ah! Uhn! Ah! You have to feel it, Michelle. Feel the beat. See the drummer playing there. Feel it. You can see the blood spilled across centuries. Feel and know all things."

Dancing. Bending and stretching to the earth, her right foot touched down, and she'd swoon in place. Then her left foot, her body yielding to African gods. Somewhere inside I knew it wasn't really funny. I felt awkward trying to dance. Something stirred in me, though it would not be named. I would dance with her until I became conscious of the stares again, and the silent reprobations would stop me cold.

Confused, I'd look back at Aunt Eloise, who never stopped dancing. She had greeted 'Legba and was now possessed by Yemaya. Or caught up in Oshun. I wasn't sure. I wanted to know . . . to dance . . . but they were looking. Their stares would reach into my awkwardness. And I'd freeze, aching to go where she was. Then suddenly, the drumming ended.

Even when the music stopped, the feeling didn't. Aunt Eloise, with new gusto, would go on talking about Africa, the beauty of black people, how Cleopatra was black and Elizabeth Taylor could only wish she was. She immortalized our heroes in the poems she wrote, and her stories left me curious and hungry for more. The walls were covered with pictures of Benjamin Banneker, Joe Louis, Phyllis Wheatley, Mary McLeod Bethune, Jessie Owens. On every spare shelf were African carvings of animals, goddesses, and gods.

"Michelle, did you know that Charles Drew invented blood plasma?"

"No, Aunt Eloise."

"He did. And guess what?" she'd say, pointing to his picture on the wall. "He died needing blood, because he was turned away from a white hospital."

"Ohhhh." I'd nod my head, not because I knew this but as a sign for her to go on. I was young and overwhelmed by the essence of her. She was ambrosia to my spirit, ever sustaining her image by the charms and magic she brought to my life. She whirled endlessly in her dreams. I drank of her. I tasted her. I savored it.

Aunt Eloise wasn't crazy. She was a sleeping lion ready to spring on cue to the moment. She was life and she was music. We only had to wonder. She knew and hoped we'd care. It was years later, after her death, that I realized I had received her legacy of love. She gave me Africa, and I love it passionately. When I hear her notes now, I sing her praises loudly, skin oiled in red earth, body dressed in the blackness of my people, soul moving to the rhythms of talking drums. She smiles, my ancestor, placated by my gifts, and returns to her throne, content, awaiting her invitation to the next celebration of life.

POPSICLE STICKS

CHERRY MUHANJI

The alley is the womb I crawl up in —
a warm thigh, a wet wood, then home.
Garbage cans are jack-in-the-boxes
with pop-off lids where flies jump out
shakin' their silly heads more content
to smother than to hover.

Buildings with kitchen windows in toothless grin
face the cracks in the cement — water canals leadin'
to the big dump — the main sewer,
where I place my boats
of popsicle sticks and rubber bands.
Folks know the canal empties into the China Sea,
where a kid sits just like me.

There's a noisy feelin' near the cracks
crowdin' me . . . slips into those long, loopin' "B's"
of Miss Garrison's handwritin' class;
they become the wire hoops I must jump through.
It spooks my alley, it spooks my play,
more nosey now than noisy,
lookin' for a tongue
lookin' for a tongue
lookin' for a tongue
to get holy in.
Who can tell this feelin' where to set up church?
Who can tell this noise where to go?
A root woman workin' . . . a mo-jo,
just to the left of my ear. . . .

People doin' a short-cut turn 'round into a mad,
'Cause white folks runnin' the downtown
don't bother to put "Dead End."
Niggahs know anyway
where white folks ain't never been.

Leakin' iceboxes in '45
wait for the cool feelin' from the ice,
as Ol' Sally, hoofin' up the alley,
leaves cream-topped milk in the ghetto.

Ol' Sally, the only horse I ever seen,
shits in the canal that holds my boats.
Ain't no horse's shit got a right to stink
and block my China Sea.

One day, Dirty John left Ol' Sally
right in the middle of my canal,
where she put her foot in the trunk
of my yellow-blue Chinese junk.

Flies did the shimmy on Ol' Sally's back,
shakin' and breakin', movin' and groovin',
keepin' time with the neon sign
Pabst Blue Ribbon Pabst Blue Ribbon
Pabst Blue Ribbon Beer.

The flies are huggin' Ol' Sally,
and she wanna just be stoppin' traffic
in the China Sea.

My friend is waitin' and I'll be late.
My boat needs repairin' and I got just enough time
to keep my date,
fo' the sun go down
fo' the sun go down
fo' the sun go down.
Then I stick a rusty end of a ol' hanger right in the
side of Ol' Sally. She jump. I choke. And Momma
starts to screamin', while she is leanin'
right from the sill of the window.

Milk sprays the alley like a fire hose on the loose.
Three winos look up in disgust.
"What the fuck!" they say,
their peein' cut short.
Bottles are breakin', Ol' Sally is wild,
an Momma is comin' to get *this* child.

The noisy feelin's still hoverin'—
a hummin' bee come to pollinate me.

What do I do with my dream?
Momma done got real mean.
How do I fix my boat?
Suppose it can't get ready.
Will I take my Teddy?
Suppose I need . . .

But I climb aboard, anyway,
knowin' I gotta make the China Sea
just for me,
fo' the sun go down
fo' the sun go down
fo' the sun go down.

MADNESS IS A SILENT ACT

KESHO SCOTT

er cheeks blushed red, as she listened to the loud voices in her head that rang like the firm pulse-beat of a six-mile-a-day jogger. It said, "Go'n, girl. Run for your life!" But how far can a woman run with her shoelaces tied? Mattie Tillman was an Olympic champ. She ran inside herself, as the world applauded itself for driving her crazy. Madness is a silent act for the victim. It attacks like multiple sclerosis to the spirit and eats her up from within. As if in a womb, the victim returns to an unidentifiable mass — the kind pro-lifers picket for.

My great-aunt used to play Russian roulette every morning, as she nipped the facial hair that grew on her face every night. She'd cut off her maleness with a double-edge razor blade. Then, as though in a trance, she'd sit on the edge of the tub. Her arm would hang in the sink like a chicken's broken neck. She'd bring the blade to her wrist and play a kid's choo-choo train game, daring her conductor to jump the track of this life and send her to her Maker. This is but one of the silent acts of madness I witnessed in my great-aunt's life as she rambled through the house, making our family very uneasy. Mattie was the one everybody knew was heading for trouble, but it wasn't defined quite yet what the trouble was and who it really belonged to. You see, her private madness didn't fit well with her status as preacher's wife. She was the mother of the church. She was suppose to be a specimen to those "once dead now alive" folks transformed by her husband's syrupy Sunday sermons. She was elevated to the level of Scarlett O'Hara but expected to go nowhere with the wind.

Mattie's older sisters were jealous of her and conspired to undermine her every natural act. They would say, "She's so inappropriate, obnoxious, and much too crisp." Mattie seemed to them like a greasy shrimp that strayed too far from the cocktail sauce. She overdid everything. When she played her music, wore her red dress, drank her booze, and giggled like Bridget Bardot from the late, late, late show, the wolves would appear. Like in Red Riding Hood's story, they would lick their lips and wait for her to take off her hood. You see, the part of the story they never mentioned is the part when the sweet thing stopped for a rest on the road and played footsie with the wolves.

"Hey, baby, you wanna tango?" says Wolf number 123.

"Why not? Ain't nothing but a feelin'. Ain't nobody gonna know as long as I take Grandma her treats. Come on, Daddy, let me curl your fur!"

Mattie visited the woods as often as she could. She played fairy-tale in her real life as if every day was Sunday. She pincurled her dusty hair, dressed her luscious body in Mamie Eisenhower suits, white lace gloves, three-inch pumps, burnt orange lips, and ceremoniously covered the passion of the woods in her eyes with the net hats of the fifties. And when it was no longer fashionable to wear those hats, age provided an escape. Her eyes were hidden underneath the wrinkles and her memories silenced to the outside world. As she grew older, the wolves howled less for her, so then she got drunk. And she stayed drunk. She needed, as the family said, "to be kept in a real cage." They said she was just plain embarrassing them with all her lying and loose talk, or was her loose talk embarrassing 'cause it was not lying?

Mattie was a ghetto anthropologist directly participating in the life of the primitive. She collected data that only brought her to the ironic conclusion that civilization kills, the way whiskey undid the nature of the American Indian. Mattie should have been satisfied like the Indians, who smoked weed and sent their minds into a dialogue with the great Sky God. Instead, she drowned in an ocean brew created by western witches. Mattie Tillman knew it was wrong to put those foreign things in her body, but she refused to listen to her southern, Indian, African ancestors. She bathed in drink, tanned, and peeled her skin in search for a new color. Soon, she needed an afternoon just to sleep it off. She knew that trying to sleep in the ocean was death. So she kept drinking, until her kinfolk signed on the dotted line like the Indians had done. The Indians lost their land. Mattie lost her mind. And both were left entering the white man's theater of reserved living.

A petri dish that houses her cut-away imagination can be seen in any museum that charges a dollar for adults and fifty cents for kids and collects other such relics from "savage" civilizations. Lobotomy is really an operation against the soul. It is an attempt to cut away that which is powerful and, thus, frightening to those without life-preserving juices.

Mattie is operational now. She eats on schedule, talks only when spoken to, and walks the pace of tied shoestrings, directly — when sent — to Grandma's house. She no longer powders her face for color. Her ashiness is permanent. Her husband smiles in her direction be fore each Sunday's sermon, and Mattie's sisters fight among themselves to escort her home. And the wolves, they sigh and remember and wait for the next Red Riding Hood to come.

Mattie was forced to give up her choo-choo train game. A simple switch was thrown, and she came to a dead stop. The conductor's detour was a dead end with no return ticket. There Mattie Tillman is frozen — in her silent act of madness.

JUMPIN' TO SUCCESS

. . . .

CHERRY MUHANJI

y palms hit the window first. And I, like the man on the flying trapeze, took to the air with the greatest of ease. "Come on down, folks, and watch the niggah leap," not from the sides of ships like my many mommas did, but through the looking glass. For I am Alice and *this* just gotta be Wonderland.

Windows see in, but more important, out. The choice is theirs. What a story they could tell! 'Bout the time Sneaky Pete was rippin' off the local Jew. 'Cause Pete knew ham hocks ain't never s'pose to cost that much. And the owner pullin' a gun, and Pete shot, and the police showin' up long after Pete done got cold. Or 'bout us kids watchin' the Chinaman and Miss Nellie through the keyhole doin' some real nasty stuff while her husband, who was really too old for her, rode his bicycle to work 'cause, folks say, he was too cheap to buy a car or ride the streetcar.

I had done myself proud. Halley's comet seen in the ghetto, right through ol' man Cherry's second-floor window. I was the talk in the old house for months, where a group of cousins, aunts, and uncles had "Never seen no crazy gal jump through no window befo'. Must be her up-bringin'. Born in the North, ya know — too much thinkin' like white folks."

My father and his father had pressed for this marriage. The women, my mother and his mother, were strangely quiet. Maybe they wished for this extra load I carried to somehow flush itself down the toilet, but this was five years before nice girls took birth control pills, and only bad girls ripped themselves with hangers. So the babies dropped out.

Passion can be a whore in rhinestone face, a magic mimic in full pantomime; passion can also be pure. And he, my boy-husband, purely loved the groan and the quiver of me coming under him. No passion pleased him more or since, than that early passion he had bought with a marriage license that read: Prize heifer — me, Owner — him. I loved those hot nights in bed, in love, in passion, until I sensed someone was in danger of dying — me. And someone else, not quite me, was trying to live. I turned and there she was. A painted smile on her face, the corners in a giant smile running from one ear to the other. She reminded me of Miss Russell, who with that big smile and a flapper hat stuffed on her head (the ones with the swirls on the sides), collected Coke bottles — all the while grinding her teeth, dipping snuff, and spitting in a can.

"What's your name?" I asked. She blinked with only one eye. One up, one down. One painted black on the lid, one painted white. "A goddamn blinkin' panda bear," I thought.

"Pick a name," she said. "The choice is yours."

She was a brazen hussy! Jump right in while I be washin' the baby diapers. Kinda rub her back up 'gainst all them nasty diapers. Or while Sarah be singin' or Coltrane jammin'. She took no never mind when she'd show up. A brazen hussy, just like I said. She'd ask the same old questions. "Who are you? And why?" And the one that always made me tense up and cry, "And what do you want — really want?" Nobody, as long as I could remember, ever asked me what I wanted. Never. Nobody. It was always decided. Everything. White folks say — niggahs do. Husband say — wife do. He want — she work. He get — she tired. He mad — she cry. He beat — no change, no change, no change.

Momma knew no change too. She lived in poverty so grindin'. Not the kind that keeps ya one food stamp from hustlin' on the street, but poverty that sucks. And you die inch by inch, day by day. Momma had left the fight a long time ago. Now when she woke each day, her eyes would pop open, like my very white doll with the blue eyes. Someone would pull the ring at her neck and she'd say, "My name is Annie. See Dick and Jane. These are my children. See Dick run. See Jane catch the ball. See! Here comes Father."

If Dick, my brother, didn't know better, I, Jane, did. Momma lived with a man, my Daddy, who slept with his penis out Sunday through Thursday and in some neighbor's wife Friday and Saturday. Her windows fallin' dark, Momma looked out on a world from eyes that were bein' snuffed out. Without touch and feelin' from Momma, my own life went dark. I felt lost, left and alone, searchin' for a seat on the bus, with Momma the only other passenger on it.

"Boy-husband, where do the wind come from? . . . Who is God's daddy? . . . Is the love of womens like what we got?"

"Wha-a-at! You sleepin' with women? Ya nasty bitch!"

Like I said, no change.

"Hang up the phone, bitch!" I had eased out of bed with his first snore, changed from gown to street clothes in the bathroom, and walked quietly down to the drugstore to make a call.

"Hang up the phone, bitch! Do ya want yo ass kicked here or home? Take ya choice."

Funny that this should be the first time I ever got to make a choice. We walked home. His fists smashed into my face, on and on and on. I'd really gotten used to his fists by now. Fightin' wadn't 'bout nothin'. I couldn't tell the difference anymore 'tween his fist, his fuck, and his fightin'. He had discovered a cheatin' wife and he'd beat her back into place, or she'd die tryin'. And cheatin' I was. Not sleepin' cheatin', but needin' cheatin'. I needed to know.

Ronnie was a frail boy with eyes that covered most of his face, ones that looked out on the world like a deer who hears danger and moves quickly. Ronnie asks me questions about God and livin', lovin' and dyin'. So, I made this call. I needed to talk. Talk 'bout what? And how could I talk in a house full of his relatives? Me, a young bride, havin' a baby, not Ronnie's, so why did I need to talk to him? And besides, I was a silly bitch, a silly hi-yellah bitch, and silly hi-yellah bitches don't talk, they purr. And this bitch, in this house, was gonna do what she was s'pose to — have this baby and not purr over the telephone to some other man. As the boy-husband beat on and on, I suffered — not from blows so much, but from no answers. Inside, I had been leavin' him for a long time and askin' questions for a long time too. S'pose, just s'pose, I thought, there ain't no answers? So, I leaped.

My palms hit the window first. The glass, stunned, felt forced entry like a rape in progress. It gave up and in. Glass cut through the air, slicing a path for this uninvited guest. Not prepared, the air, given to the flight of birds and the wings of bees, just dropped me.

I fell on top of a snowbank. Sprawlin' and cryin' with glass everywhere and me lyin' in my own funk — the funk from my own life — funk born of not enough of nothin', not enough answers, not enough choices, and not enough expectations. Me alive! Now what?

"Well, I guess you ain't dead," she said. There was Panda Bear! Right there on top of the snowbank with both eyes blinking, one up, one down.

"Wel-l-l-l," she said.

"Well what? I guess I do look pretty silly."

"Yeah, you do."

"No more than you with that one blinkin' eye."

"At least, I know how to blink. What do you know how to do, besides this crazy shit you been up to?"

"Look, I don't wanna . . ."

"Do what? Live? Well, I do. If you don't, I don't. . . . Got it?"

"Look here, you can't sit there with that shit-eatin' grin on your face and tell me what I gotta do."

"Naw?"

"Naw."

"No shit? Well, at least I got you fightin'."

AND ETCETERA
(A Tight Space a Week, Makes Fifty-two a Year)

. . . .

KESHO SCOTT

ovin' that condition. What an odd thought about how I feel about my man. Like when he's looking for me three hours after work and then reminds himself that he should have planned to spend the hours better, because it reminded him of his ex-wife's infidelity.

When the right dove flies over the black woman's head, we won't know it's a peace sign. We'll be too busy ducking bird shit.

Black women confuse need with greed. We need a man but act with greed because we want them to be everything our lives have failed at.

My thermostat on men never reaches 98.6. The temperature has never been normal. Either I have had a fever or haven't been able to keep it up. I'm only normal with myself.

Men have never been the object of my affection but the source of my getting masculine.

I can't write a love story about him and me because I've only been inspired to fall in love with myself.

My deeper desire is not to have a man that is sensitive to me, but one who can be sensible about himself in his discovery of sensitivity between us.

After we have finished his sex, my dramas, his ego, and my feelings, we both fell asleep.

All I want is for you to get a job, I said. And that was the biggest lie I ever told.

Bring me flowers, so I will know that you have practiced before my funeral. I'll be dead soon.

Don't cuddle with me after I act out on you! I don't want to be reminded that I am a black woman.

Share? Ugh! Give? Ugh! Love? Ugh! You know what you are talking about alright, but you don't know how to do it.

Opposites do not attract: You black man. Me black woman.

The white man ain't got nothing to do with your tone of voice. Or mine.

You did something that I really didn't expect. You were you.

Don't be more consistent than I'm used to, or I'll suspect you're trying to grow for us.

I can't ask him what the feminists ask — he ain't grown yet.

He said he wants me to go for my dream, even if he isn't in it. Now he's trying to change my thoughts.

My being a black woman has never been a problem for me — just everybody else's problem.

They find me attractive.
They find me intelligent and brilliant.
They aren't afraid of what others would say.
Why don't I believe them?

I love all my sugar daddies totally. They love only a part of me.

I don't want the man of my dreams because my dreams are confused.

Haven't I met you in Paris? No!
Haven't I met you in New York? No!
Haven't I met you in Cincinnati? No!
Haven't I met you before? Of course!

When I get involved with someone who loves the outside of me — the outside shows out.

Superwomen lie about more than their age.

I'm numb when he is sincere because I'm used to electrical burnout.

Either you marry me or we're through! Business is the only language we agree on.

I want men to leave me alone and bother themselves more.

Being the only black on the bus, in an all-white part of town, doesn't make me feel feminine.

The five days I'm on my period — are the five days I won't get screwed.

You want to spend the rest of your life with me? You're crazy! Let's go get pizza — I'll buy.

I boogied all night. He was so fine! I was looking good too! Nothing important happened, of course.

I send more nonverbal messages because that's the way this cookie has crumbled.

I was happy once. I was alone too!

My pussy has a better track record at getting what it wants than I do.

Suppose . . . just suppose, there were no black women in the world?

It really doesn't surprise me that you don't want to claim your kids. Faith takes a heart.

Ugly systems hire black women because ugly makes systems run.

It isn't true we can always get a job. We *can* always get back to slavery.

As feminists, we lose our color.
As blacks, we lose our sex.
As girls, we lose our power.
As dogs, we have an identity.

I know I look good because being sexy is the best quality of the oppressed.

Arrange to meet me. It's the least you can do after standing me up because of your blindness.

It would be nice to return to childhood when being a black "pickininny" wasn't a threat.

We didn't write down what we did.
We didn't hear them talk about what we did.
We didn't get scared when they did start to talk about us.
What did we do?

Stop, please! . . . is not in my vocabulary.

When I grew up I wanted more, than I wanted to be anything.

I am getting along with a man, and he hasn't lost his mind yet.

Romance a black woman and you'll see gardenias growing in a desert.

It was stupid of me to believe I could.
I should.
I can.
I do.
I must.

Answer this question, smart-ass: where are they then?

Rub me right and I'll surprise you.

Even my daddy was scared of me!

··

LISTEN TO ME GOOD, NOW

HUSH

KESHO SCOTT

ush. A word that calls a gentle halt. A word that disarms authority. Hush. More than a word. It creates a space between an ascending emptiness and spirals it like braided hair. Hush nips the biting frost beneath the cracks and settles us down to bedtime stories about our lives.

Hush was not a word used much by the women of my family. My mama has seen two hundred seasons in her lifetime and has never known the magic of her mother's hush. She has watched her mother's magic from a passenger train heading in the opposite direction. The thrill of Grandma's fireworks looks amazing from a distance.

But Mama has quilted her years into a patternless maze neatly positioned on this life's table. The seams are unsewn. Carefully, she keeps all the pieces close.

Now, it can be said that their lives, separated by sixteen years, were close, as close as ivy embracing stained-glass windows. They have shared everything from grandstands to grandchildren, but neither is able to total their sums and see that they total each other. My mother, at least, has tried to climb Grandma's Eiffel Tower ego. Once, she promised herself not to flinch when she said, "No, Mama, don't hurt me." On the inside, it gets caught in her throat, and childish sounds come out when her mama turns up the volume.

Grandma manages to hear her daughter's rumblings but reacts like a seasoned politician. She blames the people for their own drinking problems. Grandma has learned to treat Mama as a sidewalk bum. She leaves half-empty whiskey bottles on Mama's doorsteps to hold back a sober moment of reality for them to touch. Lately, as they wine and dine Jesus together, as their ages join, the painful sobriety shows in their eyes that never meet.

I grew up watching this tragedy headed nowhere and wished and wished and wished someone would be brave. I did rain dances in each camp, hoping to put out the smouldering coals. A spark or two always remained. Eventually, I just buried myself away from in between their lives. I could no longer sing.

No sounds come from them now. Not even the fussing. Not even the ever-present awkwardness of two dogs on the same side of the street. They do not attack for fear of bleeding; there is no blood. They seem transformed into roots, tangled and crammed together in a small window jar just waiting for a little warmth from the sun. Their hush brings no movement to the dark coastline between them. Instead, the tide washes ashore my own lover's heart, cracking open its bottle.

Now the hush that works for me and my lover is right because it works. It is the long and lazy kind, more of touch and posture than sound. I whirl it when his manliness decorates me in tight silk and lace and confines the world that belongs to me. My hush removes the binding off his feet, so he can leap and prance and overlap the corners of his mold. He tingles now. He whispers hush when my womanness decorates him in three-piece suits, trimmed in power that limits the spirit he has to share. His hush dislodges the blade in my throat, so I can shout and declare and nurse my wounds.

The right hush. Such a contrast to no hush at all. Remembering all the times I thought I was waiting for Mr. Right, and he all along was waiting for his mama. And both of us seeking to make life a womb instead of the roller coaster it is.

We didn't always know how and when to hush. We spent years racking our brains and learning when to use it. We climbed and stumbled until we bumped into each other's waterfall, a place we could run to bathe in appreciation. Once, he said hush when I was juggling two children, a job, a Ph.D. program, and of course, my heavy mind. That sultry sound, hush, extended me closer to my own possibilities, and I decided to stop juggling. The spokes of my life finally connected, and I am at the center of its movement.

Once, I said hush to hush a look that echoed from my lover's face, bombarded by ghosts of his past choices. He was the object of a cruel kids' game that converted loving into clowning. Now when the clowns come to laugh, they find him catching his dreams.

The right hush between me and my lover is a feeling we don't work at. It fits because we painted our own canvas long ago, and we see in it colors for us to arrange together. We arrange and hush, and manage and hush, and ordain and hush, until we behold a new sonnet.

And now my children rehearse these verses. My music lives in them and parts of me collect from the bottom up. I measure my seasons by their birthdays. They copy and gather them to wear in their hair, to portray the parts of me they claim. But their symbols cannot tailor the gap between us. I am forever mother evolving mothering. They are children multiplying the best of me by two.

I never hold back hushes from my children. We sort of do a hush-blush routine, staged from the rooms we live in. Our duets harmonize like dandelions dangling in tall, wild grass. We sway with the currents of a soft spring and make ourselves the pulp of a universal hush.

When the winter comes and catches us unprepared to make her long, dark sleep, we feel naked. Our shame suspends the open glances, and we say hush from the sides of our mouths. I feel drained and burdened and bend to winter's way. My children retreat. I'm frozen and cold. I can't find blankets to cover my edges, so my hushes are quick and thick but passionately placed between us.

Then there is their space I observe from a distance. I do not invade. I am too big and fierce-looking. I see my children sketching out our lives in baby's play. The scenes that stick in their hearts are tender and terrible and only references. One says to her doll, "Hush, baby. Go to sleep," as she plays me, playing her, play us. The other child protects.

"Hush, I'll walk you home from the bus stop. Okay?" Again, her direction, her playing me, play us. These sketches, in colors from dark to gray, from thin to faint, make sense of the shadows I feel will come from me and hang over their lives.

I tone myself down in order to tune into them more. I don't want to miss the hushes they give me. Like the alphabet I drilled into their heads, they burn memories on my flesh so I can sizzle in old age.

"Mommy, we love you so much." They hush me simply to tell me they are growing, and I can taste one less tear worrying over them. Hush makes it easy to accept the wrinkles on my face. Nature designs our bodies in the end to speak to themselves.

The loudest hush that I am learning to hear is the one I tell myself. It mimics the orange cast in an autumn sunset and speaks an Arabic dialect. The clicks and low grinding tones of its sound draw attention to my mortality. My bones respond too. They snap to the rhymes of cricket voices and tell my insides that they, too, shall pass. I have struggled against nature's gravitational pull toward an undefined center. I hear her through trees, browning grass, and dusk. Hush.

I bow to her every day and night, and she fills my mind with visions long overdue. "Hush," she says to my race. "Hush," she moans to her planet. "Hush," she tells other universes. "Listen to our ascending emptiness before we become empty containers without love."

THE LAST DANCE

....

EGYIRBA HIGH

he wide, open savannah is forever my roost. I walk among the plains aware of my full essence, the territorial privilege of one as big and bad as I. I stretch my body across the straw grass, dry-fucked by the sun. Its scratchy remains irritate my skin. Still, I manage to find a comforting groove and yawn lazily.

Turning my face to the sun, I revel in all my glory. This is comfort. It is mine. I shift to my side, one eye open, casually alert for signs of interlopers. Invisible voices, in the wide expanse surrounding me, whisper approval to lay bare my guard.

I roll over and back again, allowing the sun to wash me. Energies flow, barrier-free. A fly lands on the straw grass near my face. I eye it playfully, knowing its presence offers no threat to my sovereignty.

Slowly, my open eye closes and my body eases into familiar. I settle, then resettle myself, till I carve a warm niche in the earth. "Hmmm," I say aloud, then, "Hmmmmmmmm." The fly buzzes off, and I take notice of it landing on my hip. My eye shuts down again, and I resume my stately repose. "Hmmmmmmmmmmm."

Soon I feel myself being lifted slowly, magnificently up, a slow swing like a venetian blind going up one side at a time till it gets to the top. I am being pulled. A gentle breeze blows under me, coaxing me easily upward. Lighter now, as though my body has taken on new mass, I am relieved of the responsibility of myself. I reach the apex of my ascent and float in big, lazy circles. Black birds move past me. I am flying. I whirl and spin free to take in all that is my life. I soar uninhibited by the chains of tradition or time. Suspended by will and desire, I run through the sky, breathless excitement coursing through my veins.

I have come into being. Like morning dew on roses, I produce myself naturally. I grow in upward spirals and weave life with a needle of my own proportions. My flight sings testimony to broken chains and endless pathways.

Whirring. A buzz. Grinding irritation. Slight at first, it intrudes my dream, then my senses. Like a hawk whose flight is halted by a newly broken wing, I fall.

I try to shoo it from my world. It must be the fly, I tell myself. I shoo it blindly but the swish is in vain. This is outrageous! I am not prepared to climax myself—this "feel good" feeling. I don't know what this intrusion is, but I know somehow that it will not leave. It grows stronger, determined to invade my life with its need. A need I cannot fulfill or sustain. It must find its own way. The whirring grows, perpetuates itself slowly but steadily. Pressing on, pressing on. "Fly!" I scream, a mixture of desperation and anger. I wake from my dream turned nightmare. "Fly! Leave me alone!" My command is a threat of no substance, for the echoes grow louder still. They press on, press on toward me.

I am exposed. The security nets of my kingdom drop and reveal my invisible nakedness to the elements. I cover my vulnerability and grow guilty for my freedom.

"No!" I cry. "Not me, not now!" I grow cold in fear. I shiver the kind of shiver when something ominous is about to happen.

We are frenzied, this noise and me. I tremble, my courage caught off guard. Wobbly knees force themselves up. I turn my head wildly for explanation, signs of the advancing hunter. My vision goes from blur to steady, blur to steady. Coming in the distance a shapeless mass. Slowly, toward me it comes. The pull of its strength pins me to my now standing position. Its power grows stronger with each approaching step. A strange smell floats into my nostrils. What is it? I am rooted. I am rooted. Unable to move, I tremble. Not against the fear of it, but a new sensation — the power of it. It is coming as they all have before, to try to get the thing that is evolving in me.

My eyes blink to clear, then blink again. Slowly, slowly, it comes into view, a form known to me; I have seen it many times. But never have I confronted it. It becomes he, and slowly my fear retracts into itself. I loosen myself enough to take one step back. My left foot crosses over the right, then over again. I am stalking and stretching to the ends of this jungle. I roar, "This is mine! You keep your distance!" But on he comes. Magnificently beautiful, full of passion and power. I have seen this before. He moves with the calm and ease of a snake: with time, easy does it, and mystery. I pick up his step and move away from him. Sideways I move, then I am pulled to him. His power is deep in me.

My nostrils take in the scent of him. His skin is touched by fresh grass and raw wood. He stops. I stop. We survey each other, nearly eye to eye. His palms go up, his lifeline facing me. I answer by the touch of mine to his. We move in a slow circle dance together, then apart. He goes to the left, I go to the right. For seconds we hear the same rhythm, then the cadence of my own drumbeat comes into my vision. I turn from him to show my own power. Step. Step. I move around his long, waiting frame. A smile spreads gradually to his lips. Slowly, the edges of his mouth turn up to meet his feeling. My power electrifies him.

I bend over as I step and touch the earth. I smear it on my skin, never missing a step. I bare my breasts and quicken my pace. "You cannot have me," I dance. Up I go, then down. He receives the message and lays down his armor. We spin our energies, and he collapses. My dance ends its praises to this earth, to myself.

I back away now. I pick up the discarded weapons and sling them over my head. I turn my eyes up to watch them sail far away where they cannot harm me. I back away. Again. I lie down in the straw grass and begin to yawn. I, who am myself, can wait until he comes to himself.

LOON

....

CHERRY MUHANJI

he came . . . finally, pressed her forehead against the rounded entrance, went in and sat down. Jenny was at the back of the cave, stirring her rhymes in an iron pot.

32 dashes . . . of bitters
1 smile . . . gradual
4 children . . . quickly
and 6 rent men . . . all the time.

Jenny set the bottle down. Boone's Farm Apple. The best in the west. Guaranteed to get you through . . . the night, and sometimes, the day . . . depending on . . .

Billie Holiday leaned into the pot, sniffing . . . the vapors.

"You better watch out. Yo' gardenia gonna melt." There was Loon, sitting in the corner, scratching her ticks. Jenny/Billie was singin'. "My man done left me . . ."

"Yo' mama ain't never said you was no singer. Come to think about it, yo' daddy neither."

"Who asked ya, Loon?"

"Yo' mama." Loon starts laughing and rolls over on her back, feet up, trying to put her stockings on over her shoes. "Three-six-nine, the goose drank wine, yo' mama did the shimmy, . . ." Loon chants.

Billie Holiday bites down on a strange piece of fruit, and Jenny resumes her stirring, high now.

"I got some rhyme fo' ya, Jenny."

"What make ya thank I want yo' goddamned rhyme, Loon?" Loon cups her hand over her mouth. "Folks, she high now." Loon moves to direct the chorus of black bats who, sitting upright, begin to blink. And with exaggerated movements, she lifts the baton and taps on the rocks nearby.

"Mmmmmm. Mi mi mi mi mi mi," they prime their throats, stretching their bodies to full attention.

"Jenny's high, now." They blink, hum in barbershop harmony.

"Jenny's drunk, now." Another blink, and they shift into a minor chord.

Loon, hanging upside down, starts to counsel. "Ya betta take my rhyme whether you want it or not. Ya know I can hurt ya, don't you?"

"Not anymore, Loon."

"My ass! I sent ya through a looking-glass, Alice. Remember?"

"No more, Loon. Not this time."

"Like hell. First the man, then the babies, then the parties, and then . . . then . . . and then. . . ."

"Stop, Loon, you're givin' me a headache."

"That wine givin' you a headache. I put ya in a crazy bed, didn't I? Yo' guts turnin' green and ya spittin' up in a bottle. I can make 'em pump yo' stomach again."

Loon began to ricochet wildly, jumping from one ledge to the other, feeding herself bat droppings. She knew Jenny, not quite drunk enough, would refuse her.

"The bombs stopped dropping a long time ago, Cherry."

"Who said that? And who the hell is Cherry?" Jenny asked, suddenly aware of a new voice. She got up, straightened her skirts, walked over to the pot and took a sniff.

"That's not too bad, Cherry."

"Who's the new bitch?" Loon asked, slowly raising one eyebrow.

"Cherry, do you and Loon always fight like this?" She asked.

"Well, you know, Loon ain't real. She's just real when my rhymes git to cookin' and my head starts to spin."

"Yo' mama."

"How long has she been coming out?" She wanted to know.

"Well . . . she helped me cut open my very first doll with the blue eyes and blond hair."

"Yeah, we torn the motha up!" Loon says, as she starts to sing, "Gimme a pig foot and a bottle of beer . . ."

"Cherry, the bombs stopped dropping a long time ago," She said, trying to drown out Loon. "It's safe to come out now."

"I was lonely, then. I'm still lonely. Loon helps me make up rhymes. Besides, I've been at the back of the cave for a long time."

She moved closer. "Is that what you think this place is?"

"Well, isn't it?"

"Well, everyone outside thinks . . . we think there's some sort of show going on in here. Sometimes we hear singing, sometimes laughing and, sometimes, something that sounds like pounding."

"Oh, that's Loon bangin' her head up against the wall."

"It's a wondah my ass ain't in a sling, havin' ta live with you," Loon says, squatting but missing the top of the Coke bottle, her pee hitting the edge.

"Almost every day we hear long, long rhymes. We always wanted to come in, Cherry, but . . ."

"Who in the hell wanna come in a goddamn cave?" Loon screams on all fours now, scratching furiously.

"Cherry, you've got a whole production in here. Didn't you know that?"

"What are you talkin' about? And why do you keep callin' me 'Cherry'? I write little jingles, get drunk and sing 'em, that's all."

"Yo' tell her." Loon jumping in between them, starts to do the Slow Crawl (a dance she made up one night when Jenny was *real* drunk).

"She's got a hard head. Always did. And a hard head make fo' a soft ass."

"It sounds to me, Cherry, like you've been . . ."

"L-o-o-oonn! What the fuck are you doing?" Loon is now up at the roof with a hand drill, trying hard to bore a hole into the top. Jenny screams again. "Loon!"

"The air gettin' thin 'n' stale in here — I'm leavin'."

"How ya gonna drill through the whole goddamn mountain?" Jenny screams, all control gone now.

"Calm down, Cherry," She says. "This is not a cave. This is just your place. Your space. Your thing. Your production — the thing you do. This isn't a cave."

Jenny takes the spoon out of the pot, runs her tongue along the edge.

"Damn that's good." She turns to look at She, "I wouldn't know how to come out."

"You go out the same way Loon did — right through the top."

Cherry was alone these days. She had been there at first but no more. One day She was just gone. No explanation. Gone. Being alone, Cherry was discovering, was very different from being lonely. Cherry or Jenny or whoever she was was becoming something. A somebody. And she liked it. Well, that wasn't altogether true. There was the time when she had been at the theater with all of those lights in her face. The audience quiet — waiting — and her waiting for something to come out — something to come out of her mouth, anything. Linda was with her on stage, waiting for her cue. Damn, how does it go? Her mouth dry.

"Look. Keep yo' goddamn hands offa my fur coat. Do ya hear? I've killed a niggah fo' less. I got a ticket just like everybody else and ain't no dude in a monkey suit gonna . . ."

There was Loon, third row, center aisle, seated on her haunches, fartin' and fannin' her crotch, with no drawers on. Cherry laughed — so hard that the audience did too. Then she remembered the line. Loon never failed to get her going.

This somebody she was becoming was bigger and better than she ever imagined!

And there was Loon. When it was good and when it was bad. Just like a marriage.

"Me and Loon married?" Now that really was funny. *Real* funny.

····································

YOU MUST BE LYIN'

TALK TO THE STORM

. . . .

KESHO SCOTT

 his side of heaven is crowded and heavy because the angels carry AK-47s and bleed inside three-eyed gas masks. They speak Mayan tongue and look for the last equinox. Six-sided serpents whine in unison trying to tell us the storm is on the way.

Megan was with child and close to forty. She made all the choices career-wise white women make but finally dropped out of corporate America to raise avocados. Imagine. Raise avocados. Sounds like dog training. She had forgiven herself for believing the lies about the perfect career and the bosses' lies about just one more account . . . and walked off the job one Monday afternoon when the coffee break was just too short and her boss a bit too smug that she just couldn't do without her work. He didn't know she had invested well. He didn't believe she could set a real fire under her dreams. Now she smiled at her wrinkles and sagging boobs and early liver spots and rubbed her belly with green-stained hands.

She had learned in just a few short years how to walk on her tiptoes like children and become a blade of grass. She even started talking to the trees and maturing with the seasons. Seasons replaced "process," and visions cast shadows on credit cards. In summer, she'd change her name to Sun-netta, sleep on the back porch, eat fresh, fresh pink peaches for breakfast, wear long rainbow-colored skirts and back-out tank tops. Her color would change to sunset orange, and she'd whistle with the wind and collect avocado seeds — put them in a hope chest and pray for autumn.

Autumn was her reflection time. She'd call herself Ro-we-na, an Indian name meaning the woman who purges. Megan fasted on carrot juice, honey, and good thoughts. Took long walks until her feet blistered and lured the moon with exotic dances in her avocado skin. It was last autumn that she had met Al. Alfredo Luscanini. An immigrant who smelled and was a Peeping Tom. She was performing her ritual to the Moon Goddess — placing slim, cold vegetables between her legs as she lay face-down and oozed with the night owls. Megan noticed him one night peeping in, wanting in, and so she let him in. He made no language she could understand, but they made love in the dirt and in between the cauliflower and tomatoes and absorbed the juices of raw onions. Moon Goddess liked that and blessed Megan with a child and called Alfredo back to wherever he came from. And Megan didn't care. She knew the Moon Goddess took care of her every night with the vegetables and all the fruit in season.

As winter pressed the face of autumn into a mustard seed, Megan called herself Mecca and lived in the eastern horizon of her modest, three-room farmhouse. She memorized the Koran, spoke in its tongue, made preserves, and whispered Jungian psychology to her belly. Winter pressed her into fishbowl living and she paced her floor, making grooves for the spring ladybugs to later hatch in. All her motions in winter's time imposed on her life a discipline to reenter nature's gateway led by spring. Megan never made a sound out loud during the winter because winter asked of her nothing — and nothing was her middle name. Nothing. No. Thing. She enjoyed suffering for nature.

Spring would burst upon Megan's life with the sound of snowflakes melting to make buckets of water for her to bathe in. The cold water was exciting and reminded her of the time she napped in the avocado vines and the animals invited themselves to her skin. She lay in what appeared to be the middle of the universe as they licked her awake, leaving their animal flavor on her uncovered parts. Megan called herself Anima in the spring. She collected cow dung, bent her bare ass to the sun, and planted the prayed-upon avocado seeds.

Each morning Megan would tie up her greasy brown hair with semidry thistles and tulip limbs and wrap her seventh-month belly in a toga made of pastel terrycloth. She strolled down the rows of avocado vines she'd named after her past lovers. Peter, the priest; Jake, the anesthetist; Michael, the welder; Bradford, the neighborhood shopping cart collector; and all the rest. Tipping like Elmira, her city cat, Megan would touch each lover's head — practicing her mothering instinct. She remembered their lies and sprinkled water from her flower pot to drench out their flames. Megan had learned, from raising avocados, not men, that putting out fires was the only way they would learn to absorb and start to grow. She forgave her lovers. Actually, Megan only opened the scabs in her mind about men when she felt tight and unloved. The green avocado jackets were always tight until the sun's loving made them ripe. She freely released pee down her leg each morning, toasting the earth. The mud puddle gave way to beautiful footprints — heavier now with the weight of the child. Megan would stand in full view of Dawn, pick the heart from her lover's chest, peel away the lizard jacket, and eat. Avocado juice filled her mouth, stained her face, and embraced her waist. Breakfast was her favorite meal of the day. Yellow legal pads and lunches on the thirty-fifth floor were a faint memory now.

"I think the documents are ready for you to sign, Mr. Winged Bear. My plane will be here in a quarter of an hour. Would you mind if we proceed now? I believe our company has made a very generous offer to even agree to purchase this land."

The plane ride home was tiresome. She took one look at the mud caked on her blue suede heels and shook her head thinking, This shit will never come off. Reaching in her bag for a cigarette to blow away this last image, her hand felt something she had forgotten. Then she remembered the avocado given to her by Winged Bear's wife.

"Thank you. I'll take it back to New York with me. I didn't know you grew them on this kind of land."

Cleaning the green paste from her nails annoyed her as had the sight of women in the village reaching to shake her hand. Megan had to shake them all, of course, she thought. Each touch had left an unfamiliar residue. Haunting her. A closeness to these women that she had not known. Lumps of fright circulated up her arm and tightened her smile.

In her eighth month, Megan could no longer stay in the field and tend her avocados. Now, most days were filled with rocking chair contemplations about her child. She could think no other thought. The birth rehearsed in her mind was rote and anything rote felt like the "old her" — when she was with the firm. Pendleton-Abram Legal Associates, she thought . . . alias a butcher's shop that hired mentally ill Cherokee cleaning ladies and blue-black male studs to carry the coffee.

"Excuse me, can't you see I'm working. Leave my waste paper basket alone. Please don't come near my desk," the "old her" grumbled.

Nightair, the cleaning woman, nodded and moved to the corner of the room to scrub up the coffee stains from the carpet. Megan, annoyed at her maneuver, asked, "Do you have to be in here now?"

As though not hearing the question, Nightair spoke her thoughts: "What makes a woman like you work until dusk? Dusk divides the day. Dusk changes all women into something new. I change. I leave the life of my family and come to the life here. I wonder what you change into? In a dream, nights ago . . . I saw you wanted my help . . . but I can't take the steps for you. You start to plead. I begin to tell you the story of my mother and you turn away, I try again . . . and you say no . . . I give you the warning of the girl with the big head: life stings like a bee one day. But you turn your back to me."

Megan recoiled. She walked to the doorway, gesturing firmly outward. "Will you work in some other room," she said, pausing to control her anger. "Please!"

"Sure. I was just passing it on."

"Passing what on?"

"The message from the dream."

"What message?"

"The one that comes to me from night air. That is my name. I'll come back to clean up your stains . . . the ones that are on your floor."

Now, on these long waiting nights, Nightair's words smoked her mind and intruded upon her thoughts. There was to be no doctor, no hospital, no crying. No man to cuss out in transition, and no God-damn's to spray in the air. Megan was to crawl on all fours and have the earth cradle her child from the hole in the ground. Simple. Succinct. Elmira would be the only witness. A purring nurse with cat-bad breath telling her when to push. Megan knew Elmira was jealous of the other animals and had threatened to run them away. So she rehearsed the after-birth plans with Elmira. She would rest the entire day in the vines and suckle the child until the Moon Goddess rose in search of her daughter. They were ready. Looking down, she rubbed her tits. They kept their own hard-on.

This called to mind Moss, the coffee boy who'd rubbed his back up against her in the elevator. Her thoughts of being trapped with him caused epilepticlike spasms in her breast that ignited her lower creases.

Moss could not apologize fast enough to contain his stuttering spit before she had him fired. Five o'clock in the parking lot he signaled her and, cocky and controlled, she approached him.

"I didn't have you dismissed because of the obvious accident in the elevator. I just don't think it's good company policy for employees to participate in . . ." It didn't matter. Megan had just pulled rank on the six-foot-eight boy, who'd forgotten to remove his protest button from his uniform — a short-sleeved, starched, white shirt, red bow tie, and skin-tight tan, corduroy trousers. The thought of his uniform before Sunday afternoon naps added spice and juices to her non-business weekends. After that, Megan ignored the elevators.

By the ninth month, her lovers in the avocado vines were jealous. Angry. And began to long for the way it had been. Motherhood had robbed them of their pet.

Megan sat rocking, her eyes capturing the horizon line where the sky meets earth. Meanwhile, Elmira's ego was in need of testing. She'd customarily jumped from the porch window to the stack of boxes near the steps. Megan maintained such an intimate relationship with space that she kept all the furniture, except the bed, on the front porch. Elmira took another leap and clawed down the gray tie-dyed tablecloth that hid the television set. Megan twisted her face into a scolding nun, as she picked up the cloth. TV, she thought. It had never been unpacked. She had used its top as a table and rotated it from place setting to place setting. How long had it been since she'd turned it on? Two, three, or four years? She'd lost track. Elmira flinched and purred a grumbled message.

"Shall I turn it on, Elmira? Maybe you can see some of your Nine Lives friends?" She threw back her head, laughing. Teasing Elmira was a pleasure. Elmira took everything personally. She often would duck underneath the couch for a week. Megan reached and pulled the switch. As the black turned to green, then blue, and the rainbow spattered into recognizable images, faces with pink limbs and double-imaged noses began to fit together. Megan sat down to the faint voices coming from the dusty box. She heard: "We interrupt this program for a special message from the president of the United States."

Elmira's black hair stood up on her back. She jumped into Megan's lap and purred for her to turn it off. The announcement continued: "My fellow Americans, and allies. We have succumbed to our worst nightmare. We are being attacked. The red menace has finally come to our shores. All of our efforts to avoid this moment have come to an end. Following this announcement I will, in accordance with the power invested in me as commander in chief, employ our strategic defense system to counteract attacks already directed at our great nation. News reports are accurate. We have but our prayers and acts of moral fortitude to defend this dream of democracy that has barely lived beyond its infancy. Our enemy's inhumanity has brought us to this darkest hour — I must now . . ."

"Noooooooooooooooooooooooooooooooooooooooooooooooooooo!" Megan screamed. Clutching the arms of her rocker, she flung her neck back, becoming a curved tunnel emitting desperate screeches. Elmira, frightened, leapt away. Megan grabbed her belly and ran away from the sounds that threatened her child. She darted from the porch, never noticing the direction of her flight. Straight up. Beyond the vines, up to the top of the mountain. Panting. Perspiring. Perplexed, as her belly's weight pulled against her lungs. She was gasping and lifting now, between each step. Then it appeared. The mushroom.

Megan's body began to excrete fumes from every hole. Salty fluids created a paste over her eyes, and she fell, rolling slightly downward. Elmira broke her fall. Imitating Elmira, raised to all fours, Megan prepared herself for the child she knew was forthcoming. She reached below and a bloody mucus filled her hand. Megan cupped her birth canal, only for it to be washed by a gust of water from within. Then the internal earthquake began. She flooded in and out of delirium and dirt. Dirt and darkness. Darkness and the mushroom's image. It was moving closer. Getting bigger. Megan closed her eyes, gritted her pigtail between her teeth and her spiraling, smoky shrieks formed letters in the sky: GOD . . . HELP . . . ME! She passed out and bumped into the front door of pain. Slowly, it opened. Then came the voice.

"You must talk to the storm."

Louder.

"You must talk to the storm."

Vehemently.

"You . . . must . . . talk . . . to . . . the . . . storm."

"Nightair, is that you?"

"Yes, I'm here. I saw your smoke signals."

"Help me, please. For God's sake, help me!"

"I am here . . . to tell you that you must talk to the storm."

"What? I can't talk to a storm!" Megan climbed to her knees and stood up. "Goddamn that woman! What the hell is she telling me this for? I'm having a baby! I need help! Talk to the, ugh . . . that makes about as much sense as . . . ." The internal earthquake returned. "Goooooooooddddddddd, help me, Lord, Gooooooodddd help me!" she yelled.

The mushroom's dark overcast began to shift and take a square shape in Megan's view. It appeared like a window in the sky hung with heavy, ruby-red, velvet curtains. When the cloud was totally gone, Megan finally could focus clearly.

"It's a . . . it's a . . . stage." Confused, she put her hands over her eyes like a scared kid in the bedroom closet. Elmira ran between her legs when they heard the singing start.

"They call it stormy Monday, but Tuesday's just the same. I said, they call it stormy Monday, child-a-a-a, but Tuesday's just the same."

Megan began to feel dizzy. She had heard that voice before.

"Child, put your hands down. God don't do fire and brimstone any more. I dabble a bit in Blues. You heard this one? 'Daddy, daddy, daddy where'd you sleep last night. I say, daddy, da-a-a-ddy, daddy where'd you sleep last night.'"

Megan saw a black woman with grotesque features: a huge kinky afro; a double, buckshot barrel nose; protruding dark eyes; and a horse-thick neck. She flinched. Fell to her knees.

"Scared you, didn't I? Ain't exactly what you have been thinking you God is. I told my mother, I'd never got over the way I was looking. So she told my father to send my brother instead. When you all turned around and nailed him up . . . well . . . you wasn't gonna do the same to me. I left and went far away after you killed my brother. My folks were really hurt. He was their baby. You see, my parents were an odd mix. They families didn't want them to marry 'cause they wasn't from the same levels in the spirit. But you know how love is. They ran off in the universe and married anyway. But when we chil'rens start being born — looking like we didn't belong to the same family — well . . . they thought it best we be separated. So we accepted our differences as Gods and went our own ways. Heavy responsibility, you know! Biggest part is being sent to some hole-in-the-universe and told to create a world. That's all we Gods do. Imagine. Spending your whole existence watching what you created. By the way, it was y'all's idea to worship me. Anyway, Momma send me to the best God school, so I was a bit prepared. Earth was my first job. Not bad, I thought. You see, I had this plan: I'd start a little life from something small and before you know it — two would come from one and like all other things in the universe you'd feel the order . . . well, so far for bright ideas! I knew I was in deep shit when that boy slew his brother. I have to admit, I ran. I was never good under pressure. My daddy took the heat and got y'all to thinkin' you could e-volve. Momma laughed for days at that. She thought Daddy ought to jump in right then and correct the shit. Nooo, not Daddy. Instead, he whispered evolution in your ear and you been digging for yourself ever since. But when I heard you cry, I had to come back. Now, I know you all can't stand such a wishy-washy God, but I'm all you got. And this time I'm gon'. Megan, you can stop thinkin' you crazy. You is my chosen one."

Megan's earthquake within subsided. Everything was on hold. She felt it. She knew it. "Oh no . . . this isn't real."

"I am real. The mushroom is real."

"I mean, well . . . if you are God . . ."

"Why not, child? You referrin' to what you're thinkin', I say test me against what you are feeling deep inside. Come on, let my image fill you, and you'll know that I have always been."

Megan took in some breaths. Began to shake her head furiously, out of control.

"You only gonna hurt yourself, trying to figure it out in you head. I said feel me. I know you scared."

"If you are God . . ."

"There you go again. One of your worst traits, no faith. It ain't your fault, child, I'm gonna make it right. I sent Nightair to get you ready, and I think you are ready."

"She scared the shit out of me!"

"I know she's a bit melodramatic. Her kind's got plenty of reasons to be. Now . . ."

"But, if this isn't a joke, you are gonna have to . . ."

"What, turn the trees purple or some other fish trick?"

"Yes."

"No tricks, child. But a choice. Fact is, you white girls don't get choices. They make you think you do, but you don't. I's here to give you your first real choice. I know you want that baby more than anything. Can't you want something else? Look, do I have to teach you how to want as well as feel?"

"I don't feel my labor. Is that why?"

"Yes. You gotta feel for the whole or never again."

"I want my baby. She's mine. Those bastards are destroying the planet! I didn't have anything to do with it! I'm just a single person. It's not my fault."

"Child, listen to me now. You can't have no baby without no planet."

"I know that, but I want mine."

"Well, you can't have yours, unless they all have theirs."

Tears entered Megan's eyes as she felt herself expanding and expanding.

"That's it, child, I feel you *wanting* now. That's why I chose you in the first place."

Then God moved away. Megan could hear faint television transmissions trailing from the mushroom clouds. ". . . We cannot explain the events of the day. The experts seem at a loss. Our defensive systems have — how can I say it — melted away. We are getting similar reports from our allies — and enemies — that the mushroom clouds are suddenly disappearing. We cannot explain these incidents. Please excuse this reporter's crying. . . . I am . . . well . . . all I can say is may God have mercy on our souls."

Lifting, gripping, bending to the pain; laughing, humming hysterically to the next, Megan went waddling toward home.

Heaven is no longer crowded. There are no angels with AK-47s. Only a bushy-hair God who can correct her mistakes.

A GARDENIA FOR MISS EVA

. . . .

EGYIRBA HIGH

There ain't nothing I can do,
Nothing I can say,
That folks don't criticize me,
But I'm gonna do what I want to, anyway
And I don't care what people say.
If I should take a notion
To jump into the ocean
T'aint nobody's bizness if I do.

"Lemons today, Miss Eva?"

"Yes, of course, Mr. Jackson. Have the organic ones come in yet? I can't put just anything on my throat, you know."

Henry Jackson sighed as he studied the woman in front of him. If he wasn't mistaken, it seemed like her eyes had gotten darker since the last few times she had been in, and little puffs of annoyance were blowing themselves out behind her eyelids. "Oh, yeah. I got 'em coming in twice a week from California now."

He shifted his eyes to the lemons in front of him. He didn't want to stare, but he couldn't be sure of what he was seeing. Was her mouth twitching? Unconsciously, he picked up a lemon and began rolling it between his hand and the counter. The paint was peeling back to reveal an unfinished, beaten-looking wood. Business hadn't been the best lately.

Don't wanna appear rude, he thought. But it's such a shame. She's a nice lookin' woman. Such a shame.

Eva Johnston tired of watching him roll the lemons back and forth. "Mr. Jackson, I'd appreciate it if you'd not mash the juice outta that lemon," her voice rose a whole note from re to mi, as she tried to keep her irritation from showing through the frazzle she was feeling.

"Oh, sorry. Guess I just have a lot on my mind," Mr. Jackson apologized. That woman had a way of making him feel foolish. He kept vowing he wasn't gonna let that happen again. Oh, well, it had been going on like this for three years, ever since she moved into Charlie Hammond's old place.

He remembered the day Miss Eva came to Euclid Street. People laughed and mocked her 'cause she acted as if she was a big muckety-muck. Then the rumors started about how she was always putting on airs and was too good to relate to them. And how the inside of that house was no more than a living mausoleum. He didn't know. Fannie and Inez Evans was the largest proponents of that one. Couldn't trust them old biddies much. They poked into everyone's affairs, maintaining all the while that they were helping Jesus with his work—plucking the sheep from the goats. But after a few visits, they stopped trying to know her. She had pretended it didn't matter to her, but Henry knew that her big front masked a weak spirit. Then one day she started talking to him about her performances, how she always entertained her friends. It was peculiar how things got once Miss Eva moved in. Three years later, and no one really saw anyone in or out of that old house, 'cepting that little girl of hers, and she hadn't been seen for months now. Since Eva Johnston moved into the old neighborhood, the willows stood upright and the wisteria untwined and refused to bloom.

"Not only that," she was saying, "I'm late as it is."

"Oh, of course! I'll just get them into this bag for you. 'Nother show this evenin'?" By now he knew the answer before she spoke. It was just a routine courtesy to ask and a means of finalizing their business transaction. Then he'd add, "Of course, you want me to add this to your tab?"

And living up to her end of the charade she'd say, "Please, if you don't mind." Then she'd sweep the bag off the counter and turn toward the door in one continuous movement.

As he turned to watch Eva go out the door, Henry Jackson sighed a combination feeling. Such a shame.

Why was that Henry Jackson always standing there so dumbly when she was buying her lemons? Ordinarily, she wouldn't waste her time in that local market, but since he had started ordering the organic ones for her, she felt an obligation to shop there. And today, especially, she wasn't feeling particularly up to his lollygagging. Always looking at her so peculiarly. Wished I had never mentioned my shows, she thought. Must have lost control. Still, Eva sensed a special kindness from this man, and though she never would have let him know it, she had been lonely since Melanie was gone. She really was grateful for the comfort she saw in his eyes. And now this twitch. Had he noticed it?

It was just that she had had such a grueling day making her evening preparations, and the three-inch heels she was wearing didn't exactly give her much comfort. It was much too soon after her back surgery, but she really couldn't leave the house in those comfortable shoes Doc Warsten had prescribed for her. They reminded her too much of the ones Mama Nellie wore during the last of her days. Mama Nellie used to put them on and wear them everywhere, and when Eva had suggested she buy a new pair 'cause the sides were all run down, Mama Nellie had just said, "Chile, these is fine for my feets. You just too frivolous." She'd worn them when she'd gone out with Eva, and it had been an embarrassment.

Eva would never leave her house looking just any old way. She always maintained a special image for the public and wasn't about to change it, despite that doctor. It was bad enough that he had seen to it that she missed a Saturday performance by keeping her in the hospital three extra days. Oh, well, she didn't have time to worry about the likes of Henry Jackson or old Doc Warsten. She suspected, anyway, that they were both a bit sweet on her.

Eva Johnston rounded the corner and sighed a big sigh as her house came into view. It was her sanctuary.

"Two, four, six, four . . . it ain't gonna rain no more. Two, six, two, two . . . I don't wanna look at you."

Eva's ears perked up as she heard the voices coming into her walking range. Those damned kids from the neighborhood were always noisy, particularly when her guests were there. Home training lacking, she thought. Not like her own Melanie, who she saw to it had finishing school classes for *petite jeune filles* between ages seven and twelve. Melanie would know better than to be boisterous. As she approached the circle of neighborhood girls jumping rope, Eva pulled herself up and in.

"Hi, Miss Johnston," a chorus of girls sang to her.

"Hello, dears, I'm in a bit of a rush." No one had yet stopped her or posed a question to her, but Eva was always well prepared for that possibility. She rushed quickly past them and was relieved when she heard them go back to their singsong rhymes.

Three-twenty-three Euclid Street. Home, at last. She hurried to lock herself in from the rest of the world. It was cruel and always wanted more than she had to give. But here at home she could ease into the real Eva, the one nobody knew, because she must always protect herself from people who might try to use her. You could never tell with some folks. Eva was wise to all of their ways. They'd come to pay her a visit to see how she was since Melanie's father got custody, peach cobbler or smoked neckbones and beans in hand, but Eva knew it was just an excuse for them to nose into her affairs.

Eva never really understood the headiness she felt inside 323 Euclid Street. It was a feeling, a completeness that wasn't explainable. Besides, no one else would understand what she was talking about, and her days of trying to explain herself had long passed.

"T'ain't nobody's bizness if I do."

The music seemed to be getting louder. She worried that people might hear it. The thought fell into Eva's head as she fumbled for her keys. Where were the damned keys? She tried to calm herself because she knew the anxiety, once stirred, was hard to contain. Then it would start again.

"I need a little sugar in my bowl."

She could feel Bessie running her hands across her shoulders, holding back the anxiety. "Oh, Bessie, you're too good to me." Bessie smiled and handed Eva the keys. Eva smiled back, content that she hadn't lost control right there on the doorstep, and Bessie eased back into Eva's mind. She pushed open the door and the scent of fresh gardenias wafted gently to her nose. One thing was certain, Eva could never start her day without her fresh gardenias.

Eva kicked off her shoes and headed for the kitchen. She delicately placed the lemons in the porcelain bowl she kept expressly for holding them and her life in gear. She then set one aside and cut it into thin, thin slices and placed them in a small china saucer. Satisfied, she turned and made her way toward the stairs leading to her boudoir, though it had long ago stopped being the place where she cast her spell upon unsuspecting fellows. The giant brass bed stood magnificently in the midst of the room. Eva ran her hand sensuously over the headboard. She smiled again as she took her other hand and began to run it up and down her thigh.

"I need a little hot dog 'tween my roll."

"Aw, Bessie," she murmured, "easy, gal."

Darlene Jackson was tiring of the double-dutch jump-roping. Perhaps she was just outgrowing this circle of friends who seemed mesmerized by the rope rituals. But nothing better had come along, yet, to distract her. Frieda was getting pretty good, she noticed. Darlene watched Alfrieda Williams rock and land on her right foot to the rhythm of "Whatcha gon' do? Ya wanna get down?"

Darlene was moving her head to the beat when she noticed Miss Eva. Why that Miss Johnston so always in a hurry? Don't never have nothing new to say, she thought to herself. But when Punchie, Frieda, her, and May Jean sneaked around Miss Johnston's house, all they ever heard was some sad, strange music coming through the frame. Didn't none of them really have the nerve to hang around long enough to see what would happen next or even sneak up closer to peek in the windows.

Darlene pondered Miss Eva a moment. She found her interesting because trying to figure the older woman out made her brain work. Not like double-dutch and Frieda, Punchie, and May Jean.

"Hey, y'all, I'm tired." Then, against cries of come-on-Darlene-just-a-little-longer, she handed the ropes to May Jean. "I gotta go see my daddy," and they shut up, 'cause they knew there wasn't anything else they could say.

She turned and headed up the street and around the corner, back toward Jackson's Market, the shop her daddy owned ever since she could remember. Didn't never seem to be a time that that little market wasn't there.

"Yo' daddy always do right by us," the little old ladies on the block would take the time to say to her when they saw her in the street. "Don't never overcharge and always keep good kale and mustahds on hand."

Darlene would nod, "Thank you, Ma'am. I'll tell him."

"Alright, child," they'd answer. "You know he's our saviour." Then they'd get to fussing over her, saying how fast she was growing and looked like soon she was gonna be a woman and now she had to remember to keep her knees together and her dress pulled down. They'd dole out a whole collection of unsolicited advice. Darlene smiled to herself when she thought of the clever ways she had learned to ease away from them while they were in the heat of their chatter.

Just ahead was the shop, and no old ladies in sight. Thank goodness. She hated to stop and talk with them. Broke her concentration. It would take about twenty more steps to reach there, she noticed, since she was walking past Mrs. Evan's place. How was she going to pass the remaining two weeks of vacation? The sound of her father's voice interrupted this new thought, as it came gently to her ears.

"You alright, Darlene? Almost look like you sick."

"I'm alright, Daddy. I was just thinking."

"Seems like you do more thinkin' than you do some things sometime, baby. You gotta problem?"

"Naw, Daddy. You need any help?" Darlene figured he'd keep pumping her for her feelings, and she wasn't in the mood to talk about them. "Sometimey," her mama would say, when she saw Darlene like this. But Daddy always looked like he understood.

"Naw, baby. Think I'll close soon. Not much business in the last two hours, only Miss Eva for her lemons."

"What she do with so many lemons, Daddy?"

"Devil if I know. Anyway, ain't none of your business."

Henry didn't want to tell Darlene about how he humored Miss Eva about her "shows." Old Avery Walker always snickered if he happened to be in the shop when Eva Johnston came for her lemons. He'd see her coming, then dash quickly behind the cans of fruit cocktail and peaches to listen. After she'd leave, it was the same old talk.

"You s'pose she do something weird with them lemons, man?" Avery would ask. "Seem like she'd use somethin' a little more, well . . . a-pro-prit," he'd say. "Hell, I can help her there." And he'd grab his sides and laugh for no good reason Henry could see.

"I don't know what she do with them, and you shouldn't jump to no conclusions either, Avery. Leave that woman alone."

"I ain't gonna mess with her, I just wonder, that's all." Seeing Henry annoyed would straighten the grin on Avery's face. He didn't want their Saturday checker game postponed by Henry's being mad.

Henry knew that Avery was as harmless as a one-winged pigeon, it was just that he couldn't stand to see folks knee-deep in other folks' business and speculating on stuff they couldn't begin to prove. But he didn't want to say all that, so he said, "You just mind your business, Darlene Jackson. Hear?"

"Yeah, Daddy, I was just curious."

"Yeah, well, curious a monkey named George. I don't need no help. You go on home now."

Eva stretched her body out on the brass bed while she waited for the bubbles to fill up the tub. She especially liked the jasmine scent and the blue color that the Beautiful Journey soap bubbles made. It relaxed her, watching the tranquil blue swirl around while she floated in the tub. She would stare at the water and imagine herself floating down the Nile. Embraced by the sphinx and echoes of ancient voices, she'd relax deep into the waters, deep into time.

Anticipating the journey, Eva eased her body upright. Fine, she thought. Now what should she wear? It would be either the red satin or the green taffeta. Something clingy, she thought. It felt like there would be a good crowd tonight. Eva always based the crowd size on her feelings. And with thoughts of the Nile and a little bit of Bessie's help, her irritation of the day had melted away. When she felt good, a packed house was assured. This would be one of those evenings. She decided on the red satin. She felt extra good. Let 'em get their money's worth, she thought.

She took the red satin out and hung it over the portable valet she had purchased. So much easier than having real help to pry and poke their noses into her affairs. Eva dropped the robe from her shoulders and stepped out in her bare skin, except for the long strand of cultured pearls she was wearing. She never took those pearls off for any reason. She walked to the bathroom and closed the tap. The jasmine enveloped her, and she could hardly wait to step in, till a thought caught her off guard. Did she put out the programs? She dashed quickly downstairs to make one last check.

Downstairs, in the living room, a slight chill came over her nude body. She did have a lovely home. Daguerreotypes of all kinds decorated the walls and small tables. Shots of Alberta Hunter, Ethel Waters, Florence Mills, Freddie Washington, and Bessie, all her girlfriends stood proudly in her midst. They were such old photographs that it seemed the glass was filled with smoke. Some hung in the room and protected her camelback couch and Queen Anne chairs. Intermingled with the photographs were bronzed baby shoes and little glass and porcelain figurines, which also lined the windowsills and spare shelf spaces. A sea of white lace doilies decorated the tables, chairs, and couch.

Eva lit some Night Musk incense and glanced in the direction of her Victrola, her most prized possession. A quick check and, yes, the records were all stacked in order. She had seen to that last night. The programs sat neatly stacked on a small table between the chaise lounge and the dressing screen, which partitioned off sections of the room. She hoped she wouldn't have to take them down. If folks brought extra people along she could run out of drinks, and folks always wanted extra drinks when someone's songs poked them in the heartstrings. She took a final glance and dashed back up the stairs to the waiting barge.

Darlene had turned over twice on her bed and was still feeling edgy. She had spent the rest of her day watching television and reading Brenda Starr comic books. She had even cleaned up her room and still wasn't tired. Her room contained all the things a twelve-year-old girl could want, and yet, she felt empty inside.

Darlene got up from her bed and crossed over to the window. Woodward Avenue, the big street, was perpendicular to Euclid Street. Weekends, the street paraded a whole different atmosphere — a party atmosphere. "A wild place," her mama called it. The sounds of passing cars and the voices of the night people were starting to get louder.

Henry and Doris Jackson always took every opportunity to remind her that the night people were no good, and she better not get any high ideas about their kind of activity. Darlene knew what they meant. It was no secret that some of the sixteen-year-old girls from the neighborhood had taken to hanging out with some of the fast men and found themselves in deep trouble. "Fas-tails," her mother would call the girls. "You better watch yourself, Darlene," she warned her daughter.

Sticking her head out of the window, Darlene could see the neon lights of Buddy's Bar flashing. They flashed excitement. They flashed fun. They flashed something to do besides staying holed up in this house on Euclid Street. She listened to car horns blow, people cussing, and bottles breaking. She was just about to pull her head back inside the window, when she noticed lights going off and on in Miss Eva's house across the street.

Miss Johnston. Darlene wished she could figure out what it was that interested her about the lady so much. It was like she was hiding something, but what? May Jean had speculated that Miss Johnston was a witch, and Frieda and Punchie just said, "un-huh," echoing May Jean. They were such babies. Didn't have enough nerve to try to find out what was true and what wasn't. Then again, neither had she.

Darlene pulled back inside. Then, she tiptoed to her door and listened for movement in the house. Doris and Henry usually went to bed early. She couldn't hear anything. Quietly, she opened her door and, after checking in both directions, tiptoed out into the hall and down the stairs. She knew what she would do. She'd go see for herself. Grabbing her key from the hook by the front door, Darlene Jackson snuck into the night.

Eva Johnston sucked on the remaining lemon slice. The bath had been a well-needed tonic for her frazzled nerves. She guessed she had better get ready. She abhorred tardiness in anyone except herself because she was, after all, a star. And it was fashionable to keep the crowd waiting just a little bit.

The red dress was clingy. Good. She remembered how her voice had been a little off last time. Maybe this time she could divert their attention in case it happened again. The neckline of the satin dress plunged into a sharp *V* in the middle of her chest. Yes, she thought, this ought to do it. She reached up to the shelf of her closet and pulled down a red flapper hat. She adjusted it just so on her head and patted down the feather. She wound the strand of pearls double so that they rested just above her cleavage. Then she reached for her rhinestone slippers.

Eva whirled around to take one last look in the mirror. She still had her looks, thank God. Only this twitch bothered her occasionally. She would give some more thought to retiring soon, while she still had her face and figure. She wouldn't want people to remember her as some old, worn-out woman. She looked at her crimson cheeks, lips, nails, and toes and smiled approvingly at her reflection. She had class. She placed her hands on her hips and slowly moved toward the stairs to her waiting fans.

> Gimme a pig foot and a bottle of gin
> Send me daddy, move right in
> I feel like I wanna shout . . .
> Give the piano player a drink
> Because he's knocking me out.

The sounds floated up to Eva's ears. She could tell that folks were already starting to have themselves a good time. She knew Percy Markham and Ella Evans were cooting. She could hear the laughter and encouragement of the crowd. "Don't break it. . . . Make him sweat, Ella. . . . Get her, Percy. . . . Rock it, y'all." It was nice they were having a good time, but she was on her way. Cigarette smoke was drifting up toward her nose. She couldn't stand it, but if it made them feel better, let them smoke. Who was she to argue with her paying guests?

"Hey, Eva," she heard someone say. "Baby, you lookin' good." And another voice, "Uhn, uhn, uhn! Give me some of what you got now, woman!"

"Aw, y'all just love me," she said casually, beaming inside. "You all got enough drinks and food? Then, let's party!" and with that, Eva walked over to the Victrola and pulled out Bessie Smith's record. She placed it on the turntable and watched it go around. Then she tuned up and started singing.

She sang her heart out. She knew she was on fire 'cause the red was flashing out from her. You could hear a pin drop. Nobody said a word. She sang and screamed and sang and shouted and sang and sang until she was dizzy. Then she passed out on the floor.

Darlene Jackson couldn't believe what she was seeing. Maybe all those things that folks had said was true. Miss Johnston all dressed up from head to toe, screaming at the top of her lungs, saying stuff like, "Did y'all like that song? Well, what do you want to hear then?" Darlene had tried to see in the room better, to see who she was talking to, but as far as she could tell there wasn't anyone there but her. She could see empty tables and chairs and programs on the tables. Miss Johnston going over to the record player putting on different records and taking them off. Just watching the record go round and round, then taking it off and putting on another one. Then laughing hysterically.

Darlene's eyes bucked and her mouth gaped open, no sound coming out. Miss Johnston, laughing like a hyena and cackling like a witch.

Oohweeee! Ooh! Miss Johnston, Darlene heard herself whispering. She jumped up and down wanting to shout at her, "There ain't nobody there but you." But she didn't. She just put her hands over her open mouth. She watched Eva laugh and roll around on the floor. Darlene started to shake, looking through the glass doors that were covered only by sheer curtains, watching Miss Eva Johnston and shaking her head. She caught her breath and grabbed her chest simultaneously. She hadn't really ever seen no crazy person before. 'Cept Otis, the wino, who hung out by her daddy's store. But he was a wino; nobody really believed he was really crazy. Darlene backed down the stairs of the porch still clutching her chest, still panting. Her legs were wobbly underneath her. She turned and ran.

She knew it was in the direction of her house, but she didn't care where it was as long as it was way away. Miss Johnston, oh, Miss Johnston. The scene flashed in her head over and over and over. Miss Johnston with that feather hat dangling from the side of her head, legs wide apart, dress torn to her navel. Darlene ran up the stairs two at a time, into the house, and slammed the door. Crazy Miss Johnston.

Why, Eva thought, had she passed out? What had happened to her? She couldn't continue to lead this kind of life; it was wearing her out. She was tired. She lay on the floor trying to regain her strength. She noticed that folks had left. "Aw, let 'em," she mumbled. It really didn't matter anymore.

Eva Johnston struggled to her feet. She made one last trip through the room where she had spent the last three years of her life. She looked at all the familiar faces smiling down from the walls. She saw the same sad smiles on them that she always saw. "There really isn't much to say. Y'all tried to tell me," she said to them. She went around the room, turning out all the lights. "Goodnight, ladies. See you in the morning. Have me some fresh gardenias, now." Eva Johnston turned, grabbed the programs, and staggered back up the stairs toward her boudoir.

CENTER STAGE

. . . .

CHERRY MUHANJI

 he pool table is center stage. One single light-
bulb hangs, hooded, over the table — a single
flame pushing back the darkness. Green velvet runs in all directions, edges the table, then
drops off into the unknown. Sounds of clink-
ing glasses in the darkness . . . the match has not begun. Soon,
though. . . . The air is heavy and someone or something is sucking it
from the room — a muted monster standing in the corner spooking
everyone. People speak in short, muffled sentences as if afraid.

"Is the ol' man here yet?" someone asks.

"Yeah, he always here. Somewhere."

"Where the young punk that gonna take him on?"

"Probably somewhere whorin'."

"He ain't takin' this at all serious."

"You ever seen him shoot?"

"Naw."

"Then shut the fuck up, because the boy is ba-a-ad, real bad."

The ol' man, pulling a silk handkerchief from his back pocket, stopped and unfolded it carefully before shaking his head in disgust. He started to wipe the smoke haze from the bathroom mirror. He had learned pool up in the big house when he was a boy. While Sadie had ironed shirts for Masters Brown and Smith, he had cleaned the spittoons. White men, with fat bellies held in by Sadie's starched shirts, came to play "the gentleman's game," as they called it. Rooms filled with blue smoke. The chalk-blue tip of the cue, the smell of Cuban cigars, and the feel of money had made him know what his game and his life was gonna be. And it was. He started hoboin' from town to town learnin' not to play billiards, but what niggahs played: pool. Much faster and he liked that; then the money could be made faster. Besides, white men would never let him at the big money. He had come north where the factory money was. He considered himself an expatriate of the South. The North was another country, with its grim gray buildings and niggahs with no class. Niggahs who worked in the factories by day and chased women by night.

He looked in the mirror again, straightened his Panama straw, opened his silk shirt at the neck, and checked the shine on his shoes, all in one easy movement. It was time. How many matches was this now? His mind drifted back to the knickers worn at the knee, his first pair of long pants, and the broken pool stick. Sadie took some wild berry and jigger juice — and soon, the stick was healed. Wood always responded to her touch. She said it was alive, just in a different way than people.

"Only colored folks know that, though, 'cause white folks spend all they time buyin' and sellin', not feelin'."

He could still smell the wood from that stick. His very own stick! No matter how much he paid for his sticks now, and they were all imported, none ever felt the same. He could hear . . . cussin' . . . Ed "Wild Bill" Smith leanin' low to the table . . . too low. He knew from the first how this game had to be played, how this lover had to be won, when and where she would respond. At least, most times. There would be days when the quarrel would go long into the night, and she would refuse him, a cold back against his hot hands. Oh! But the days she did turn on! Those balls would dance and spin, a nymph with a siren's call darting from one tree to the next — into the side pocket, on cue, on time, in love forever this time. He would smile at his lover, she would curtsy, and he would run the table. God, it was good!

"Ol man, ya 'bout ready?"

"One minute," he said, disturbed by this intrusion. He examined his early morning manicure. He'd have to talk to Geraldine; she was getting a little sloppy with the clear coat. Now, to work the talcum powder through his fingers. Not too much. The bar was full and niggahs draw heat — he needed to keep the feel of the stick fluid in his hands. He lifted the stick from its private case and felt for the wood grain, moving along the stick, up and down, an unconscious gesture triggered by some sweet-smellin' memory driftin' in from long ago. As he rubbed the long, sleek stick through his talcumed fingers, he felt, just for a moment, the pinch. Then the pain started from wrist to elbow. His hand stiffened. Not now, you bastard! Not now! Thoughts of Mary filled his mind. She would know what to do; she always knew what to do. He flexed his hand again and again — better — yes, Mary would know what to do.

"He learned to live for his pool and for it only," Mary had said. She didn't understand . . . the arguments, the "What bitch you got, now, keepin' you gon' all night?" Finally she left, leaving him alone. The pain started. This need for her — the first feelin' he could remember since Sadie died. He kept his game going for as long as he could. But he could see it was off, and she hadn't returned. So he went to find her. When he found her with a daughter, he beat her.

"That won't get me back," she said.

"And who gives a fuck?" he said.

"You do."

"I can make it."

"Then why you come?" He raised his hand again.

"Don't try it. That was your first and only time you gon' hit me. The next time, I'll kill yo' ass."

He remembered Sadie sayin', "Don't have no woman ya got to beat to keep."

"Mary, understand what I need. Ain't no other woman. Just me and my game. Understand how it is. And I will try and understand what you mean."

"I understand the cause of the game. Will ya understand the cause of the baby? Both is 'cause somewhere we is lonely. And in our lone-someness we need an expression. You got yours, and I got mine."

She came home after that, and he made room in himself for the baby. . . . Yeah, she would know what to do. And Emily, playing nurse, would try and make him all better. He smiled. Suddenly, he was impatient for this thing to be over.

"Ol' man?"

"Yeah?"

"Jimmy Joy just came in."

"Yeah, I smell the oil in his clothes." Niggahs with no class. No excuse for it. Why do niggahs play a gentleman's game with dirt under they fingernails?

The young man was nervous, stopping briefly to speak to people, eyeing the back of the bar where he knew the ol' man was. And Jimmy Joy knew the ol' man was watching him. He hadn't slept well, hadn't eaten. His hands were already sweaty.

"If I beat him, I'll be king. Hustlers would come for miles just to see me and take me on. I would be the best! The ol' man would finally be finished."

He knew, if the others didn't, that the pain was increasing in the ol' man's hands. Since he was a boy, he had watched him play off and on. He knew every line in his face, every muscle in his arms. His timing was impossible to beat. At least it used to be. He knew where the balls were going before they did. Jimmy Joy remembered the match between the ol' man and "Wild Bill." Bill played pool like alley kids play alley ball. Put 'em in a school arena and most of 'em can't adapt. But the ol' man had learned to adapt, and not only that, his instincts kept his game always alive and kept his opponent on edge, off balance. He played 'cause he had to. Not for fun, but because he had to — just like he, Jimmy, had to. Yeah, him and the ol' man understood. It was time; his time now.

He was the guest. He broke the balls. Wham! Real sweet. Just the way he liked it. He started to run the table. "Six ball in the side pocket." He could hear the sound of his own voice keeping time with each shot; a song meshed together by the sound of the balls slamming against the side of the table. It was always like making love for the first time. The sweet piece of the self given over to something bigger and badder than you — the whole. His pace quickened, his breathing labored. Sweat started to bead on his forehead. He paused to wipe his sweat; one pearl could burn his eyes and kill the shot. His grip tightened. He could feel the move start in his legs. Rising. He let out a groan, then another, his energy spent. Pearls of sweat were everywhere. Under his arm, on his stomach, in his groin. "Damn!" The turtle had won the race, because the hare had come out of the gate too fast. He missed.

The ol' man bent low to the table, changing positions here and there. Checking and double-checking. First the table, then his stick. And, finally, the weight of his gaze fell on Jimmy Joy. He handed him the empty wine glass, gave him a salute, and went into what had become his trademark: talking to the spirits. The ol' man was on! He bent low, leveled his stick, the crowd hushed, he drew back . . .

"Daddy, Daddy!" The sounds came from a little girl who had somehow gotten into the bar. The crowd groaned, annoyed. "Who is that kid?" someone said. "And how did she get in here?" The ol' man seemed to short-circuit. Jimmy Joy's eyes raced through the crowd. There was Wild Bill, Smoky Joe, Rack'em Eddie. All of them had come in for this match. They shook their heads. Smoky put his toothpick back in his mouth and, giving Jimmy Joy a salute, walked out. Wild Bill started small talkin' to Rack'em Eddie, "Damn!" No matter what, Jimmy thought, just before he picked up his stick again, I'm still one down on the ol' man.

"Momma wants the car keys." He lifted his body from what seemed a great weight and smiled slowly.

"Henry, get the lights please. Meet my daughter, everybody, who don't give a damn about this match tonight."

He reached into his pocket and threw the keys right on top of the balls. Some scattered. The clambering child pushed the balls out of the way and picked up the keys. Looking up at him, she felt something was wrong, but what?

"Tell your mother I'll be home for dinner. This time, on time."

"Okay, Daddy."

ELLA BAKER

. . . .

EGYIRBA HIGH

he turned and looked out the window. The waves washing up on the shore were relaxing. Very relaxing. She needed to relax. She needed soothing, and the rhythm of the waves helped soothe and numb the memories. Soon it would be nine years since Bernice died. Damn! What was the point of coming all the way over to Jamaica to forget, if she was going to allow the dates to creep into her mind as a constant reminder? Ella shifted her body and tried to still her parading thoughts by nodding her head to the rhythm of the waves washing ashore. Catching the beat, she rose from the bed and crossed over to the balcony door.

As she took in a large lung-full of ocean air, her hands ran back and forth over the balcony railing and on the exhale, Ella let out a small cry. She knew suddenly that she was never going to forget, never going to stop blaming herself for not trying hard enough or long enough. The seagulls' strained song overhead cut into her daydreams and momentarily diverted her attention from the ritual burial thoughts she participated in every January.

She had driven Morris away with her neurotic passion. He had tried. For the first three years he had automatically assumed her major responsibilities during December and January. Before she asked, he answered her every request. It would begin simply by him taking over the dinner dishes and two weeks later, right after the New Year, he would be floating in soapsuds, house dust, and kid dirt. He would guide her to her room and encourage her to rest. He screened her calls and visitors and brought fresh tulips to her bedside daily.

"Morris, oh . . ." Ella sighed, her voice trailing off. "First Mama, then you. . . ."

Years four, five, and six went pretty much the same, although Morris's winter face began to show the strain of living for two. He still brought in the tulips, but a touch of longing now froze in his eyes like the coming of the winter icicles.

By the seventh year (ironically, the seven-year itch, she thought), Morris had packed his bags and moved into a hotel for the four-week period to startle Ella out of her persistent grief. When, however, she took the move personally (and not as the loving experiment Morris imagined it would be), she let herself go totally, and the four-week drama crept gradually into five, six, seven, and catcalls. . . .

It was true. That seventh year had been ambiguous for Ella. Morris didn't have to leave her like that, though. She could get around and fix meals and look after the children, but soon she hadn't cared to. When Morris had moved into the hotel, it was complicated to be alone at first. She had moved silently among the children, who found their mother strange. After the first four days of Noodles Romanoff, followed by six consecutive days of tuna noodle casserole, plus three more of Chili Ella (in which she added leftover tuna), the children had called their father, who promptly removed them to their grandmother's. Ella didn't protest. She thought it was a battle of wills and only temporary. She was sure of it. But when the kids stayed into February, then March, Ella got nervous and her behavior became definite. Soon, after that, she didn't bother to get dressed at all and took to parading around the house butt-naked

*when all the curtains were open. She never combed her hair and it stood
out over her head, the right side of it matted down and tangled. Her nose
accustomed itself to the lingering, musty scent of her body, not pungent
at first but lingering, determined that she would take notice. Ella never
noticed. The kids spoke to their mother on the telephone or peeked in and
waved shyly from a distance when Morris stopped by to check the mail.
She took to eating cheese sandwiches and when the cheese ran out, she
dined exclusively on the next thing she saw, until it, too, ran out. Sar-
dines, Vienna sausages, tuna, chunky soup, and boxes of saltines and
crisp Ritz crackers.*

"How can you leave me, Morris?"

*"Look at you, Ella. You're not caring anything for yourself. This is the
seventh year and eighth month since Bernice died. In the last three
months, you've bathed yourself about ten times. You don't comb your
hair or even wash out your mouth. The kids can't live with a person who
doesn't give a damn about herself, the way you don't. They're confused
and scared. Ella, please, get some ... why won't you get some help! I don't
know what else to do, baby."*

"But you know it's always hard for me during this time of the year."

"Yes, Ella, I know. But how long?"

*"Morris, I-I-I-I do try ... the pain ..." Ella's tired whine hit the icy
air and met with sullen indifference.*

*"Morris ... Morris, I need ..." but the sound of the closing door
bounced the words off the walls and back into her mouth. She had cried
herself to sleep.*

Ella turned and stepped back inside the room of the Hotel Tropica,
stopping in front of the mirror. Moving up closer, she studied her
reflection. She was still an attractive woman, but these last nine years
had crept into her eyes, furrowed into her skin, and pushed her thirty-
nine years to look more like fifty. When had she really ever looked at
herself?

Never. She had never known an Ella, only a strange woman on the
other side of the glass. She had never cared to know any more than
that and now, seeing the etched lines on her forehead, she wondered
where the lost years had gone. Ella lifted her hands and tried to
smooth out the wrinkles. The stubborn lines only seemed to get
deeper. Her frustration turned into rubbing, and Ella went dizzy re-
calling the lost years. Ten years passed, and she kept on rubbing. Back
into her early days of marriage, before the kids, when she and Morris

had spent every weekend in bed. Five years, then back further to her teenage years, sneaking behind Mr. Perry's drugstore and heavy petting with Morris. Rubbing harder, she tried to blot out more time. She rubbed, unleashing her passion, and when she exploded, she was certain she was looking into Bernice Williams's eyes.

"Mama, please! Please, come!" Ella whispered. The space about her was blurring now. Ella tried to block out the voices. She shook her head vigorously from side to side.

"I told you I didn't approve long ago. Why are you begging me, Ella?"
Ella didn't know, except what kind of wedding would it be without her mother? But Bernice Williams was the kind of woman who rarely changed her mind, once set. She had come at her husband's prodding. And so, she sat in the pew, rigid, unmoving, and without comment.

Ella knew it was Claude Williams's urgings that made the difference. She could hear his calm, soothing voice, "Oh, come on, Bernice." And later, "Ella, don't worry. Your mama will come. Don't cry, sugar." He had pulled her close and held her tightly that day. The wedding day came and by nighttime, Ella could not relax. The muffled cries of pain that Morris mistook for passion were, in reality, cries to Bernice for forgiveness of some unknown transgression.

Ella shivered. The pain was as raw as the day it all happened. She staggered to the bathroom to wash the tears from her face.

I I

Strolling along the beach, Ella looked at the lovers lying in the sand. Finding a place, she lay down on her forearms and steadied herself, as she picked at the sand with her brown toes.

"Something to ease your mind, man? Cocktail, thirst-quencher, or fresh fruit?" Tilting her head back to find the source of the delightful patois, she smiled up at the brightest smile she had seen in some time.

"Yes, triple vodka and lime, please." He smiled. His nametag said Eric. She watched him stroll back to the bar. He had an easy gait. The deliberate movement of his hips and the way he steadied the tray on his raised arm was an invitation. For a moment she thought she was rolling with the waves again. Her head rocked from side to side, and Ella found her thoughts privately in between the rhythms.

As Ella contemplated the rhythm of his hips and the coolness of the man, she saw her vodka and lime come into view.

"If I can be of any further help to you, man, I'd be happy to oblige." He smiled and two nearly perfect rows of white teeth flashed at her like diamonds.

"Thank you, that's all."

He bowed in deference, turned, and made his way back toward the bar. Ella wondered what it might be like to make love with a man whose body said there were no time restraints. She shook her head. The drink was slurring her thoughts. She had come here to make peace with herself.

Ella turned the drink up to her mouth and finished it in one quick gulp. She watched him move among the patrons. From time to time, she noticed that he was looking at her. When she'd look him squarely in the eyes, he would wink, and she'd blush and turn away.

"Was ya drink to ya liking?" His shadow fell over her.

"Yes, it was just fine. I'll take another, please."

"Another triple?"

"Yes, if you don't mind."

"No trouble at all, man." He strode to the bar and just before reaching it, he turned one last time toward her and smiled slowly. He took his time making her drink, his eyes watching her over the glass.

He asked her out and she accepted. Dinner and dancing. She needed to do more things for herself. When he arrived that evening, dressed in a white summer suit and matching white shoes against coal-black skin, she was pleased.

"You look ravishing, man." He put the emphasis on the second syllable of the word. Rav-*ish*-ing. The night, the man, the dinner, the dancing were just the touches she needed. And when she said good night to him at the door, he simply smiled once again, then turned and left.

I I I

The porcelain vase. She was dreaming of the expensive vase again. Pieces. Sections. Scattered all around. Blue and white designs. Pieces of herself scattered and spread on the floor with the vase. Bernice using parts of her to collect the precious bits of her prized possession. Ella screaming. Cuts. Blood.

Nausea welled up inside Ella, and she sat bolt upright in bed. Sweating, she reached for the light. She was shivering. She scooted down a little under the covers, her teeth chattering. It was always so real, this dream. She needed sound. Music, laughter, voices, anything. She picked up the remote control and turned on the television. A blur of people paraded across the screen. She flicked the buttons from station to station. Nothing.

Getting up from the bed, Ella went to the bathroom to get a glass of water. This is ridiculous, she thought. It's only a dream. I can handle it. She shook the images from her head and found an old movie to watch until she got drowsy. She flicked it off and went back to sleep.

Eric was intrigued with this woman. He took a hotel passkey and let himself quietly into her room. Softly closing the door behind him, he took a deep breath. He watched her from the doorway. She was sleeping. He could see her naked shoulders and in the shadow of the moonlight, the rise and fall of her body beneath the covers. He slipped out of his shoes. He quickly peeled off his clothing and stole toward the bed.

He slid his body into bed beside her. His nose tipped her shoulder and the smell of her skin filled his senses. Like anise. He was overcome with passion. He placed his palm on her stomach and rubbed gently. Then his hand moved upward to her breasts. Round and full. He bit his lip. Ella moaned. He placed his hand between her thighs and stoked her softly. She was a mystery he would unwrap one step at a time.

Ella turned over onto her side. She curled her legs and drew them up to her chest. She could feel the heat in her body. She felt warm and secure. She imagined she was dreaming again. A pleasant dream this time. She turned onto her back again and groaned.

Now was the time. Lifting himself up and balancing on his hands, Eric moved his body over hers. One smooth stroke and he was inside. Aah, he thought silently. Ooooh. Slowly. Slowly. In, then out. In, again. He was climbing the falls like he had as a boy. Out, slowly. Sliding down the handrails in school. In, in, in. Out, out, out. He was home.

Ella moaned softly. Yes, this was it: the warmth, the feeling. This was how it should have been all along. From the very beginning. Why had it taken so long? She began to rock to the movement of Eric's thighs. Yes, like this. The warm feeling built up inside her and burst. Oh, so good, so good. Yes, it was like building castles in the sand and baking cookies together and wearing look-alike outfits and off to Grandma's. Not like the broken vase scattered all over.

"Oh, Mama, like this, like this," Ella cried out. "This is the feeling I have waited for, Mama!"

Eric stopped. He stopped cold. Mama? she called him "Mama." What? Was this some sort of joke? Her mama? No. She must be mad or queer or both. He pulled out and away from her. Ella didn't notice. She kept writhing on the bed, calling for her mama. Eric watched in disbelief as he pulled on his slacks. He pulled his shirt half over his head and grabbed his shoes, moving quickly to the door. Like a bitch in heat, he thought, but howling for her mama!

Ella climaxed. Opening her eyes, she looked around the room. Nothing. A dream? No. No, not a dream. Where are you, Mama? Mama, where are you? I know you are here. You must be hiding. It was supposed to be like this. This way, Mama. I was supposed to be born and you were supposed to love me and it was supposed to feel good like this, Mama. Ella stood up and looked around the room. The moonlight shone over her shoulder.

"Mama?" No answer. "Ma-ma? Come out, come out . . . please, come out." Still nothing. Ella began to whimper. Small sobs. "Uh, uh, uh." Then again, "uh, uh, uh." She clutched her knees and started to moan. "Ooooooooooh. Oooooooooh. Ooooooooooooh."

She lay in a heap in the middle of the floor, rolling and rocking herself. The cries of the seagulls circling overhead blended with her moans. Together, they became one long reverberating dirge.

SHADOWS OVER SHADOWS

....

KESHO SCOTT

nti Communists would sleep tight tonight if they knew what we do in the dark corners of our lives that abort revolutions before the crack of dawn. Rebels come in all breeds. They live and die for the smell of fresh-inked leaf-lets, paper illusions. Ginger is a part-time file clerk and rebel and her spice has a fuse.

I first met her at the Free Medical Clinic downtown in Main and Middle Urban America. The town was in its winter clothes, and we waddled in thick blue parka coats, underneath a mountainous regime of bulk. There we were — rows and rows of women — clutching empty prescription bottles and holding empty gazes, eyes lost in the details of indoor-outdoor carpet and shit-brown paneling. Clinics, like bus lines, collect those who miss the main street of life. Women swinging passively between illusions and dying and staying sick to live.

Ginger straggled into the clinic with the other regulars I knew and took a number. The nurse gave her that kind of don't-ask-me-no-questions look and directed her to take a seat. She hesitated for a moment before seating herself next to me. Her hesitation drew our eyes to read the story on her face. I tensed up. I flinched, recoiled, and readjusted my attention to the floor. This goddamn blood pressure medicine has me seeing double, I thought, to resynchronize my insides to the routine sniffles, sighs, and sterile silence.

I dropped my prescription bottle underneath the chair. As I weaved in and out of chairs to regain it, eyes met mine, sympathetic and annoyed. Kelly stood up and moved her chair. Our previous conversations flashed through my head . . .

Girl, my husband wants to fuck all the time. Lord, the man done started coming home for lunch and pussy. What am I gonna do? Doctor say I should take something for my nerves and calm down. My man say, "Woman, you don't give me enough!" I feel like I'm losing my mind. I'm tired all the time. Ain't got no children. Ain't got no energy to have none either! I'm so tired.

Her mouth, now decorated with a pile of fever blisters and her legs sprouting hair, made the perfect picture. I nodded so she could set her chair down.

Doreen asked, "Did you find it?"

"Yes, thank you."

"Give me your coat. I'll hang it up," she said. "That way we can get a little more room in here."

As it was, we were strangers sitting back to back on cold, hard, caramel-colored, cast-iron chairs. I felt grateful as I had when she lent me the cab fare home two weeks earlier. The woman barely knew me, but she knew the bus ride would kill me. "Oh, by the way, I've got your fare to return to you."

"Keep it!" she said abruptly. "I might not need it. Doctor said I might be dead by next week." I had heard that "What the fuck!" tone weeks ago, when her baby son of sixteen was shot in a stickup and a month before anticipating something would go wrong with her daughter's graduation from high school. Doreen talked real fast, as though afraid she wasn't gonna be able to get it all out before the nurse called her number. And when called, she always jumped up like an attentive five-year-old, smiling tightly and marching — knees high, step one, two, three — in line to the doctor's inner office.

My eyes surveyed the room checking all the debutantes from the end of the bus line. There was Vida, the swinger who lived downtown — and uptown on something. She was twenty-four and drunk on daylight. Vida was always talking in a kinda in-between rhythm: "Yeah . . . baby . . . honey . . . darling, and what's it to you, sugar?"

She alternated between filing her long purple fingernails and fits of chipping the paint from the chairs.

Willie Mae sat two seats away dressed in her starched white uniform, clutching her pocketbook with cash register fingers. She didn't like Vida.

"She's a hood!" she'd say under her breath. "She don't need no doctor. She need to go somewhere and get straight."

"I don't know, Willie Mae. You're being kind of hard, don't you think?" I asked.

"So what! She'll knock you in the head like anyone else." Vida could make Willie Mae close her legs tight and turn her nose toward other irregular body smells. Willie Mae just didn't like undefined things going in the body because, as it was, she couldn't keep her own IUD in place or in peace.

Mrs. Shelton, with the bleeding skin rashes that came from eating colored folks' food, said very little most of the time. But twelve noon would signal daytime soaps in her head and the entertainment would begin: "Erica is sick. The boy done gave her a house, a car, and a bunch of clothes, and she just can't be satisfied. Now she's chasing Antoinette's husband, Arthur, who they think gots something going with Michael. Erica is about to give me a heart attack. I just wish I could tell her . . ." she'd say. And on and on and on.

I asked her once how she was coming along with the treatments.

"They cost too much. The doctor suggested that I eat supermarket baby food. I've been trying it a month now, and I really can't feel no change."

And, of course, there was Crystal and Sue. Crystal had the voice of an angel and three hundred pounds to keep her falling from the clouds. She always gave me and Sue her church programs with her name in bold caps: CRYSTALLE and no last name. Sue, we called her Lady, sat in the corner and ran dialogue with herself in full verse. Her lips moved to the caricatures of Al Jolson and, without paying admission, we got our money's worth of showtime. Lady Sue, often tripping over her doughnut-roll stockings that hung over combat boots, sat with a three-inch smile, drumming her foot.

Ginger spoke first, not to me but to Lady Sue. "Lady, you all right?" Lady Sue turned away and increased her own silent volume.

"Uhn! I've been here at least a hour and a half," Ginger snapped, attacking the silence.

I peeped my head around my huge school-diaper-grocery-bag purse and said, "The doctor won't be in until after one."

"What do they think we are, a motherfuckin' herd of cattle? It's a goddamned shame there's only one doctor for all of us. We pay taxes! If this office was down on East Lafayette, we'd have a red carpet and lunch by now, ain't that right? One o'clock, my ass! Do they think all we have to do is wait around all day? We should all just get up and leave. Uhn! How would that son of a bitch make his money then?"

Our eyelids caught themselves in their sockets as we heard familiar words. Lightbulbs went off in our heads — she was right of course — and to her sermon, in order of succession, we splattered upon the silence a series of "yes, Lords," "A-mens," and "well, well, wells." Lady Sue shifted her seat toward the center. I stopped fiddling in my bag and turned off my reoccurring nightmare. She stood up and asked one of those politician questions, the kind people asked after Bobby Kennedy's death. "Well, what's it gonna be, people? Liberty or death?"

Back then I was saying good-bye to my childhood and running smack dead into waxed living, an American skateboard to slip and slide beyond one's resources and below one's potential. The sixties tuned out the fifties and turned on my agenda: BURN, BABY, BURN! Everything was in full color: afros and red-necks, po-lice and suburbs, Mal-colm X and John-son, Viet-nam and De-troit. Street people were claiming major victories. Afros had replaced tulips and cussing brought forth detente. Kelly, Doreen, Vida, and Willie Mae were on the front lines then. Crystal was directing them in a chorus of Curtis Mayfield's song, "We're a winner . . . and never let anybody say . . . you can't make it 'cause an evil mind's in your way." Mrs. Shelton didn't have no skin rash then, 'cause her and Miss Rosa Parks were churchgoing friends. And now Ginger had just lit the pilot and boiled our memories of talking back to white folks, to men, to the FBI, and protecting our sister, Angela.

The nurse, caught between her color and calling, rang her desk bell and broke our collective déjà-vu. The sound lured us back from the hills where rebels hide out. Ginger, seeing the group in danger, made her move toward the nurse, hollering: "Enough of this shit! We want that motherfucker, right now! You know where he is, Y'all always know where he is . . . !"

My soul stepped completely out of its container, and I watched a part of me drop to the floor like an old coat. Startled, I looked around, and we were all standing, right behind Ginger. ". . . I bet he's been eating his lunch all the goddamn time!"

"He's finished. Ginger, you may go in now."

Ginger slipped through the door. Poof!

Silence filled all the spaces between us. I found myself another spot on the dirty indoor-outdoor carpet to plant my gaze and drew a big fat blank. I was a walking, talking time bomb firing blanks, anyway. Free clinics give permanent residency to my kind.

"Somebody's in there whimpering," Lady Sue said, putting sounds to her words for the first time. I turned to Kelly with the hairy legs, dropped my prescription bottle on purpose this time to get everybody's attention.

"It sounds like someone is crying to me," I said.

Vida, nodding out, said "Yeah . . . it's the one . . . with the big mouth . . . shi-i-i-i-it! They must be whipping her ass."

"No way! It must be somebody else in the doctor's office," Willie Mae said, straightening her collar.

Doreen, thinking they had called her number, jumped up, stopped, then sat down again. "I didn't see nobody else."

"Neither did I," Mrs. Shelton said dabbing her oozing skin rash with her Sunday hankie. "But I think it's her. She's been crying since she went in there."

We all looked over to the other side of the room where Crystal had begun humming "Precious Lord" as Ginger's whimpers turned to screams. Our aahs and oohs and shifting body sighs commenced when the screaming settled down and the door opened. Ginger walked out and placed her chart in the rack and left. Looking for the smoke to appear, I responded to the nurse's "Next," and moved toward the inner door. I paused for a moment to catch the silence in the room, and my eyes locked onto the words on the doctor's chart. *Diagnosis*: Ginger is sick. *Prescription*: She needed to cry.

MISS RUSSELL

. . . .

CHERRY MUHANJI

iss Russell dips snuff and spits in a can.
Sometimes she forgets, stalls, then spits,
missing the can or ignoring it, and that's
what the Hollyhocks hated. It was like,
they murmured to themselves, she made
a special effort to spit on the hem of their dresses. "Heifer!" they said.
They were dependent on winos' pee for a good growing season. And
they were doin' good, ever since the war was over, and so many of
them who went away came back flinchin' in their heads — wind-up
toys with broken springs, oilin' themselves with Cask 59, maybe some
Muscatel. And the Hollyhocks wanted to keep it that way. Winos can
be choosey where they pee, they knew — exchanging privacy for a
clean spot in the alley. They wouldn't pee on no ugly snuff stains if
they could help it.

The Hollyhocks stood ready. The pee makin' a difference between pretty red flowers, or fadin' pink ones. They grew just at the edge of the alley where the cracks were widest. They would tunnel up through the concrete despite the best efforts of the people downtown, who felt that their good and loyal coloreds should have decent alleys to connect their neighborhoods. The record books downtown listed this alley as Sherman Street, so any summer week jackhammers could be heard cuttin' into the underskirt of the alley, gettin' it ready for a new pour of cement. The coloreds of this city were gonna have decent "streets" for their children to play in. "Or else," this administration said, "heads will roll."

Miss Russell had taken up crazy just in the last few years, the Hollyhocks knew. Before that, she had been a real southern belle. But now . . . collectin' bottles, sellin' all exceptin' Coke, the ones with the fragile green tint, countin' and recountin' them. People was re-luctant to take up with an ol' lady countin' and collectin', sellin' and savin' bottles. Smart thinkin' ones knew that folks who was "tetched in the head" best be left to they own musings.

"She ain't that crazy," the Hollyhocks argued. "She ain't got no reason." None that they was gonna accept, anyway, for spittin' on the hems of they dresses, and not in the Maxwell House coffee can she carried for that very reason, or so she say, they said, she say. "Why," they asked, "don't she just spit in the alley?" Not take the time to find them to spit on. Who did she think she was, anyway, movin' down the alley just like she owned it? No sir! She never own nothin' exceptin' that old house on Maybury Grand, the one she had kept closed up all the time, the one nobody went into and she, the onliest one ever came out of, the one the people downtown never checked into. Instead, they preferred to keep tearin' up the alley every time the sun got hot — but we knew some very strange stuff was goin' on in there. Yeah, she was a sly one alright, even the Willows, with they worryin' self and all, knew she used to only come out that house for bottles and then sold all of 'em, exceptin' Coke, and was heard at odd hours cussin' and laughin', hummin' low and singin' inside the old house on Maybury Grand.

The Poplars told everybody who would listen 'bout her comin' up from Luzana after the first war, with her southern ways and it-si bit-si manners, wipin' her mouth on a napkin (and a cloth one at that!) after each bite. Why she even drank wine at breakfast! They had heard her clinkin' glasses, but with who?!

One day she just pulled down the shades and that was it. No more nothin'. Laughin' and cussin' sometimes, hummin' low and singin', but no more nothin'. Still, she wasn't so hot, and besides she didn't own nothin', not anymore, exceptin' all the Coke bottles in the world and that old house on Maybury Grand.

"Where is she now?" one of the young Hollyhocks asked.

"Child, let me see, if memory serves me right that was in 19 and 50. I hear tell she down in that ol' shack by the railroad tracks. Been there fo' some time. At least if a body can put any stock in what dem uppity Elms say."

Annabell Lee Jones Russell *did* like Coke bottles best, the ones with the fragile, green tint. After all, in 19 and 50 fragile was very necessary. There was talk of another war, and she hadn't got used to the last one ending. Joe had left soon after that. And Jessie . . . what could she really say about Jessie?

Yeah, she liked Coke. The glassy green tint reminded her of magnolia trees — her daddy sipping mint juleps high up on the veranda, while she, home from college just for the summer, was seen, regarded, and duly noted by her family. What would they have said if she had said straight out what she wanted? No. She couldn't. But it had hurt to leave Jessie alone in the hot dorm all summer, with no place she could go. What else to do? They both needed to finish. Then Harlem, Chicago, Detroit — some place north — a place to get lost in. But it didn't happen, it just didn't happen.

What to call it? How to call it? No good-byes. No ending. No way of saying now what you meant to me. You opened me up, Jessie. Made it all happen. I remember. Still, it was so long ago. So very long ago. But Jessie, I remember. I remember touch. And what touch is. And what it is not.

I couldn't get up before ten. You up working. The sun spilling through the doorway. Warm. As you were. Bent over your work. Frowning. Trying to make it work. Never thinking it did. But it was working, Jessie, and we were, we were working. But it was you. It was. Risking. Patient. Thinking I'd catch up. I was young. You were the artist, not me. I was all you. And couldn't understand why you couldn't be all me. And Bapu, your African elephant, was being born. He grew up between us. Munching sweet grass, etched on an African savannah, patterned in zebra stripes with ears that tricked the eye. You asking me what I thought, how I felt about an elephant in zebra stripes, with ears that waved. Me, not aware of just how good you were. Bapu, our elephant. I can still smell the cypress, sage, and sweet grass — and you, Jessie. And I learned. But not for years and not before Joe.

Jessie made Millie Jones uncomfortable. Why, she didn't know. After all, she was a well-bred Negro woman. Her family was "niggah rich" — not like white folks, but better than the better part of most coloreds. Her daughter at Spellman. She had gone there herself. It was not a place for the coloreds. So why had her daughter brought home this strange, dark girl, much too dark, who made her perspire — no, sweat. And that girl knew it. That smug smile. That niggah! How dare her!

Yes, Millie Jones understood college. Nice southern girls went, some until they finished, knowing they had a better time of it than many men. But most stayed only until they could meet and marry well. And she, Annabell Lee Jones, knew what "well" meant. A nice hi-yellah husband, so she could do her part and help the race refine itself. A nice, dull hi-yellah husband, with nice, dull hi-yellah manners, and they would have nice, dull hi-yellah mannered children, and all live together in a nice, dull hi-yellah, well-mannered house. So when she saw her mother was serious, she exchanged the yellow and dull for the black and gold.

Joe was black as a raven with one gold tooth in the front of his mouth. Like a beak, it filled his face and set her focus. How to live with Jungle Boy, for that's what he called himself. Marry him? Why would she do that? Well, she would if she had to. He was, he said, going north. She casually mentioned it to her mother, who screamed at her when she announced his intentions and she declared hers. *What career as an artist? Where had she gotten such a notion?* From that dark girl, no doubt. And who was Joe Russell? What family? Do we know them?

Maybe Joe just got tired of Detroit, the ghetto, the neighbors — me. He knew I was an artist. What kind, he never cared to know. Can I paint? Not like Jessie. But maybe.

Joe had been in the first war. In Paris, France. Such stories. Nobody believed all those stories. But he had been to Paris, France. He finally came home with the flat hard helmet he wore in the picture. America, he said, was no place for colored people. But if you had to be here, let it be in the North. God, let it be in the North. He stayed, longer than he would have in Louisiana, because of her. But then, he said, "Come, Annabell, let's go."

And after they married and moved into Black Bottom, he whispered, "I am the man, man," and spoke obscenities under his breath as he went down between her legs.

"What are you looking for between my legs, Joe?"

"Hush, Annabell. Women ain't s'pose to ask questions like that."

"Why?"

"A woman is a woman and 'why' ain't what they needs to know."

"My ass."

"Annabell Lee Jones! (He never called her Annabell Lee Russell.) I don't like no talk like that comin' out yo' mouth."

"You cuss, Joe."

"Ya mean when I . . ."

"Yes, when you fuck."

"Annabell! Besides, that's diff'ent."

"How?"

"There ya go again."

"Joe, at least I know what I'm looking for."

"When?"

"You know when."

"Not that again."

"Yes, that again . . . when I slide . . . down between the ridges . . . inside the fragile, green . . ."

"Now ya hush, Annabell! That's crazy talk! Nobody can git inside a Coke bottle."

"How many times do I have to tell you, I do? What's more, I know what I'm looking for. Not like you — struggling between my legs — looking for something you can't name."

"Annabell, what do ya feels when I does go down . . . between yo' legs?"

"Curious. What, I repeat, are you looking for?"

"Annabell, ya sick."

"No, Joe, you're sick because you keep looking for something you can't name."

"Can ya name what's inside of a goddamn Coke bottle?"

"See, I knew you believed I could get inside — when I wanted."

"No, Annabell, I know ya cain't, and I know you speaks sorta crazy sometimes, but I be lookin' fo' . . ."

"Something you can't name."

"Naw. That ain't right. I can so name it."

"Is it feeling, Joe? Why do you look for it between my legs?"

"Because that's . . . that's where I find it — sometimes."

"Did it ever occur to you that good feelings can come from other places?"

"Like inside a goddamn Coke bottle?"

"Yes, Joe. It's like finding . . . finding God."

"Annabell, you a crazy screwed-up bitch."

"Joe, you get a feeling you can't name, a feeling some people kill for, themselves and others, a something they won't name, that is beautiful with so much feeling and love and . . . I know what touch is. . . ."

"Annabell, nobody finds God in a Coke bottle! Nobody!"

"But it's alright for you to find Him between my legs?"

"Annabell!!!!! Stop yo' blasphemin'."

"Joe, you're an asshole. Just like most people."

Joe left just as the second war ended. At first, she was angry, then silent, and finally, indifferent. What could she tell the neighbors? She couldn't just say he had gone somewhere. Where exactly was somewhere? So she said nothing and, finally, they stopped asking. Northern coloreds, she learned, after they see you're gonna survive, accept silence. Survival was the thing, the one sign that everythang gon' be alright! And that's the only real miracle they knew about in 19 and 50, in the ghetto, in Detroit.

Joe, she remembered, was always mumbling about "the man." "The man" this, "the man" that. "The man ain't never gon' give nothin' he didn't take back. Ten, twenty years down the road. Shit," he'd hiss, "we still ain't got our forty acres and a mule."

Joe didn't wait for "the man" to take it all back. He did. All the war bonds he bought at the plant. Well, not all. He thought he took them all. He stopped counting after the first ten or so. For every one he got after that, she'd hide one. But he did take her two good pieces of jewelry and three foxes with the rhinestone eyes all clumped together and each other's tail still in the mouth.

Money was a problem now. Now that the second war was over. She had had money during the war. Everybody did. Now her shades were down and she was quiet, the silence so real sometimes, she could hear it. And she laughed. And kept laughing. And when she felt the deep hum in her throat, she laughed again.

Jessie, see! My lips move making your name. See my lips. Jessie, darling, good morning. I've been up for hours. Such a sleepyhead you are. Coffee? Bacon, warm toast, and marmalade. Eggs, sunny-side up, right? See, I remember. Come, sit. No, the paper isn't here. And yes, I love you before you ask. We went to the summer country last night, don't you remember? Before sleep — high on a hill we were — the stars pecked at us . . . me, intoxicated, drunk inside of you. My eyes, flame . . . you, all in velvet, ran your tongue along the edge of me. I could not breathe.

You did not move after the last star burst. Your sleepy mouth found my nipple . . . and you slept. And me? I slept. Finally, but not before I reached again, inside the warm well of you. Suddenly thirsty, I drank again. You came. And I grew like a flower.

The day dawned hot in 19 and 50. And cool, green, and fragile were very very necessary. The sky heavy. Haze. Haze that held the sunshine in. The sun would finally free itself but not before it took revenge.

It's hot as twin bitches in here. Better not work so long on top of the ladder. I'm getting kind of dizzy. If I fall . . . but it's almost done. Jessie, you proud? You damn better be. I'm working my ass off. So, what do you think, Jessie? Yeah, I think so too, I'll get the glasses. Hold on a minute. I know you're excited. But wait. Let's do it right. It deserves a toast. Wait till I pour, will you.

The doorbell rang. Is it Saturday, Jessie? It is? Damn, I forgot. I didn't hear them blow. Did you? I didn't think so. You laughing? I love to hear you laugh.

"Hold on, I'm coming." Miss Russell raced for the door, reached for the knob. It moved. The bell again.

"Yeah, I'm in here, wait a minute."

Where did he think she was? She went every second Saturday to the market on the neighborhood bus with these nosey neighbors.

It was not the time to be careless and let him in. He had once — well, he had looked in once. No more. It wasn't time, yet. Where was she working then? In the living room? No. The dining room. She had pressed the door shut leaving him in and out, stuck like an animal caught in quicksand, with terror and the scream still stopped in the throat. He was careful after that and so was she. She reached for the knob again. This time it turned, but now there were three knobs, now five. How could she be sure she had the right one? There were so many of them — bobbing and weaving up and down, up and down just like the buoys on the Detroit River — moving all the time but going nowhere. Nowhere. . . .

"Was that the bell again, Jessie? Shhh!!! Stop laughing he'll hear you. God, how I love your laugh."

The door flew open. And that's the last thing she remembered. And *this* was 19 and 50 and all she knew. . . .

Stories traveled fast in Black Bottom. The local coloreds, high up on they own porches, could spin a yarn faster than Miss Nitty could bake bread. But the Hollyhocks down by Maybury Grand still tell the story best.

"G-i-irl, they finally had to take her away."

"Girl, hush yo' mouth. When?"

"Kickin' and screamin', I bet."

"Ya kiddin'? Not that southern belle."

"Who took her out? The cops? the white folks downtown — who?"

"That Danny boy, the one use ta live near dem uppity Elms, the ones still got all that sickness, who keep they noses in a pinch, anyway. Seem like they woulda got off they high horse by now, seein' they ain't nevah got much bettah. Must run in the family."

"Will ya git on with the story. A body ain't got all day."

"Well ya can try and tell it yo'self. Ha! But ya cain't. Ya grew up in the neighborhood later. After she done already left. Ya don't know it all after all, do ya Miss Fast? Well, like I was sayin', fo' I got so rudely disrupted. Danny went in."

"What ya mean went in? Blossom tell me ain't nobody ever been in that ol' house since fo'ever."

"Blossom! That strumpet in the streets! She don't know her ass from a hole in the ground. Danny got in, I tellin' ya. And I don't know how. Do ya wanna hear the rest of this story or no? Well, Danny blows and blows. No Miss Russell. So he goes in. Well, Sam, who tended to dem ol' and slow folks down in the hollow on Maybury Grand, gits tired of waitin' in the bus, so he hops out to see what done happened to Danny. If ya ask me, and nobody ever do, Sam was just 'bout the nosiest man I ever knew. Always tryin' to git in other folks' bizness. I can still see how his tongue used to slide over his lips when he finally done got a chance to see what got Miss Russell so holt up in that house. Well, ya know what Danny be doin?"

"No, I don't. Remember I weren't there. Blossom say all y'all been tryin' to look up under the shades fo' th' longest kinda time."

"There ya go again, bringin' that strumpet into decent folks' bizness. Danny lets up the shade I tells ya — that's when we seen the holy ghost got a hold of him."

"Have mercy! Was he jumpin' and shoutin'?"

"Honey, hush! I'm here to tell ya that's just what he was doin'. Then he stopped. Looked up and went to rockin' back on his heels. Callin' on the Lord. Hummin' "Deep Jesus." He a preacher man to this day. Do ya know that song? Learned it as a girl."

"Will ya *please* git on with the story?"

"Sam stop too, and was lookin' up, and then went tearin' through the whole house just like somebody half crazy, shoutin' fo' everybody to git outta the bus, and come see what been happenin' in the ol' house on Maybury Grand. Well, wouldn't ya know it, Big Bertha was the first one off the bus, Sam's wife. That heifer! Always lookin' fo' somethin' to see. Well, when she swung dem big hips through the do', Big Bertha stop dead in her tracks too. There was Miss Russell out cold on the flo' with everybody steppin' over her and dem three gon' to glory. Well, not Sam exactly, fo' he unglorified hisself and was runnin' from attic to basement, basement to attic just like some rat spinnin' in a cage. Which caused Sam's wife to commence to movin' faster than she ever done done in her whole life. Upstairs, downstairs — nippin' at Sam's tail all the while."

"Girlll! what be the mattah wit 'em?"

"Well, we heard her shoutin', 'Looka here! Look yonder.' And then she started testifyin'."

"Testifyin'! Have mercy! Was she speakin' in tongues?"

"Let me finish. First of all, I ain't one to believe everythin' I hears, like so many other folks 'round here. So, I peeks in real good and I just be damn! There we all was — on everthang."

"What ya mean on everthang?"

"We is on the ceilin' and on the walls and in the bathroom and in the kitchen and on the kitchen cabinets and, and . . ."

"She paint us on everthang I tells ya. My flowers coverin' the whole ceilin', even when I don't look so hot. Ya know, like when they was all gon' to the big war and then the bigger one, and we ain't gettin' no real good waterin' then."

"Yeah, I heard tell them was some hard years fo' y'all."

"Yeah, but she paint us real pretty when we was high on the hog *and* when we wad'nt. Ya know how I am. I ain't nevah cared fo' them uppity Elms, and I ain't nevah thought they looks so hot. Not as hot as they always thought they was. But, shiiit! Even they looks good. And the Poplars, with all they talkin' and givin' way other folks' bizness, look real sweet — sweeter than the Lord at his last supper. And the Willows that be teary all the time. Even they look like they finally got it all together. Birds be comin' and goin' out they hair just like they does fo' real. We all touched by the Lord hisself! She paint us friends, the winos, too. Even paint Melvina, with her mumblin' self, cuttin' through the alley on her way uptown to visit her sistah Grace. Ya know Grace? She give her money fo' that cheap wine she drink all the time. Ha! Mumblin' Melvina drinkin' her Silver Satin."

"Get down, Melvina."

"But it kinda funny when I commence to talkin' 'bout them ol' days. 19 and 50, huh! But we all looked just fine. Somehow. Real fine. Huh! Now that we talkin' real honest. We did look kinda funny all over the ol' house. Ya thinks that's what she mighta been laughin' and cussin' 'bout at night inside the ol' house?"

"Well, I don't know. I weren't there, remember?"

"She even painted herself up there."

"How she do that? She cain't tell what she look like. Could she? 'Less she painted while she looked in the mirror. Can ya paint yo'self? To hear ya tell it, she musta lay on her back to paint y'all on the ceilin'."

"She wad'nt the first ever to lay on her back to paint toward the heavens."

"How she do that?"

"All I know, she done it. And naw, I cain't paint myself. I ain't no painter, but I pretty 'cause I sees myself fo' the first time, like I seen by others. And I ain't nevah knowed I looks so."

"How a body look like anythang on the ceilin' and the walls?"

"Miss Russell musta thought so. 'Cause she be workin' on us fo' a long time."

No one saw Miss Russell rise from the floor and leave. After everyone went inside the house "Amens" and "Yes Lords" were heard when they entered Jessie's room. Where the altar was.

They all stopped suddenly when they saw all the Coke bottles.

Jessie loved Coke — their long slow afternoons filled with each other and Coke with the fragile, green tint. . . .

Jessie, stop, I'll get the Coke. Why don't you come in before your arthritis starts acting up? What? I know the light is good today. Are you ever going to get used to working up here and so close to the railroad track? You've been working all day. It's getting cold outside. You want me to bring your shawl? Better yet, I'll start a fire. Besides, I want you to come see what I've been doing. Is it that late? You're right. Here comes the five o'clock right on time. . . .

LITTLE FAITH

....

EGYIRBA HIGH

espite the sense of foreboding that Marilyn was feeling, she attended the wake. She stopped at the door of parlor number three, and stared at the casket in the room. For once, in all the time she had known her, Faith was calm and collected. She was dead. From the crowd that was gathering in the inner room, Marilyn heard whispers and muffled, jerky sobs. She felt a quick chill through her body. Maybe she shouldn't have come.

Marilyn signed the register by the door and stepped into the room. She made her way down the nearest aisle, not able to look at the body. First she would gather her thoughts, then press the memories to the back of her brain. There weren't many people, but there was still time. At least forty-five minutes before the wake was officially over.

Marilyn moved all the way to the rear of the place and sat down in the last row. The cold, metal folding chair made her flinch. In a few minutes, the heat and humidity would make her unstockinged legs stick to the chair. She decided to stay twenty minutes, no more.

Marilyn didn't recognize anyone. She guessed that the people most disturbed in front were Faith's parents, but she wasn't sure. Well, who else could they be? She chided herself for not being more certain. Of course, Faith's family would be here. No telling who would show up. Faith was a distant, introverted person, and no one went out of their way to get to know her. At least her parents must be here, she thought. But a second voice inside her head asked, why must they?

Something was amiss here but Marilyn couldn't name it. There were about ten or fifteen people in the room and yet, the desolation of Faith's life (and death) jumped out at her. People moved into the parlor quietly and spoke in hushed tones. The minister tapped his fingers on the podium and checked his watch periodically. Marilyn thought about what Faith must have meant when she asked what she was living her life for. But Marilyn had brushed the question aside. Everybody felt that way at some time or another. Marilyn thought that it was just another thing for Faith to complain about.

The more she thought about it now, the more she sensed something unnatural here. The grief of these people seemed rehearsed, more a timed display for public appearances than a sense of real loss. Marilyn wrestled with her negative thoughts. Of course, Faith's parents were grieving. What was going on with her today? But she remembered back to the few times she'd heard Faith talk about her past. And the disdain she saw in Faith's eyes when she talked about her family. Where were her pleasant memories? Marilyn had asked her. Pleasant memories? Faith had repeated the question and had laughed. Leaving home was the pleasant memory. Home had been hell. She couldn't wait to get away from the place. Faith's words struck a feeling in Marilyn that she couldn't quite name. Now, as she sat among people she didn't know, in a place where she shouldn't have been, she realized that Faith hadn't escaped entirely. Still, despite the evidence of Faith's body, Marilyn found it hard to believe that death was the only solution.

They had found her body swinging from a rope that was tied to a plant hook in the ceiling. Twenty-eight years old and dead by hanging. Fortunately for the authorities, there had been a note that read

I'm tired. It's been all I could do to get this far. I don't feel like explaining. Ask my momma. Ask my daddy. Ask my friend downstairs. I give up.

They took the note from the pocket of the vest she had been wearing. Marilyn wouldn't have known so soon of Faith's death if the police hadn't knocked on her door to make some inquiries. She was the friend downstairs. No, she had told them, she couldn't think of any particular reason Faith would want to take her life. Well, they weren't that close. She had lived there about a year and a half. No, she didn't think Faith had many friends. No, she couldn't remember seeing anyone ever really come to visit Faith. Faith had always said that she couldn't trust people to do anything for her or to be there when she really needed them, that her cats were easier to trust, because they loved her. Yes, she had talked a little about her family, but she was sure that distance had alleviated much of the strain. She wasn't sure why Faith liked her. She supposed that she had to talk to someone. Yes, she would cooperate in every way.

Marilyn shivered in her seat. The only reason she had tolerated Faith's constant pessimism and complaints was because it helped to dispell some of her own loneliness. Now that she had been saving money to go home, she missed Cecilia more and more. How had things gone wrong between them? When she found out she was their mama's favorite? Marilyn, the dependable daughter. Did everything right. Cecilia had withdrawn from her.

Talking with Faith about her family reminded Marilyn of how she and her sister had loved each other as girls. She did feel sorry for Faith, but Marilyn had avoided asking too many questions. Faith's burden was heavy, and Marilyn could think of no way to soothe her fears.

The body was so still. There was an eerie feeling here. Marilyn shut her eyes. She felt nauseous. She wished now she hadn't come. She didn't belong here. She wasn't a real friend to Faith. This should be a private affair between Faith and her family. She would leave.

"Are you Marilyn Agee?" Marilyn opened her eyes to find a dark-skinned woman standing over her.

"Yes, I am."

"Well, I am Faith Walker, little Faith's mother."

My God, Marilyn thought, little Faith? She got stuck for a moment.

She looked at the older woman. The glasses she wore could not hide her mole-covered face. About five foot seven, she stood towering over Marilyn. It was not that she was heavy, but her gigantic breasts pointed at Marilyn like a scolding index finger. Here it was. The something she had felt.

All the conversations that she had had with Faith ran through her head. She got dizzy. She thought of Cecilia, then Faith, then Cecilia. The nausea swelled inside her. This was Faith's mother, not hers.

"I said I'm little Faith's mother," the voice repeated itself. "You are little Faith's friend, Marilyn?"

Coming here was definitely a mistake.

"Uh . . ."

"My husband and I want to talk with you about little Faith. Can you tell us anything? What could've brought my baby to this? Can you help us, please?"

The woman stood over her waiting. Waiting for an answer that she was not prepared to give, now or later. How did this woman know who she was, for heaven's sake? Faith Walker was a grown woman, and here was her mother standing there looking down at her, wanting to know about her little Faith. Who, Marilyn wanted to ask her, was that? But she didn't ask. She could only feel irritation at this intrusive woman. She placed the flat of her palm over her stomach. Next time she would follow her feelings.

"Uh," she tried to answer again. The woman appeared to be frowning. She's upset, Marilyn, the voice inside her said. You're not helping. "Uh," she said again trying harder to answer, but the words wouldn't come. She closed and opened her eyes. And again, "I . . . uh. . . ." The face of the woman was pressing against hers, demanding an answer. It seemed to Marilyn as if big Faith was both judge and jury and about to pronounce both verdict and sentence on her. She opened and closed her eyes again. Go ahead, tell her, the voice said. The woman was losing patience, she could tell.

"I don't know if I can help you," she finally found the words to say. The woman did not believe her.

"Wha-a-a-aat? I said my husband and I need your help."

"Mrs. Walker, I was only Faith's neighbor. I talked with her a little and visited her sometimes, but I really don't know . . ."

"But she talked about you . . . she said . . . oh, Jesus! Frank!"

Marilyn flushed. What had she said wrong? A pale-skinned man, slight of build and balding, came running down the aisle. Mrs. Walker was clutching her heart and rocking on her heels. A few of the other mourners followed close behind Mr. Walker screaming, "Faith! Faith! Lord, Jesus! Faith!"

It was all happening so fast Marilyn didn't know what to do. Jumping from the seat, she heard her thighs squeak from lying bare so long. But it wasn't fast enough. Grabbing the backs of two chairs in front of her, Marilyn retched and retched until there was no more anxiety inside.

I I

When at last she opened her eyes, Marilyn was lying on a cot in the funeral home. One of the family members sat beside her, watching. She told her how she had thrown up, then fainted and landed in it. That was why she wasn't wearing her own clothes. It was such a mess. Such a shame for little Faith. This was her funeral, after all. Seemed disrespectful, somehow. Marilyn groaned. She wished the woman would go away. But the woman went on chattering that Faith wasn't even in her grave and there was trouble. Marilyn closed her eyes. Maybe she could make the woman think she was really sick, then maybe she'd shut up.

"But Faith just couldn't believe what you were telling her, that you wouldn't help her and all. She said little Faith had told everybody you and she was the closest of friends. Imagine not being able to help your closest friend's mother. . . ."

"Ooooooooh," Marilyn groaned, turning over on the cot.

". . . Faith says that little Faith wrote home telling how you all was gonna go to Africa together, that you was a teacher and all. Faith always liked teachers," the woman trailed off. "Said there was nothing more respectable for a Negro woman than to be a teacher. Anyway, little Faith told her family how you all traveled together and socialed together — how you even dated men friends who was friends to each other. Sounded like you all was tighter than the seams in a handsewn quilt. Even told Faith how much alike the two of you all was. Told her mama that there was somebody else in the world like her."

Lies. All of it, lies. Marilyn couldn't take anymore. She had to get out of the place. Looking down, she saw that she was wearing a choir robe. Where were her clothes? She felt so weak. If she could sit up, she could get her bearings. Then she could get out of here, hail a cab, before anyone would notice. If she could only send this babbling woman out of the room. She couldn't stand to face any more of these people. Faith, oh, Faith, why? Why me, Faith? But as she said it she knew why.

"Ooooooooooh," Marilyn groaned.

"Are you alright, sugar?"

"I could use some water. My stomach . . ."

"Hold on, I'll get you some. Lord, Jesus, what a day!"

Marilyn watched the woman move toward the door and out. She tried to sit up and fell back. Gotta get out of here. Up again. Back down. Oh, help me get out of here, she said to the empty room. She rolled over on her right elbow and managed to sit up on her arm. She swung one leg off the cot, then the other. Taking her free arm and placing it by her elbow, she was finally able to push herself up. She had to get out. The air was stifling. Finally, struggling to her feet, Marilyn crept toward the door and opened it. She could hear loud sobs coming from a nearby room. It had to be Mrs. Walker. Marilyn was torn. Maybe she could think of something to say, any little thing to make her feel better. Damn! She was caught between two brick walls. She felt to blame for not listening enough to Faith and here was Mrs. Walker, crying 'cause she didn't have more to say. She ran.

Down the hall. She had to get out. She had to. Run, run, run, the voice was telling her. Run out of here. She ran breathlessly down the long corridor, a blur and shock to mourners in different viewing rooms. She heard gasps of "Did you see that? . . . My God! . . . What was it? . . . Woo, a ha'nt! . . . Jesus, Jesus, Jesus! . . ." Out the front door she ran. Down the stairs, a streak of lightning. She didn't stop running. Faster, faster. Away from this courtesy turned horror. Moving. Was it fast enough? She didn't know. All she knew was that she couldn't stop now. They might catch her. Might even tie her up and do something crazy. They couldn't make her talk about something she didn't know about. Her panic was overtaking her. But she could last until she got home or somewhere safe. She was making it. She had gotten way away from the funeral home. This wasn't my fault, she cried. She gained a second wind and ran like a sprinter going for the gold. She ducked and darted through traffic, still huffing, still frightened. This would be behind her soon. Running. Telling herself every step of the way what she was gonna do when she got home. She would call Cecilia. Today.

Cecilia. Things didn't have to be like this. Running for her life. She moved into high gear and envisioned how things would be. I'm coming home, Cecilia. I'm coming home. But Marilyn didn't see it coming, and neither did the blue Oldsmobile sedan see her, until it was too late.

A NEEDED VIOLATION

. . . .

KESHO SCOTT

he one I named after humanity pushed me off a cliff. In the blink of an eye, I fell into the universe and bumped into a frightening feeling. A need to have a woman.

Sacha and I were carrying on like daughter and mother, servant and master, jerk and superjerk one Saturday morning. We were jumping around in the waterbed and talking way too loud. Her birthday had been the month before, and I realized that my commitment to her had survived eight long years. The day of her birth, at the age of twenty-four, I had said, "Sacha, this is the sun. It will always shine for you. I am your mommy. I promise to take care of you until . . ." The pregnancy had been a liberated woman's nightmare and the labor—well, words like "miracle" popped in between my a-ha's, sending just about the right amount of depth to my slapstick commercial life.

"Momma, let's go to Venice one day. . . . Okay. Shall we take your sister? . . . No! . . . Sacha! . . . What? . . . Do you think I should marry James? . . . Yeah, Momma!"

Here we were east and west winds circulating to a Saturday morning pace. Jumping around on the waterbed. Fun. Giggling. Happy. I reached and grabbed Sacha, and we continued to play. We wrapped our arms and legs around each other. Laughing. So real and so silly Sacha made me feel. I forgave her for all those diapers, and the time she swallowed a bottle of cough syrup, and her "little lying" about eating up my pecan cookies, and putting my expensive cologne on her baby doll.

An hour later, sleepiness infringed upon our play. We had been absorbed. My once-pregnant belly-object maneuvered to my shoulder. Coming up from the twilight of sleep, I felt myself stroke her hair and take in her aroma. I noticed that she had finally lost that total baby smell which had been the symbol of my artistry. Missing the smell, I visualized rituals of the past when I awaited her, this, my creation. I remembered the highway sounds outside my window during those after-work afternoon naps the doctor had prescribed. But now my attention focused on our togetherness and our natural and syncopated rhythms. Sacha's breath followed mine and I chased hers, out of rhythm and with the movement of the waterbed. The air in our stomachs made two white camel lumps in the cover, one going up, one going down. I started to count the rotations in our orchestrated movement . . . but the math and the magic of the moment lured me to sleep.

I was finished falling in my dreams when my eyes completely opened. Mother's instinct or the attraction of like-molecular energy — something drew me immediately to the fright on Sacha's face. She stared at me as if caught. I was so close I could see, in her glasslike, Chineselike, brown cornea, my face. Masked. An illuminated totem. We had crossed into the utopian dimension of female Amazons. A secret society intoxicated by love. Dances in the blue night. Moonlight. Curved bodies drooped, swaying our tight, twisted skin to the ground. Mixtures of sand and leaves discolored our skin and luscious rumps, as the nipple-to-nipple contact erased biological imperatives and tattooed us as irregulars in nature. We blinked. Shifted. Adapted. And got lost in our tunneled imagination.

Why did Sacha and I try to pop the spring that holds back the living and loving between everything that is the same in nature? Why had we tried to unwind existence as it was by child's play? We had been zapped into an eerie velocity, traveling at the speed of fright. Exposed. Ambushed, but charged, I felt fear. I felt her fear. Resistance. My stomach swam madly, turning my juices poison. Perspiration appeared in my hairy places. I felt seasick. Sacha's almond eyes filled with water, and she acted as if I were the engineer of her tear ducts. Confused, afraid, I turned my head the other way and ordered, "Sacha, it's time to get up and cook dinner." I spoke in the tone of an inhabitant of another world. She moved in a sleepy slow motion out the door and down the stairs. Never looking back. I put the event of the morning out of my mind. Discarded. Barricaded. Secure again, I avoided looking into my child's face, Sacha's face, for the next few months, and when the coast was clear, I even hugged her — in front of an appropriate crowd. But I knew we must never imitate aborigines again.

This incident left me unraveled. I did not know how to direct the misplaced passion of my dreams for us. The nervous energy, absent from our play, found a home in consumption. Compensation. Gluttony. I had noticed that my head was getting smaller as my body was undisguised, like dandelions on new spring sod. I did not know where the weeds were going to plump up next. Also the months of adjustment to a new town, new people, new routines set a collage of emotions working underneath my skin — all at the same time. Mirrors began to give me back other people's images: John Blubber Butt and Martha Phibbs with the King Kong Tits. Those were the kind of jokes I told on myself in the cafeteria at work. So with little pageantry, I sniffed out the gym. It was in the middle of campus and needed a major facelift too. Women's gyms. How boring, I thought. I dragged myself up the dingy hall to the locker room. Tennis shoe marks and a lost-and-found box demonstrated its previous use. But it was empty of people, and the lack of noise had me looking over my shoulder every five seconds. Secretly, I wanted to posture myself as the who's-fatter-than-you queen. Instead, I sat alone judging how much fat lay on the bench. My fat. I always had hated my thighs. They were like ornamental turkey legs. No one ever eats them. I was told I could do some leg exercises. Ae-ro-bics. Sounded Greek to me. It was for white girls, not soul sisters who ate soul food and protested against international apartheid before it was a fad. So I chose the sport that was a real struggle for life. Swimming. It was also at the ghetto price. Free suits. Free towels. Free manicures — the chlorine could get out all the dirt between my toes and nails. Free illusions in the water. Lost in my negative thoughts about myself, I suddenly heard footsteps. Taking a far-sighted view, and with a quick snap of my neck, I saw a white image advance. A towel on her head and butt naked, she walked directly to the locker next to mine. Shit. Of all the weird things. A zillion lockers and she had the one next to mine. I turned my back to draw an invisible line and sign: this is my space. Do not enter. An inch or two was between us. She did not intrude. Good. She had gotten my message. I continued to undress. One stitch at a time. Shirt, pants, undies, earrings, watch, socks, until I felt the warmth of two laser beams on my bare back about the exact distance apart as a pair of eyes. I enjoyed the aerial massage. She did not make a sound. Between us existed the silence of motion that makes the music deaf people see. I kept my back turned to feel powerful and in control. My mind returned to the directive seeping from my fat — exercise.

I was in a tug of war with my leotards when I smelled a smell that was intimate in my memory. Jungle Gardenia. The smell created a flash-card effect in my cerebrum cortex. My memory corridor told me it had been Grandma's favorite. She wore it with a vengeance. And she used it to remain puppet-master. By its smell, my mind could simulate our afternoons lost in fantasy and could bring back the images my small eyes had seen.

I would be in low form, moving one branch after another from my pathway. Tall bushes snapping back into place, as I moved them back one century at a time. My ancestors in skirts tried to woo me faster to my destination. Come closer. Come closer. Running now. Running faster and faster. I fell. Looking up to the hole in the pink sky. Adventure and danger tantalized me and synthesized me to the private hymns I sang as an unspeaking child. Crying got warmth. Wet got warmth. I did both in the jungle. I was lost. Lost in the dark hanging weave. And ten long warm snakes would not calm the lust within. I stood in the middle of the warm dark cave and moaned as memory shifted away from childhood. . . .

The locker room did not sprout jungle gardenias from the cracks of the army-green lockers. The smells did grease my loins and unloosen my mind from its rusted parts. The smells told my body to turn. But there was no movement. I was hyperventilating now. The smell repeated the command. Turn. Ignored again. Every letter in JUNGLE GARDENIA followed a cocaine line to my nose, and it lay prostrate and in spasms. As if icing my brown cupcakes with rum was not enough, she began to sing her lyrical poetry. "What a difference a day makes . . . twenty-four little hours . . . brought the sun and the flowers . . . where there used to be rain. My sunny, sunny nights are blue, dear . . . today I'm a part of you, dear. . . ." She sang in a low nasal southern tongue. Sing the song again, Momma! I thought, as my nerves flickered from head to foot. Feelings of ownership, of warmth, clouded my mind. I could see the sequence of her movement again from my peripheral senses. She was dancing. Entertaining me. It was time to gape through the curtain of my back.

I fiddled for my combination lock to lock away my possessions and lock out her hold over me. Our proximity felt promiscuous and familiar. I stood with my head against the locker and heard another command. Turn. My body did. My conscience split a second later. The ticker tape in my brain answered the dictum floating in midair. Look. And I did. Into a large pair of polka-dot sunglasses! And then at all of her. She was without garnishment and acted upon a cue from my inner luster. Taking off her sunglasses, she called me to a-tenn-hut. Frozen. Alert. Ready to come to order. She banged her hand on the locker, and I reacted and felt entered. Somewhere. Somehow. The cymbal hung between my hips absorbing the sound. Bang. Bang. Bang. Startled. Frightened. She moved closer. Erect. Intense Jungle Gardenia scent flirted with me again. This time adding a moist humidity to rows of army-green lockers and to me. My skin hairs elevated to the snake charming sounds my heart was making. She ran her fingers through her long, long, long, curly brown hair which, when parted, concealed what I felt. I followed the red hue that moved from her face down to her feet, up my legs, and to my forehead. We let out a sigh together, which flung me back to another time. Light from memory crept in again. I remembered way back when there was no line between us. Me and Momma. Me and girlfriends. Me and God. Remembering this made me dizzy, as I heard footsteps like marching combat boots. She drew the line this time. A cliff appeared. I dropped. I wailed. No. No. No. An atrocity. I suddenly lost my smell for flowers.

"How many onions should I cut up for the dressing?" I asked Mimi.

"We've got the same number of people we had last year — you should know by now!" Grandma's heavy tones piped through the spaces in between her twisted sentences.

"I know, but that doesn't mean I know how many onions to chop up."

"Use your heard, girl!" Tension as usual. We couldn't even follow the twenty-year routine of cooking Thanksgiving dinner without the customary game of verbal tennis. Backward and forward, baited slips of tongue that collect dark stains at the top of the small kitchen ceiling. Mimi. The name brought up the way I hated fish smells, welfare lines, and teenage homicides. Never any rest from her assault.

"How I wish upon a star." Jiminy Cricket would appear. Smile. Woody Woodpecker would appear too and say, "That's all folks! HA-ha-ha-ha-ha-haaaa!" Feeling like a cartoon frame, I'd ask again, "Mimi, how many onions?"

It wasn't always like this for Mimi and me. Easter reminds me of being eight and having my hair pressed and having a new pale blue bonnet fixed on top of my carefully cut Chinese bangs. Chinese bangs. How I had begged Mimi to make them for me. She had. We were going to get in trouble when Momma got back from down south.

"I'll handle your momma. You hear!"

"Yes, ma'am."

"Besides, it's time a girl your age got some distinction! You know what I mean?"

Did I? No. Did it matter? No. Did she know I really didn't know? No. We were equal in our understanding. Mimi was the helmsman of my crusade out of childhood.

"You look beautiful child. Never gonna be a moment like this again. Remember it, hear!" Her words began their journey throughout my veins and made a circular travel that had no final destination. "Now come here, I got a special surprise for you. I've been waiting till you got old enough. Bought it when you was born. Yo' momma thought I was crazy. But I knew my granddaughter was a queen. Sit here at my vanity until I go get it."

She had never invited me to her throne. That golden stool of Ashanti women adapted to four-room apartment living. Mimi's throne had a looking glass, as large as heaven, sitting upon its shoulders. My moment, I thought. I sat. Transformed. Transfixed. Transferred. Remembering when she seduced me as a child. I had sat at her feet as she dressed. "These silk stockings got to be put on straight or the seams gonna be crooked in the back. You must always remember these things for a real lady ain't got no excuse for keeping herself a mess." Mimi had stretched her beautiful legs across the top of the rainbow and pulled the stocking to her garter belt. It hung in symmetry on her waist. She had draped herself in layers of fine silks, taffetas, and other articles from the treasures of the Orient. When she finished, Mimi would turn toward the mirror of the sky and would, without God's help, place angel dust on her face. Instantly, mystically, she was beautiful. Striking a Lena Horne pose, she'd blow herself a kiss. "Goddamn, you are beautiful," she'd say. I nodded and knew she was deeply in love. With herself. And I was too!

So I sat and waited until Mimi returned. Trying to find a woman to be in love with. Me. "Here it is child, I had it buried in Granddaddy's trunk for years. Almost had to pawn it once 'cause we was short of making ends meet. No sir. I was gonna keep it for you." I opened the box no more than an inch or two, feeling restrained. Good feelings for women contradicted the rumblings inside. It was a ruby, ruby, ruby, red brooch.

I screamed. "Mimi, for me? For me, Mimi? Oh, Mimi, it is magnificent!" Panic. Panic seeped from out of my joyous broadcast.

"Here, I'll show you how to put it on. Got to know the right way, or you'll look like a fool." She crowned me. The brooch perched on my chest. I could only believe the sight of such perfection for a brief second. Closing my eyes, I sunk my head into Mimi's chest for safety. Resolution. Tutelage. She lifted my head, saying, "Child, love yourself, 'cause that's the best and safest kind." I grabbed her close.

But then the intrusion. I heard what the kids in my neighborhood would be chanting. Mimi heard them too. "You are a sissy. You are a sissy." She pushed me away. Suddenly. Affirmatively. I fell into a crevice and watched my childhood love ooze and freeze into Cassandra's oracle. Mimi's face registered a journey I already knew I had to take. Opaqueness. Dreaming. Faraway visions. Nightmares about chasing and being chased ran behind the screen in the background of our moment. Ignoring Mimi and the mutant shapes from the distant ashes of queendoms unthought of, I found, instead, the woman I was to love. Me. I pricked my finger with the brooch and made myself my own sister.

"Look, if you don't want to cut the fuckin' onions, just get out of my kitchen!" Reality. Pain. Mimi. Synonymous. Where had we parted the universe?

"Sacha, I've got a gift for you, honey."
"Yeah!"

"Yeah! Come here and give me a hug first." She followed. I knew she would. I knew she'd catch the scent.

"Momma, you smell good."

"Thanks, baby. Here." Opening the small box she sat on the throne — my lap. I hummed and hummed and plastered a criminal smile upon my face, reminding myself of the penalty for a needed violation. "It's perfume, like yours . . . Jungle Gardenia!" Sacha screamed. I could hear the Amazons in her voice. I grabbed her tighter. She sprayed and sprayed. In panic now, and in search of a mirror in the sky, she turned to find it in my face. From my heart. Reparation. Renewal. The one I named after humanity now knows she needs a woman too.

DELORIS DELAINE PUGH

. . . .

EGYIRBA HIGH

er sign read: PLEASE HELP ME AND
MY CHILD. With thoughts of steamed
rice and shrimp in her head, Deloris
fixed her attention to the placard in
front of her. She wanted to blot out
the reminder that she'd hardly eaten in two and a half days, and what
she had eaten, hadn't been much of a meal. Having to stand in line for
food handouts was wearing her down. Not that she had much of a
choice. In the name of expediency and thrift, the government had decided that feeding the poor three meals a day was more economical
and practical than turning over food stamps. She, and a whole city,
had exchanged the welfare lines for these food lines. So it was: stand
or starve. It wasn't for herself that she was so anxious, but for Stacy
LaTuan, whose cries of "When I'm gonna get some more, Mama?"

bludgeoned her hourly. The desperation Deloris felt hovered around her like death, beckoning.

Stacy LaTuan was sleeping. All Deloris could do now was sit and try to blot out the smells from the fast-food Japanese restaurant across the street. The workers at the Brotherhood of Man Mission were good to the mothers and their children who ate there. Children were always quickly singled out and brought to a section where they would get immediate attention. There were so many women coming into the mission, that often there wasn't enough to go around. The mission also fed the winos and homeless, and Stacy LaTuan always cried for more. Deloris sighed a heavy sigh and shifted her body where she sat on the doorstoop of the York Hotel. Looking down at Stacy sleeping peacefully, she sighed again and relaxed. It was a moment when all seemed well, a peaceful and undemanding moment. It would be bliss for about thirty more minutes, and then Stacy would open her eyes, and Deloris would find herself back in the living hellhole that was her daily routine.

Glancing across the street, she watched the well-dressed business-people dashing in and out of Mr. Sushi's. Each day had become a ritual for Deloris of sitting in the dusty doorway, watching people stream to and fro, able to make a choice about their noonday meal. Soon, Deloris would have to start walking again — pacing up and down the streets, Stacy LaTuan underfoot, holding the sign in front of her: PLEASE HELP ME AND MY CHILD, and hoping the people would drop their spare coins (and some that weren't) into the can she taped to the side of the placard. She could tell from the faces of the people that passed her, especially those that averted their eyes, what they thought of her and the whole situation. On some, it was hands tightly clenching coins in their pockets, grimly determined not to aid an able-bodied person, flashing a why-don't-you-get-a-job-nobody-gave-me-anything-when-I-was-your-age look. But she was able to look them in the eye and say in a second of a glance do-you-think-I-like-having-to-do-this? It wasn't a matter of pride anymore. Deloris had lost that a long time ago.

Then there were the faces of the people who took one look at the little brown girl tightly clenching her mother's side and, after quickly sizing up Deloris, would drop some coins in her can. Their eyes would meet for only a second and the donors would keep stepping, confident that their charitable acts would reconcile their consciences at church the coming Sunday. Fourth Avenue was a street in the business district of Seattle. Each day, the very rich, the workers, and the poor moved up and down, absorbed in their daily routines. Large, shiny, mirrored skyscrapers sprang up everywhere and the old, well-built buildings decayed slowly around them.

Coming into view now was Mr. Stanley. Perceval Edward Stanley. Known as a ladies' man when he bloomed like forsythia in the spring of his youth. Now Mr. Stanley was alone and got most of his solace from Muscatel. Still, he managed to stay semisober and never a harsh word out of his mouth, at least not to Deloris. In fact, Mr. Stanley was pleasant and always whistling a tune, despite the fact that he had to get around with a cane and was the constant prey of young thugs. "I'm just a mulewalker . . . walkin' all day long," Mr. Stanley sang.

"How do, Miz Pugh?" Mr. Stanley tilted his hat at her with his free hand.

"Not too bad today, Mr. Stanley. And you?"

"Gettin' on, just gettin' on. And the little one?"

"Oh, she fine — quiet right now."

"Well, you take care of her good, now."

"Oh, I will." And with that assurance, Mr. Stanley would glide on down the street singing. "Yeah . . . said I got me a lady who don't care if I stay or go."

Deloris would listen to his songs until he was out of ear range. The words always seemed sad to her, but Mr. Stanley never complained. Such a nice old man, she thought. He wasn't no better off than she, and many times he had given up his mission meal or brought her something extra when he could. It was more than Charlie ever did for his own flesh and blood. Charlie couldn't be depended on, once he was out of her sight.

"Uhn," Deloris mumbled to herself. Thinking of Charlie could turn her mood from pleasant to nasty. She didn't want to dwell on him. He was only good for one thing and that was trouble. Still, Charlie plagued her dreams and hopes when she allowed herself, for just a fraction of a moment, to think about the possibility that he might change, knowing all the time it was merely wishful thinking on her part. Charlie Simonds had a way of working himself into her imagination and keeping himself there against her protestations. The bum. Deloris smiled. She was remembering the last time Charlie was in her life. Seemed he never was, except to get in between her legs and leave her with a baby when he was finished with her. She thought of how it took nothing for Charlie to talk her out of refusing him.

She wasn't going to let him screw her no more. She had said that. And she had meant it. But he had grabbed her wide, flabby buttocks and squeezed, reducing some of her will by proportion. "Baby, you know I need you, don't you?" he breathed into her ear, gliding her slowly back against the wall. And before she knew what was happening, she was parting her legs and releasing her will to him. Then with some skillful movements, Charlie pulled off her panties, held her above the floor, braced against the wall, and she was all his. "Oh, Charlie, do you love me?" she'd ask, throwing her legs around his back. He'd answer by easing himself inside her, and it was all over. "Uhn huh, baby . . . yeah." And Deloris Delaine Pugh would once more find herself pleasured, pregnant, and alone.

No, she thought, no more. No more Charlie Simonds to leave her begging on the street for the rest of her life. Deloris looked down at her stomach. She was barely showing, yet the baby was due any day now. She'd lost the last one. Was kind of a blessing. She had sworn that Michael Gene (that was the name she had given him, even though he lived only two hours) was the last one, but here she was again carrying a load she knew would sink her deeper and deeper into the pit.

Stacy LaTuan stirred and brought Deloris out of her thoughts. She stroked Stacy's hair to keep her still. Stacy was a pretty, brown angel. Smooth, black hair framed her small, tan face. She wasn't as dark as Deloris had imagined she'd be. Charlie was, after all, the color of Alaga syrup, the kind Mama Lou (his mama) served with her pancakes. Deloris had asked Mama Lou not to give too much syrup to Stacy, but she had ignored her. "This is a colored child, Deloris. I know what I'm doing." And that would be the end of the discussion. Deloris would snap her mouth shut, 'cause Mama Lou would always find time to remind her that no matter what she thought or felt, she still wasn't black. Mama Lou was all they had, her and Stacy. She was all the friend Deloris had in the world. She wouldn't risk Mama Lou's ire, so she'd fade back into herself, while Mama Lou went on about the herbs and root cures she used to practice in North Carolina.

Deloris winced as she remembered how Mama Lou had tried to warn her about Charlie from the beginning. "It ain't nothing personal, honey, but he's a good looker and ain't gonna tie hisself down to just you, just 'cause you white. I thank you better know that now."

"Yes, ma'am. I don't wanna tie him down."

"I'm just telling you. I seen plenty womens get hurt by pretty boys like Charlie. They think maybe they can change him, like they got some special kind of mojo they gonna work between their legs, but them boys just go and find some other gems to polish."

At first, when Deloris heard it, she as insulted. Her and Charlie was different, and anyway, who was this old woman to tell her this? Then she realized by her cloudy eyes that the woman didn't mean her any harm, so she sat, quieted her insides, and listened.

· "Dexter Denby was his name, and he had the young girls sighin' and pantin'—breathless from the sight of him. He lit fire under his feets tryin' to court me, but I never paid him no mind. I was busy learning the roots. When I was workin' with them, wasn't no greater thrill. My hands would feel the life in them plants, and I knowed God never spoke no greater language. Somehow, I always knowed that. Never had no time for no courtin'."

Deloris wondered if this was to be one of those lectures that would find her sitting in the same place by sundown, but she fought the urge to be bored. Hiding behind those cloudy, gray eyes was a message. She knew it as Mama Lou's eyes opened and closed, remembering the sweetness of youth and its necessary foolishness.

"One day I was out to the woods to collect me some Mother roots. Bertha Simpkins was about to birth, and we needed lotsa squaw vine to smooth her labor. Just going about my business singin' to the trees, I always sang to the trees 'cause my heart was glad, when Dexter Denby come from out of nowhere and put his hands around my waist from behind."

Deloris watched Mama Lou stifle a smile, as she pretended annoyance with the memory of Dexter Denby.

"'Oooooh!' I screamed, 'I know you wouldn't like me to throw this pail of dirt all over you, now would you? Get away from here.' But he just smiled and said, 'C'mon gal, you know there's more to life than these here plants. This ain't all God made now.' Next thang I knowed, we was rollin' around the dirt, and Dexter was plantin' kisses all over my face and tryin' for my neck. Next thang I knowed, it was something else 'sides gatherin' roots every day, to be concerned about."

Mama Lou's voice trailed off, and her body rocked back and forth in the rocker while her mind floated back to Dexter Denby, North Carolina, and times when innocence was goodness. Deloris shifted in her seat slightly, not wanting to break into Mama Lou's thoughts nor appear impatient for her to finish the story. Mama Lou had to be near seventy if she wasn't already, and Deloris had learned you couldn't rush old folks. Deloris found Mama Lou's story interesting, but Charlie wasn't Dexter Denby.

"We became like pigs to slop. Couldn't nobody separate us. That was what I thought. I was younger than you is and we didn't know that much, and the more Dexter Denby whispered in my ear, the more I became convinced that workin' roots was just a diversion waitin' on him. I got in over my head. Slipped him my maidenhood, let him take it from me practically. Naw, gave it to him." Her voice trailed off again remembering her foolishness. "Coulda, mighta, shoulda said how you want it, on a gold or silver platter, Dexter? But I didn't ask no questions, just give it to him straightaway. Times was different then. We had to sneak to steal a kiss, let alone some special time. But mens always been the same. Soon as they see they can suck your sweetness outta you, they gone on to look for some riper fruit. Dexter took it, then he took his curly-head self and started after Precious Canfield. After that, it took me a long time to work back up my interest in roots. I worked hard though, got a firm hold on 'em after that and ain't been tempted to forget how it was since."

Mama Lou sighed and folded her hands together in her lap. Fifty-five years passed between them and wove a silent bond. But in the next instant, she sat straight up in her rocker, looked Deloris squarely in the eyes and said, "But I'm sayin' all that to say a pretty man can't be bought with your sweetness."

Deloris hadn't known quite what to say so she had sat and nodded. Then Stacy LaTuan was born. All Mama Lou said was, "Bring me my granbaby," never once mentioning an I-told-you-so. There was no reason to rub salt in the wound. That was evil, the way Mama Lou saw it.

Al of this was ten years ago when Charlie had brought her to meet his mama, and she could remember it all like the day she heard it. Mama Lou took her in and made a daughter of her, and Deloris loved her more than her own mother.

Stacy LaTuan looked up at her mother. "It's hot, Mama. Can I have something to drink?"

"You better go on in to Mr. Evans and ask him for some water."

"But I want something different, Mama. Can't I have a cherry slush?"

"Girl, what did I tell you? You know we . . ."

"I can't never have no slushes!" The little girl stalked away into the lobby of the hotel. Deloris was weary. Everyone was out here asking for something. The religious folks, the political folks, the beggars, the handicapped, everybody. They were all vying for the attention and patronage of the passersby. Some would yell louder, some dressed provocatively, some adjusted their bodies to catch the attention of prospective donors, like throwing out their chests. Deloris, caught up in the flurry of competition, found herself looking more pitiful or thrusting her sign out farther in front of her whenever she noticed more coins clinking in the cans around her. But she didn't do too bad.

Destitute mother and child. Sometimes it seemed like whoring to her, the way Peaches described whoring, except it wasn't her body but her sorrow she was selling to anyone who would buy some. She had sorted out her choices. When she had decided on begging, it was because she was completely and solely devoted to Charlie. She couldn't imagine opening her legs for any other man, even to survive. Peaches had said she was just being an uppity white woman.

"Everybody need some extra dough. You need to get off your high horse. After the first couple a times it numb you."

"Charlie wouldn't like it if I was laying up with some other men, Peaches."

"Girl, you better wake up and see the daylight! Charlie! What is that mothafucka doin' to help you and your future child? Grow up! This ain't no joke. You know anywhere else you could make forty dollars a night free and clear for a few hours' work?"

"Naw, I don't."

"Look, honey, maybe you think that white skin of yours gonna buy you a special ticket outta here. Ain't no white prince rushed in to save you from despair and big, black dicks. By now, you shoulda learned that white or not don't matter. You still here living in this hole and for all intents and purposes you black. Think about it, now."

She did. Peaches was wrong. Deloris had settled for asking for handouts, and it was going alright. So far. But Peaches had cooled to her after that. And because of Peaches, neither Mayrella, Esther, or Gloriette would ever say more than "Hey" when they saw her. Except for Mama Lou, the old ladies had always looked away from her, remembering Mobile and Meridian. And the old men could only sneak a smile under the watchful eyes of their wives in the way of an apology. Here in this place she was the island that no man ever was.

Born and raised by an alcoholic mama and a gamblin' daddy. Coulda been different from the beginning but for the chance turn of events. When her daddy lost his arm in a foundry accident and spent all the compensation at the poker table, her mama kicked him out, and Deloris never saw him again. Mama turned on the bottle, and Deloris turned eleven and took to playing kissing games with the little boys in the neighborhood. The years passed and like the neighborhood, the little boys grew old and changed from white to black. And she changed and grew and found herself settled in a place where she didn't really belong. Down deep, and deeper into this place, like the roots of an oak tree. It might of been different, except her daddy fucked up and her mama died drinking, leaving her suspended and floating in a sea of color.

She hung between worlds till Charlie. Then she took up with him, and what whites was left in the neighborhood disowned her, and the old black ladies clenched their jaws even tighter and shook their heads vigorously in disgust. Now Mama Lou was her only friend, and Stacy was her only person to love and hold onto. Charlie was a dream that would never have a happy ending. So Deloris had made up her mind to fight for Stacy and for herself. For now, this was all she knew how to do.

Stacy LaTuan appeared in the doorway. Deloris brushed her hand over Stacy LaTuan's hair a few moments, then pulled her closely to her body. She cocked her head to look into the eyes of the little girl beside her. "Did you get your water, baby?"

"Un-hunh."

"You ready now?"

"Yes, Mama."

Deloris reached for her daughter's hand and pressed it a few extra seconds. Reaching for the placard and can, she stood and adjusted it against her body. She gathered together the memories and hope, and with Stacy LaTuan at her side, Deloris took her place among the bag ladies and winos, street musicians and religious crusaders. With shuffling footsteps, she dedicated her life to the balance of the day.

HER

CHERRY MUHANJI

ouses collect — things, old newspapers, junk mail — her. She had come under cover of night, a stowaway with Brother's child tucked in the bottom of her belly, the only ticket in with no way out. He had stuck his Alabama outhouse, dirt farmer finger in her Detroit urban ghetto, Ford Motor Company hi-yellah hole, and she had gone from somewhere, to nowhere, somehow. She understood somewhere, it had been up against the house, inside the 1959 Desoto, or under a blanket at Belle Isle. It was the being nowhere, somehow, that was confusing. It had come, this "thing," rolling down the alley, fierce, forever fragile, needy, and necessary, unwanted and wanted, cursing the night, then seeking benediction from the day. Now, here she was — a winner, somehow, going nowhere.

The house grew people. Real cousins, arthritic aunts, nervous uncles, and Aunt Marion's boy, the one with the tie-tongue. They had come, each trailing a dream from behind, like a peacock in mating season, in full color, from plantation to plant in one easy step. It collected them in bundles, separating them into rooms, where the women moaned at midnight; not from the men jacking off inside them but from the remembered dirt between their toes, the smell of honeysuckle that fondles the nose, sending sweet orgasms into the mind. "Sweet Jesus," they said, while the men smiled and grunted in their sleep, and the women sat behind the glow of cigarettes way past the midnight hour.

"This her, Momma."

"I know who she is, but what she wont?"

Brother didn't understand the question and neither did she at the time. She heard it roll out toward her, enter the stream flowing in and filtering out through her mind, but she wouldn't undress and bathe. Best to ignore it. She knew she wanted sweet potato pie, red velvet furniture, and Brother's finger in her hole. Brother's momma didn't ask "but what she wont?" like she was gonna run out and get the pie and buy the furniture and special-order Brother's finger for her hole. Miss Charlotte suspected her of something, but what? No, "but what she wont?" lifted her skirt, like Bobby Jenkins did in the first grade, intent on enjoying the mystery, if not the meaning.

Her, the piece-a-yellah-throwed-away, niggah nose, niggah lips, nappy hair that said don't ya comb it and don't ya try. Better that yellah skin on a narrow nose, small-lipped brown gal . . . with straight hair. Brother knew, as Miss Charlotte said all the time, the hi-yellah ain't worth much, and that was exactly why he wanted one. He could swing in on vine or rope, over the alligator pit, quicksand, and pointed stakes with her under his arm. They would escape together. She would be glad — then grateful. He could stake his claim then. Put his thing in. Her. He, Brother, king of that mountain he humped, could claim her, not because she was there, but simply because he owned the mountain. The hi-yellah's, Miss Charlotte raged on, "Plumes and fumes over the toilet water but not over the toilet." And when he told her he was gonna do the good and right thing and give the baby his name, Miss Charlotte said, "Damn that, how ya know it yo's?"

"It mine alright!"

"Why ya gon' pay such a price fo' bein' a man? Ain't no man ever cared 'bout my black ass, even if I knowed 'bout or wanted any toilet water, not even yo' father. King Solomon is some cheap chicken shit bird. He gonna try and ease past Saint Peta one of these days, with his pockets still bulgin' carryin' the first dollar he ever made, so he can say he really took it with him.

"Girl, come here."

"Yes ma'am."

"What ya momma say 'bout this hurry-up marryin' y'all done done?"

"Momma ain't said much. Daddy did all the talkin', drivin' us downtown to face the judge."

"Then I done said too much."

Miss Charlotte would reach into her "nowhere," toss her an easy rope, then let her drown, all in the same breath, in the same sentence, and with the same sweet scorn. "Let me rub yo' feets down with some camphorated oil, child."

"Thank ya, Ma'am, but I feel fine."

"Ya carryin' the baby in yo' hips; a knot-head boy fo' sho'. What ya wont, child? A boy or a girl?"

There it was again: her move, the flower waiting to be picked. The one planted among the mint and licorice roots. The one to draw through the nose. The special one, the one the women planted near the doorstep.

"I want what Brother wants."

"Don't I smell yo' soup scorchin', child?"

The house unhinges its face at night, places it on the nightstand, and starts to unpeel its politeness — like a prostitute taking one silk stocking off at a time as the "John" who can't "get it up" sits transfixed in the corner. Like Beverly — the Easter-egg Man, who was always tranfixed but seldom in a corner; who found himself that way as he watched the roll of her hips and the slit of yellow thigh exposing sunrise. He felt on the edge, a lost somebody. His eyes hung like lost words in midsentence, trying to remember what they were supposed to mean or what they were supposed to spell or who they were addressed to. His mind rolled around those hips, caught between the yellow of them and the blackness of his dick ready to fuck sunrise.

"Is yo' real name Beverly?" she asked Easter-egg Man.

"Yep."

"How ya git a name like Beverly?"

"It's the name she gave me."

"Who?"

"My momma."

"Yo' momma give ya a name like Beverly?"

"The name's a slave name just like yo's. Ain't no difference."

"But I ain't got no boy's name, like ya got a girl's."

"It's still a slave name. Look, white folks did the namin' and nig-gah's did the pro-claimin'. Like ya house niggahs did. Told ev'ry time we was gonna 'scape. When that baby due?"

"Doctah say June, Miss Charlotte say May."

"What ya say?" he asked.

Her move again. The pawn to his queen. "Well, I don't know."

"Y'all Miss Anne's all the same, open a niggah up with a whip or a smile, dependin' on. And then actin' like ya ain't — held him open and planted row after row of pussy up and down his mind. And when he come to harvest, ya holler rape or act real dumblike and say, "Well, I don't know."

The house sat forward, knees pressed together, hem neatly tucked in place. It remembered, with slow excitement, the rub of the Easter-egg Man when he placed the palm of the paintbrush up against it — moving up and down, up and down. With the slap of many licks, the house felt the beginning of a shiver, slight at first, then an increasing timbre. Each slap of the brush against the wall was slow and lingering; swish, swish the brush moved, the sound steady, slow, and low, wrap-ping the house in lullaby. A soft hum with each stroke. A yellow stroke (for Miss Charlotte loved yellow). Long strips of paint that covered his face, arms, legs, and thighs.

"Ya sleepin' in there?" asked Miss Charlotte, knocking on the door of the bedroom.

"Yes, Ma'am."

"Well, unless ya talk and answer in yo' sleep, ya wake."

"Yes, Ma'am."

"Brother warmin' up the car. He gon' take me to work. If I can ever get him away from Easter-egg Man. He graduate with Brother, but all he is is a jack-leg. Doin' a little of this and some of that. Seem like he would take some pride in hisself. Huh! Handyman stuff; what Brother see in him beats me. Anyway, Easter-egg Man be comin' 'bout nine. Make sho' ya let him in. I wanna get the hallway painted. Cousin Levi on her way north."

"Yes, Ma'am."

"Stop callin' me 'ma'am'. This here the North, ya know. And I ain't as old as all that. Ya been here all yo' life. Ya thank all I know 'bout is the South and 'em slavery time ways?"

"Yes Ma'am. No Ma'a . . . Miss Charlotte."

She pressed her lips together and snatched all the "yes ma'ams" out of the air, pushed them back down her throat. She was choking.

She could see the slow curl of the tail, the weight of the rattle pressing the tongue forward. Jarred, she moved from the dream. The doorbell. She pulled the weight of her body from the bed, too slow. The doorbell rang again.

"Is Charles at home?"

"What?"

"Is Charles at home?"

"Naw, he ain't here."

Standing on the stoop was George. A blue-black mountain man with a body that looked like a sledgehammer and gestures that poured tea from fragile teacups — a geisha in Wrangler jeans. The voice like amber, low. It made a sound like wind chimes in the distance.

"Tell that moth'r fucka I'm lookin' fo' him. And his ass is grass. No son-of-a-bitch is gonna lick my ass one minute and steal from me the next."

"He's workin'."

"That niggah ain't never worked a day in his life. He steals and lies. Ya just tell him what I said." She shut the door. Pressed her back up against it. Heaved a sigh, then smiled. Aunt Marion's boy trying to lick a mountain's ass. Now that was funny. Did the tie-tongue get in the way? she thought, amused.

"Do ya always go to the door like that?"

"Beverly! How did ya git in?"

"I always get in — where I need to."

The house blushed and cupped its hand over its mouth.

"But . . ."

"But nothin'. Look at ya. Nitegown ridin' up on yo' ass."

"The doorbell kept ringin', and Miss Charlotte said to make sho' I let ya in. Besides, I'm pregnant, Beverly. Nothin' fits anymo'." He started to tug at her gown. It tore.

Her stomach loomed like some silly balloon that didn't know what it was supposed to do. Balloons are free, not like people, who lock themselves into the heat and sweat of other people and get trapped.

Even Miss Charlotte's grandchildren knew that. They would come with their balloons. Just as soon as they could, the balloons broke free and took off for the second floor, then the third. And with the shuffling of shoes and the clambering up stairs, the grandchildren would go after them, pull the string too tight or hug the balloons too close. Then pop! The end!

When Miss Charlotte cared to see how the grandchildren had grown, they arrived with their mothers and their balloons. All wanting a spot — a place to be or be from. Someplace or somebody to say, "Ya done done yo'self proud." Somehow the grandchildren knew they were supposed to want something from Miss Charlotte. But what this was, this place their mothers pushed so hard for them to be in, remained a mystery.

Miss Charlotte would look them over, pulling their legs up like she did when she was south and knew the horse needed shoeing. Then she would tell them all to take off their shoes, if they had any on, to see and comment on if they had Sippie feet. Nobody was quite sure what Sippie feet were. It got real hard around the holidays because no sooner had the grandchildren got their shoes off on Thanksgiving, there was Christmas then New Year's. How much could their feet change from Thanksgiving to Christmas to New Year's?

The truth was, Miss Charlotte didn't care for any of them. Babies made her nauseous. She would call the mothers when she felt herself getting sick and say, "Mothers, yo' babies is callin' ya and my stomach is callin' me." Her eyes would cease then to hold them, returning to an inward view. And she would laugh about nothing in particular and to no one special — just laugh that private Miss Charlotte laugh.

The women who had her grandchildren were all filled with men. But no real woman took men seriously, Miss Charlotte would muse. They were for endurin' and fuckin', not for any serious arrangin' of the mind. To move the mind was, after all, what thinkin' was suppose to do. And these women moved their minds around men, like stirrin' lye in an iron pot; the clothes got clean alright, but the lye ate them up. Miss Charlotte would ponder this sometimes. But never understanding these women, she would dismiss them. First with a smile and, finally, with indifference.

King had had money when she met him. He owned something — a farm, so she loved him. He talked with reason if not in rhymes. She missed the rhyme of black men, and King had somehow failed to learn them, but his reason had served him well. He had managed to work in the fields only long enough to employ others to do the work. King had an eye for the ladies, she knew, so she planned the sons carefully. Three would hold him at home; any others she killed with the horse medicine Miss Ruby used at foal time. She killed the girl child first. No sense lettin' in yo' competition. Miss Ruby had let her know it was a girl, by the way she carried it, real high up, stuttylike. She told King she fell at the well, the pail being too heavy for her to carry. He went and put a pump in the house, as she knew he would.

She knew 'bout mens and their daughters. Only takes 'em a minute not to tell the difference 'tween them and her, she knew. Then there's two bellies in the same house swoll with nobody tellin' who did the doin'. King wasn't no talkin' man, 'bout daughters or nothin' else, but still no need to bring the storm into yo' own house. She could wind up an extra kettle on a full stove. No sir! The next time she would be more careful. Heedin' the moons and seekin' the conjure woman early was a smart move. She only had to kill the fourth boy 'cause that time Miss Ruby got drunk and mixed the wrong stuff. Her womb went hollow.

The gown tore into jagged edges, just under her belly. She looked like an overstuffed cupie doll — like the ones you win at the circus who, being too big for the dresses they wore, stood mute with frozen smiles on their painted faces. Their bellies, round and ready, stood at attention like they did, waiting to be rubbed. Waiting to be wanted. "Come here!" Easter-egg Man said, finally, after standing and looking at her for what was a long moment.

"Ya yellah bitches finally got what you deserve.

"Black is beautiful, baby, and no black brotha ready for the re-volution gonna git off no more on yo' yellah asses. The revolution is for black people not for some trumped-up yellah bitches who sleeps with whitie.

"Ya house niggahs spoilt every plot when us field niggahs, the real blacks, was makin' plans north. All y'all wanted to stay with 'The Man' and give up the brotha. How ya gave up this dick fo' that no-dick mothafucker?"

Easter-egg Man was pressing up against her now. His breath fell, hot, to her shoulders, then her breasts, and finally her stomach. His hands were moving round and round her belly, and she? Why she was on the merry-go-round riding the red pony with the big teeth and holding the gold harness as she rode and rode. Until she was told she must get off, for it was late and she had been too long on the spinning horses. "But I wanna stay! I wanna stay!" she heard herself saying over and over again.

Just then the door opened. Miss Charlotte came in. She stopped so short that Brother, who was right behind, bumped her. Miss Charlotte said nothing, turned, and gave the situation over to Brother — all with one look. Which said, "Where's yo' manhood boy? Take care of the bitch!"

"What the fuck!" Brother said.

"Ya need to keep the bitch tied, man," Easter-egg Man said, bending quickly, giving sudden attention to his paintbrush lost deep inside the can of yellow paint.

"Oh, Easter-egg Man, I need ya to have a look-see on the second floor." Miss Charlotte said, pressing Easter-egg Man to pick up his buckets and brushes and come with her.

Brother had pushed her into the bedroom already, his tears starting to fall. "Why? Ain't I tried? Ain't I? Ain't I? Ya ungrateful bitch!" Wop! The sound of Brother's hand up against her face sent the house into pain. It placed a hand over its eyes and groaned. It had heard these sounds before, but it wondered at her. She made no sound.

"Send a cab to 1448 John R. Street. My car had a flat. I'm already late fo' work." Miss Charlotte said in low tones into the telephone.

The only sounds heard in the house, if one cared to listen, were the whistle of Easter-egg Man already busy on the second floor, Miss Charlotte hanging up the phone, and Brother drying up his sniffles.

She looked into the space of the tiny bedroom. From floor to ceiling, from ceiling to floor, from right to left, and left to right. To the crib waiting in the corner for her to unload her belly. To the large stuffed animal that cousin Marion's boy, the one with the tie-tongue, had already bought for the baby. To the round belly that had brought her there.

....

SAY IT AIN'T SO

AIRBAG

KESHO SCOTT

hat is the truth? Do you have to be a Socrates or Plato to know? Does it come from the meanings of shadows on caves or long soliloquies about freedom and choice while someone else is cleaning your house and watching your kids for minimum wage? Is truth truth because it really really happened the way you said? Or the way the police said, or because you could get the metaphor to work right in the story? I couldn't tell you and I didn't know.

I just got up and took my three credit cards, car keys, and passport and walked out. No one in the kitchen bothered to say a word. They just kept throwing verbal darts at each other and pretending it was just family, a normal family routine. I don't know why this Friday night like all the other Friday nights of the past seven years was different, but I stopped and looked at them. Quickly I recognized the "perfect looking enough" children and the "perfect looking enough" husband and the "perfect looking enough" home and the picket fences of my life. And by some instinct alien to the usual me, I obeyed the "it" in me and walked out.

I had really been gone a long time anyway. I seemed to be the only one who had noticed me . . . being me. At least, no one mentioned that I had been acting strange or looking sad or that I seemed ravenous for something. I just felt . . . not there. Not anywhere. Maybe scattered everywhere. So, I walked out in the way runaway moms do. I walked back into the garage, took out the groceries I purchased before lunch while at work, deposited them on the floor by the door, got into my car, and drove away. It was painless — no blood rituals. We were not cutting our wrist and painting our faces. I just walked out and the car was waiting with open arms to take me wherever I wanted to go. My car was smiling the way she does when I go too fast and get away with it. She was my Thelma and I her Louise, and as I arranged mirror, music, and pulled out maps, we laughed the "fuck 'em" laugh — out of sight, out of mind — and headed for Chi-town.

Passing familiar exits and mile markers I settled into an easy road pace with adjacent car sounds of driving sixty-five miles an hour soothing my tensions. It was early dusk and the "get off work" music and traffic watch reports were almost over. Always attentive to such reports about the weather in the past, I chuckled under my breath. I knew that no weather patterns, no matter how tough, were gonna stop me from making this journey this night. I thought of the times I didn't go to Rita's house when the weatherman said the roads were 20 percent visibility and the Doppler was something I didn't understand and to stay off the street. Reports like these in the past would stop me in my tracks and my task! But not this evening, I thought. And with the flick of my wrist I shut him off and switched on American lite 104.6 and heard Sister Gladys . . . "Can it be that it was all so simple then," and with an emotional editorial, I noted, "Hell, fuckin' no!" "Or has time rewritten every line . . . if we had the chance to do it all again," and another editorial outburst, "I do . . . I really do," "tell me, would we, could we? Memories maybe beautiful and yet" and I tuned out Sister Gladys, who was getting too close for comfort. Just where did she get off asking me about my memories?

I glanced at the odometer and noticed I had gone about sixty-six miles, and had half a tank of gas left when I heard the bang. "Aw, shit! Oh, no! Ugh! Ugh!" I looked into all the mirrors and headed off on

the shoulder. I turned on the flashers. I knew this sound had flat written all over it. I had never had a flat in this new car. Why would a car
less than a year old have a flat? I thought. The question didn't change
the situation one bit but asking it in my mind gave me a feeling that I
was rational, even as a tornadolike rage was forming in my gut. When
the car completely stopped I jumped out to the music of "What you
want . . . baby I got it . . . what you need . . . you know I got it . . . all I
asking . . . is for a little respect," and I was so mad at Aretha I could
have shit! The tire was indeed flat. I flipped the trunk switch and began to wonder where the jack was. I searched. I found it carefully
rolled up with its new-smelling directions that looked like a computer
printout for the gifted and talented. In other words, not me. I
dropped them back into the trunk, shut it, and returned to the front
seat. I sat for a while until I saw the light — the red, flashing, bright as
helicopter lights — behind me. Two officers approached. I rolled
down the two windows and only one spoke while the other poked his
head in my car. It didn't take us long to communicate — flat . . . tire . . .
woman . . . need help . . . help . . . jack . . . found jack . . . hike up car . . .
pull out spare . . . attach it . . . put the toy of the boys in blue away . . .
say our thank-you so much, and of course, we are glad to help you,
and be careful this evening — and head off the shoulder to a gas station to get the tire fixed.

It all went too fast — watching them bend over in their tight blue
police pants and shiny buttons and police caps turned me on. I always
liked or was always turned on by those navy blue pressed pleats and
their "procedures." Oh, those procedures! And I loved the "yes,
ma'ams" that police were fond of saying. I often wanted my husband
to "play cop" and arrest me . . . handcuffed to the bed . . . I could report him to his superiors . . . and then I caught myself down this fantasy lane. This was not my reality. I was nurturing a divorcing. Hubby
and I weren't on playing terms and definitely not on sexual terms.
There were absolutely no terms of endearment. I hadn't spoken the
word with the big "D" yet because I was overwhelmed by what it
meant to end a fifteen-year marriage. Battles over child custody, divided property, and living with the smells of a second failed marriage,
oh, no, I was nurturing an affair beyond work, beyond food, beyond
my own family values. I couldn't handle any reality. Truth. And I was
called back to Whitney Houston's version of "I will always love you,"
which jerked my mind back to the present moment and the police-
men's presence. "Oh, yes, I will be careful and get this fixed immedi-

ately, sir." With that the boys in blue with pink faces and can't-tell-if-they-really-mean-it smiles said good night as I drove off.

"You got here just in time . . . we close in fifteen minutes," was all the gas station attendant said as I nodded with a smile and motioned that I would be in the bathroom or the coffee shop next door. Thirty minutes later, I was counting the stars in bloom; the evening light had turned completely pitch-black now. I felt my destiny ahead of me — in the dark, in the night, in the words of Patti LaBelle now coming out of the radio, "You are my friend," and I rocked myself in the seat until the leather seat comforted me like a gentle hand on my shoulder.

Now having driven another two hours I was feeling the strain in my neck. I had eaten all the breath mints I was used to keeping on the dashboard. I was very hungry. I wondered what they had cooked for dinner at home. Would they fight about it, or just do the thing they always did — someone would cook what only she or he wanted, and everyone else would bitch in silence the way the lonely girl at school with flat feet does at the dance. Remembering just then a granola bar I had in my glove compartment, I reached over to open it. But I reached over a bit too much when the car swerved to the middle lane. "Shit!" I thought. Then I felt it — only the wrapper was left. "Shit!" I said again. It was one of those teens . . . the kind that used the mayonnaise and leaves the top unscrewed on . . . use up your tampons and don't replace them and when you ask them to let you use the phone a minute . . . (since they have been on it since 3:30 right after they got out of school and it is now 10 P.M. and it is after all your phone . . . you pay the bill) and they ask in the defiantly wrong tone, "How long are you gonna be, Mom?" Or it was the teenagers . . . the scum of the earth . . . the prehistoric man in every proper family . . . driving parents to distraction.

I remembered my lecture on the strains of the "empty-nest syndrome" on women in Wednesday's class. I had couched that talk with the inevitability of it to women's lives and transitions out of the family caretaker roll. What I really wanted to tell a room full of nineteen-year-old pimple faces was that we parents can't wait until you fuckers are gone. That we don't want to share not a damn thing else with you. We are sick and tired of you and please go. And maybe, for a few seconds, a very few at that . . . we will feel the pangs of another child gone . . . a quiet house for the first time in eighteen years, cooking smaller meals and lots of leftovers . . . and part-time momism . . . overall, we jump for joy . . . because we can be naked in body, words, and thought because you are not in our home. Knowing I'd get fired for this nonscholarly interpretation of the data and countless interviews with other teen's parents, I slammed the glove compartment, wishing I had crushed their heads in the crack when I heard another bang!

I jumped in my seat. Looked immediately behind me. I had not been hit. But the car was slowing down fast so I immediately turned to the shoulder of the highway. I immediately jumped out and I immediately saw again that I had another blown tire. Not the same tire. Not the same side of the car. Not the same end of the car. But flat as a door and burning rubber. I looked at my watch. It was late. It was close to midnight. I immediately started to curse the car . . . whose grille didn't show the earlier smile we had begun this journey with. She (the car) didn't do her "Thelma act"—dumb white blonde car . . . and I didn't do my Louise act . . . "It is okay, Thelma. We are great girlfriends." . . . I kicked the tire wall and got back in the front seat. I turned on the emergency signal and got out. Locked the doors and with purse in hand, I started to trudge to the nearest rampway not thinking of the works of the soul sister . . . fuck 'em . . . 'cause I couldn't get no satisfaction!!! I needed a melody out of this nightmare. I'm scared and pissed and the songs came easy . . . "Bali High will find you," "I'm gonna wash that man right out of my hair," "Doe, a deer, a female deer," and "Oklahoma where the wind comes sweeping down the plain." The songs were working a white mojo on the night and on me . . . and suddenly . . . I was . . . strictly . . . a female . . . female. "Some enchanted evening . . . you will meet a stranger . . . you will meet a stranger . . ." and I knew it wasn't across a crowded room. He had jumped out from the viaduct . . . he was gritty, greasy, and grizzly. This was my knight in shining armor? It was my Prince Charming? Oh, fuck no! But he would fix the tire. "On the road again. Just can't wait to get on the road again. . . ." Willie Nelson's words. Patsy Cline . . . "Crazy, crazy for feeling so lonely . . ." and I decided to turn the music off.

The silence had done me good. After an hour and a half, I had figured out my game plan. I'd get to Chicago about two A.M. Get me a cheap room at the Days Inn, take a good hot shower, and sleep till noon. I'd have some ribs at Fat Daddy, get to the airport by two, buy my ticket, and be off to Cairo by five. Yes, this was a good plan.

Pooooow! And I'm struggling to keep the car from going in a ditch. It does! And it wasn't tire number one or tire number two! And

I knew trouble came in threes. The airbag almost smothers me and my head is aching. My blood pressure has gone through the sunroof. Tears come. And I know I got whiplash. Not the fucking hospital again. Not Dr. Randolph with the surgical fingers. Not three months of physical therapy and three more months of chiropractic adjustments by a woman who has a gleam in her eye that lets you know that she is enjoying this a little too much. No more sessions about my inner child. Or shrinks who write prescriptions for Prozac when they can't think of anything else to do. I can't fit another twelve-step meeting in my life . . . no more . . . simply no more!

And with a mounting number of my protestations . . . I notice that the airbag is standing outside of the car. I shake my head to the left and so does it. I shake my head to the right and so does it. And I know it must be the impact. I shut my eyes and it's gone. I struggle out of the car, glance at the bare rim and pieces of tire everywhere. I say to myself, "only God can save me now." I turn and the airbag isn't an airbag. Oh shit . . . oh no . . . oh oh oh . . . no! Not me! Not now! No *Star Trek* tonight. Please! Oh! And airbag points to the car and it levitates onto the shoulder. Airbag points to the tire and it fixes itself. Airbag points to me and points for me . . . to go home. And I do.

ALL ON A SATURDAY NIGHT

. . . .

EGYIRBA HIGH

Here we go loop dee loop
Here we go loop dee lie
Here we go loop dee loop
All on a Saturday night

Ah, yes, and the dance continues. But it is so like the child's circle game that has been abandoned because the poor darlings still nursing ruffled feelings find the game less fun. It was not like this at first though. There were no questions of why I would want to write about you. Your letters were not grist for the mill; I was not hungry for story lines. I did not need to cull, cultivate, or collect a moment in time, nor coddle you into a dance to lay a trap for you. Nor did I need to coerce your heart from the solitary chamber where it beats a melancholy rhythm for something it fears it may never ever have. No, none of this was needed to coax a timid imagination into lyrical expression.

No writer's sensibility was needed to love you. I did not need that then. I do not need it now. What I need is to make sense of what happened, to see it from all angles. I am a writer, so I write. And I wonder, "How did we get here?"

In the beginning when I met you, there was a flame. At first, only the hint of warm embers smoldering in charcoal passion, then a quick blaze. Aflame in Eros, who, disguised in a robe of filial love, bid us draw closer to lust that should not be spoken into existence, we drew closer. I was becharmed. You felt more like kin to me. Your words still come to me, rivulets of desire, of longing, of what-could-have-been. In the center of my head I can see you. At the center of my heart do I feel you. Round the center of my soul you are wandering, a beggar, frozen and hungry, so unaware that you are not alone. If you look up you will see me, open your ears, hear me whispering. Free your heart. I am beating in you. There somewhere beyond space and time, we are dancing still, the music of compulsion our seduction song. Ever present, though you pretend not to hear it.

No, it was not like that when I met you. Then it was fast becoming clear that you were affecting me and falling quickly yourself. How did it move so swiftly from the realm of fun to those recriminations of which you always spoke? I hated that word because you used it too much, bandying it about at moments of intensity, growing a wedge between us. And so I ignored it because it felt like a game in which you were leveling the playing field. And though I seldom play games, I could at least be effective sometimes, I'd think when I tried. "What do you want?" you would ask me frequently. "I don't know," I would say.

When I read your personal ad on the Internet I knew there was something special about you. In between the lines of bullshit I could see you clearly. And though I should have turned away, I could not resist despite the numerous red flags and yellow lights that flashed all over my brain. I ignored them because I glimpsed such élan I had never seen in a black man of my acquaintance. I could not resist because brains have always had an aphrodisiac effect on me. Urbane and charming, sensitive and poetically articulate, there you were. Um. How *could* I resist? Between us we had good minds, strong desire, deep passion, and intensity. You seduced me and I nibbled the bait because the best challenges are always those that appear only slightly out of reach. I let my newfound affection for you douse any idling "be carefuls" still flickering at my ears. I fell in love deeply. And so did you.

We spent long hours and days, and days into months in conversation, weaving a world between us from the scraps of our tattered lives. Yours: a twelve-year-long prison you were dying in, bogged down as you were in domestic living and a fear of being really really close. Trapped. Despite yourself and all your good intentions, you told lies to the heart that would not give you rest. Trying to loose the rope of marital fidelity knotted round your mind, you drowned your heart in denial by pretending you could leave at any time. You never got it when I told you that the only freedom there really was was in your mind. While you struggled to out-picture in your actual life your bold ideas about relationships and love, you sought meaning in quasi-intimate relationships that guaranteed you the right to ease away should the weight of a familiar feeling press your neck again.

Mine was an ill-considered trip down "Matrimony Lane," for the heck of it, to play a role as second wife in a marriage where there was already one wife too many. Despite the crazy circumstances I married him because I felt like I could belong to something, had a purpose, that I was needed. My own boy was all grown up. A man! Finally, off to college I now felt the lonesomeness that an empty nest bears witness to. I never noticed how hard I tried to blunt the mothering impulses still fluttering inside my womb. I would smoke, eat, and computer myself into a frenzy that would help me forget that my work there was through, that I was getting older, and that yes, it was now clear, I would not finish my doctoral dissertation. In panic, then, I married. Now either unwilling or afraid to close the chapter of that book, I looked askance and there you were: diversion.

We did not bother to work out the details. We delighted in easing our mutual loneliness, delaying the future accounting with which we would have to contend. "Why don't you know now?" you kept asking. "I don't know," I still answered.

Then you said, "Your heart is safe with me," and to the promise in those words my heart clung with desperation so fierce, and yearning so flaming, it sent you running. Not fast at first, but the kind of getting away that happens when you want to be polite — you look for an opportunity to exit, and boy, then do you take off! You ran like that. I hungered for intellectual, spiritual, and creative compatibility with a man, the full sense of which I understood only from my well-rehearsed girlhood fantasies. With a starved passion and secret lust buried so deep I could not recognize them as mine, I preyed upon your heart. You were not ready for the promise you found and still long for. For now you nurse your wounds. I imagine you thinking,

"Boy, was that close." For a moment, though, there is sweetness, a rose-pink river between my legs that flows from my heart, having been born in your eyes. It is divine. For a moment there is the possibility of transcendence.

Jasmine cautioned me. But what does she know anyway? She has no practical knowledge of men. From her vantage point it was never clear why an intelligent black woman — any intelligent black woman — would put herself in such a situation with a man, would place herself in harm's way then refuse all help out. "But you know me, Jasmine," I told her. "You know this is something, this is different. You know I really love him. He sets my soul afire." It is amazing how many times she took your side, her Libra drive to get the balance in a situation always prevailing. I love her for this even as I shudder in my skin because of it.

"I know what you mean," she said. "But it's not different. *You* are not different. I know you love him but you deserve to have someone who is totally available to you. Why are you settling? He'll come here, and when he finds out you're just like her, he will feel deceived. I love you," she told me, "*Please*— love you, too."

Even when I try and explain it to her I hear how foolish I sound. There is no real way to justify the impossibility of it all. Just the what-if? to keep me trying. "What if this is the fruit of a lifelong unconscious desire now coming to harvest," I ponder aloud. "How can I resist that?"

You fly to me and I know I am right. At the airport I take in your delicious burnt brown skin covering that strong, slim frame of a body of yours, which moves toward me with long, easy, open strides. This is right, this is right, I tell myself when I gaze into your dancing eyes. I am sure of it. Then you hold my hand as we walk down Jefferson Avenue, eyes only for me, and again, I am right. At the Eastern Market, we walk through aisles of fresh fruit, and flowers, dream and meditation at the Detroit River, and later, when we select a choice bottle of wine from the wine-seller, you want to give me everything. "I am in love with her," you tell the pretty Lebanese waitress serving us humus and lamb, who unaware of me would like very much to have your attention. If you notice, it does not show. You leave your seat across the table and move beside me, smiling all the while, staring deep into my eyes.

Later you pull me to yourself and kiss me over and over (oh, we did do that so well!) as we wait in the theater line to see *Soul Food*. You are delighted at the happy girl you see inside of me. I giggle as my flowery gauze dress billows around me, your kisses staged to excite, as people passing by stare at us. I know I am right again. I am never so carefree in public. And for a long moment we create a world of our own on the day you return to England. At the airport again, there is no space for lovers wanting to say private good-byes, so we find a seat on the floor around the corner from your boarding gate. You lay your head in my lap, your eyes saying all for words that are inadequate, and my heart cries yes, this is it! This feeling, this deep joy is all I have hungered for all of my life. Still, even the divine magic of these days is not enough to transcend our days and years of unquenched desire, nor its promise of fulfillment. The longing must go on as the heart plays the illusion with a sleight-of-hand befitting David Copperfield. Inevitable obstacles lie in wait for us.

When I think of it now I know that it could not have lasted, given who I have been. It has never lasted. This need to believe, to place my trust in someone else because the hope keeps me alive, betrays the truth. And girlhood dreams are meant for girls. You would say it is because I need a flowery backdrop upon which to view and understand life. You are right, as you often are, though yours is rather plain, and dull from my way of seeing. I wonder how you find a place for the joy that is in your heart? What do you do with the color that wants to cascade from your soul and spill into creation birthing something so magnificent, so brilliant it thunders the spirit in ecstasy — an orgasm of the soul? I ask these questions in my mind but I do not want to think of this. I do not want to speculate upon the answers. Instead, like all the times before, like all the men who precede you, I give my heart away. I do not yet know that though I am dancing with you, you are really only the mirror of the relationship I am having with myself. I think it is you who make all the difference but you are simply the manifest reflection of the love that is in my own heart. But I do not know this while we are weaving and dancing. I do not know how to love my own self enough. Trite as that may seem, it really was the case.

And so I say, I do not know if you can hear me but I pray you are listening anyway. What we shared was very real, and not a pipe dream. It was too scary, too soon, too much to move beyond that moment. There were too many encumbrances. Now there is a wall of icy distrust between us. I reach out to you, extend my hand in forgiveness, in friendship. I want to make real sense of things so my soul can rest, at peace. While love is suspended in suspicion and doubt, I know all I wished I had known then. It is me. Despite the many efforts I made to abandon myself, throughout the many days I could not see rightly, *I* was happening all along. Recovered and self-aware there is no returning to the darkness, no place to hide my glory newly born. I move to clear remaining brambles of confusion still lying in my path.

You wanted to dance with me and so we began. We blazed a fire dance, a holy conflagration that excites the gods. We lit the flame in each other's soul. In an eternal moment we are dancing, still, in that place where all intangibles exist without complication. The music of compulsion our seduction song.

But will I write about you? I still have not decided.

COMING OUT AND
INTO THE NEW AGE

. . . .

CHERRY MUHANJI

 psychic told her once to help make some sense of the flashbacks, lying on a hard-back table, chubby little legs up, arms outstretched [Stop. Smile. Camera. Click.], whose mollycat was being scrubbed clean by her mother, that it was her Momma's way of trying to ease, erase, numb it.

[Stop. Smile. Camera. Click.]

This'll take the smell out of the rose, the blue blue out of the sky, and the mint out of the leaf that's growin' wild 'neath the front step. No sense in moonin' over the peck of stars, my daughter, you a hi-yellah gal! Chances are you'll team up with somebody's sooty black boy. To take on a feeling? A good time? Equal out all that yellah? Ha! What it'll get you is ababyayearababyayearababyayearababyayear. That's all the creatin' that needs doin'. Turnin' gray the only three to depend on is the Father, Son, and the Holy Ghost ... have mercy! If I scrub you clean now, it won't matter when black-skinned black girls throw arrows, 'cause they ain't you, my cream-colored baby. Now open your legs real wide for Mommy.

[Stop. Smile. Camera. Click.]

Jenny was all the things to love — Tonka trucks and tennis balls, hairpins and bobby socks — divided between a clever mind and a curious one, with lips that would never tell and eyes, even then, that made you stare. Star-bright and stormy. She never told you that at times she could see the end of things at the beginning, did she?

What if I told you that all she ever really wanted was to be the girl in her dream? Would that surprise you? Did you know or could you have ever guessed that it was her imagination that kept her alive — innocence — participating in life but not the daily living of it? Would it surprise you if I told you that I know much more about her than even that?

She's a funny one, you know — like funny girls are in funny dreams. Where somebody *is* funny or some*thing* is but you're too nervous in this dream, because a girl like that in anybody's dream can wreck it. I know because she can make you think that she is all the things you are not. Yeah . . . she's the one who sends deep color into this dream and moves your eyes toward that victorious V nestled between her thighs — not seen, even by me, but promised. You suddenly hope, as you have never hoped before while being ushered to your table, and soon offered her nibbled bread stick before the meal, that this dream never ends. Later, I imagine she offered you her forefinger dipped in red wine, right? Whispering suck, perhaps? Toward the end of the dream (and you know it's about to end), when both you and she are sipping strong black fragrant coffee all too sure that this time everything's just right, till you up and spill your coffee all over the white linen tablecloth tumbling over the thick heavy cream. Still, her eyes forever smiling perched atop her coffee cup, seem afloat in some exotic air, somehow watch while you try not to frantically wipe away coffee stains with only the tip of your napkin plunged into the crystal goblet of iced water. That gesture only egged her on, I bet, moving (to your surprise) her stockinged toe up against your nyloned thigh. [Stop. Smile. Camera. Click.] In the dream, because it is your dream, after all, she did something for you that no one else knows about, I bet. Like watching in silence as you, moving your fork to the right side of the plate even though you are ordinarily left-handed is always sparked by a sense of loss. Silent still as you move your knife to the left — that you never do that without a flood of memories of your grandmother tying your left hand behind your back—getting you ready for a white world—because you didn't need one more thing to overcome. Pursing her lips and cupping your hands she told you all very sincerely that she understood. But then the dream never failed to jump and you would experience yourself—despite your best efforts, blowing out a candle, while slowly taking the stairs one at a time, that going to bed, no matter how many times with anyone else besides her means going alone.

Jenny (not of the dream), wouldn't dare. Her life wasn't like that. That Jenny allows. Keeps her head down, always looking for the shiny penny, but never finding it knows only one thing: that it's too confusing to ask in a black-and-white world in the middle of Detroit, where the only miracle is survival, any questions. Certainly not one like, is this all there is?

Surviving the waking world without quaking (ha, that rhymes), took all that she had. But it was in her to be a girl like the dream Jenny. I know that confuses some people. Cherry isn't. Ask her. She's the one pressed up against (penned in is more like it), Jenny, and Jenny's boy-husband more nights than either one intends to remember. But on a particular night, I'm not remembering what month—day, when Jenny (not of the dream), letting go just the tiniest bit realized that what she was really doing—had been from time to time, was trying to get used to all the somebodies in the bed. That night she and boy-husband were into that giveaway sex, the kind you're always giving away because you don't know what else to do with it. Well, what she was really having trouble with was Cherry's angst, which was smoldering just beneath the covers. It became "like something done in fever, when nothing fits, mind into mind nor body into body . . . when nothing meets or equals—when dimensions lie and perceptions go haywire."*

"Why ain't ya' doin' somethin' that both of us enjoy?" Cherry asked. "I don't care that this is your wedding night. It's not as if you're Cinderella and he is Prince Charming, ya' dig? You're already pregnant, God help us one and all. This give-away sex—may hold some promise for you, Sugar, but not me."

When he finally rolled off of Jenny and she eased out of the nuptial bedroom, and down the hall careful not to wake him, muttering

* From Walter Benton, *This Is My Beloved*.

to herself for the very first time: is this all there is? Cherry was too thorough. That's when I made my move. The air became like thick soup. The night rhythm changed. I showered Jenny (of the dream) down on both of them, and as Cherry looked up she froze. While the top of the house opened I lit a match and set a canopy of stars on fire. The night sky was ablaze. Then too, I've been known to do other things like plant worlds, harvest them, and hear while in the mix of all of that the sound of a heart breaking.

A Dream Jenny can be anybody, go anywhere, and do anything. Like making a long-distance train whistle sound like Miles's trumpet. Eat an apple every day for a century. Even make you think that loving was what was happening in that room between Cherry, Jenny, and boy-husband. But it's more than that, I think.

Even I ask myself sometimes, wonder even, as I watch the spin of moons around planets you do not know, or witness suns nova, is all of this just a matter of movement? That nothing is allowed to stay as is? That move we all will. But rhythms of the universe, or multiverses, or even the rhythm of Jenny's moonbright thighs wrapped around boy-husband's back, or a million and one nights like that — with all the parts of Jenny colliding with Cherry nightly, or even the rhythm of this story, will move us somewhere to something — make us more than we were, or maybe, god forbid, less.

Finally, I found Jenny (now of the dream) examining the mirror, pressing her face up against it nose to nose with Cherry in that tiny, tiny bathroom at the end of the hall. She didn't know yet that this was a cosmic call, that I had heard her, seen her night visions, and heard her rambling through her daylight madness — longing for nightfall, experiencing her desperation.

I could hear Cherry whispering, "Put your tongue up against the mirror." Jenny began licking at the glass, rubbing her hands all over Cherry's face in the mirror, moving her eyes all over Cherry, sure, not sure, who this other part of her was. But licking at her wounds for the first time felt good, as beads of sweat began forming and her breasts began lifting and her breathing could be heard down the hall. Finally, whispering in a little-girl voice, "Mommy, it's feeling so good. It's not hurting anymore."

Cherry was stunned. "This isn't what's supposed to be happening is it?" Cherry asked still breathless.

The Dream Jenny just laughed and laughed. A question like that begins worlds. And ends others. It moved them away from that house, the boy-husband, the curves and squares of that tiny, tiny bathroom, the baby girl on the hard-back table and into the night, where nothing ever meets or equals. But it's in the night sky where Jenny's off-rhythm and Cherry's on-rhythm appear nightly, colliding with stars and forming the worlds they want.

All you got to do is look up.

[Stop. Smile. Camera. Click.]

SELECTED SINGULAR LIVES

The Anti-Warrior: A Memoir
By Milt Felsen

Black Eagle Child: The Facepaint Narratives
By Ray A. Young Bear

China Dreams: Growing Up Jewish in Tientsin
By Isabelle Maynard

Flight Dreams: A Life in the Midwestern Landscape
By Lisa Knopp

Fly in the Buttermilk: The Life Story of Cecil Reed
By Cecil A. Reed with Priscilla Donovan

In My Father's Study
By Ben Orlove

In Search of Susanna
By Suzanne L. Bunkers

Journey into Personhood
By Ruth Cameron Webb

Letters from Togo
By Susan Blake

A Lucky American Childhood
By Paul Engle

My Iowa Journey:
The Life Story of the University of Iowa's First African
American Professor
By Philip G. Hubbard

A Prairie Populist: The Memoirs of Luna Kellie
Edited by Jane Taylor Nelsen

Snake's Daughter: The Roads in and out of War
By Gail Hosking Gilberg

Tales of an American Hobo
By Charles Elmer Fox

Tight Spaces
By Kesho Scott, Cherry Muhanji, and Egyirba High

Unfriendly Fire
By Peg Mullen